Katharina Stern or Tell Me If There's No One in Heaven

This book is loosely based on historical events that transpired fifty years ago. Any resemblance to actual persons, living or dead, is purely coincidental. Real places and historical figures are depicted under artistic license.

BRIGITTE ZEPLIEN

Katharina Stern
or
Tell Me If There's
No One in Heaven

Translated by Kylee Carlson

Bibliographical Information of the Deutsche Nationalbibliothek
This publication is listed in the Deutsche Nationalbibliographie of the
Deutsche Nationalbibliothek; detailed bibliographical information
can be accessed under http: //dnb.d-nb.de

© 2017 Brigitte Zeplien
Translated by Kylee Carlson (Minneapolis, USA)
from the German Original "Katharina Stern oder Sag mir,
wenn im Himmel keiner ist"
Printing, Production and Layout: BoD – Books on Demand,
Norderstedt
ISBN: 978-3-7448-4250-1

PROLOGUE

The young woman tore through the pulsing city's glittering streets in a panic. She pressed on through the unfamiliar surroundings like a hunted animal, unthinking.

Jeanne Alien soaked up the evening, the city seeming to her like a bright shining star spreading the heady light of its bustling center out into the warm darkness of the outer boroughs where people lived. "Like a star," she thought. "Can I really find heaven here – after escaping from hell?" She felt the first tiny seeds of love for the city start to bloom inside her. Hamburg was a lot like her beloved Montreal in Canada, where her parents lived. It seemed as though the cool spring evening wanted to tuck a blanket over the secrets that slumbered deep within the city.

The attractive young woman cut a sleek figure. Her blue-black chin-length hair was smoothed expertly in an expensive haircut, in perfect keeping with the style of the day. Her slender hands looked elegant with a salon manicure, tiny patterns on the tips. Yet her anxious gaze and fluttering hands did not match the perfectly groomed eyebrows that accentuated her dark eyes. Nor did she quite fit the smoothly tanned skin that should have maintained the facade of beauty.

The small suitcase hadn't held much.

"I really only need clothes and a pair of underwear," she concluded silently, and went into a brightly-lit shopping mall, where she was immediately greeted by glowing backlit ads and enormous mirrors in the entryway. She deliberately walked slowly over to them so she could casually check her reflection. There were the first greying roots glinting distinctly out from under the black. "I really ought to get those dyed. Preferably right here somewhere." She looked around uncertainly. Who could she ask? Everyone was speaking a language she didn't know, but they'd understand her English. The nearest hairstylist was right around the corner; she was, after all, in the most expensive mall in Hamburg. "Credit card?" *Kreditkarten? Natürlich.* Of course. Here, at last, she was in a city of the world. The international scene was all around her. Not just the hairstylist, but every single store offered unlimited possibilities. Hamburg, the home of her company's headquarters, welcomed her with open arms.

She would never go back to that backwater town in Italy, to that awful family of her Italian husband's! In a mad rush, she'd fled and gotten the very first train to Hamburg. She would ask if she could be transferred from the Italian branch to work here.

She also needed a place to stay. A woman on the internet had offered a furnished room for 995 Euros a month. It did not occur to her how much that would add up to. She went straight there, though she had no idea where she was going to get the money from.

"No matter. It's better than nothing. I've got another credit card anyway. And Maman will support me." Her credit card did the trick, even though she hadn't been in good standing in ages. Far away, Maman was tearing her hair out.

"She and her husband were so happy when they were a young couple studying in Montreal!" thought Maman. "But all those years playing the traditional housewife with that Italian family made my little girl's life a living hell."

Jeanne ran away several times during her eight years of marriage there, though she had learned to love the Italian language.

"That awful family haunts me in my dreams," she told a friend over the phone. "They make me cook and make them Italian food. My husband took my credit card, suspended my account, and started rationing my money out to me. That was the worst. It was so degrading. We owned a really nice expensive condo. But all my income was going just to that, paying for the interest and mortgage, with nothing left for me."

She spent six months in Japan – everything was fine there! When she had to come back, hell broke loose inside of her. She was miserable, even more so with alcohol.

"You can't go on like this," her mother-in-law scolded her. She ended up in the hospital with severe alcohol poisoning. Her life was on the line. If she had never woken up again, only her mother in faraway Canada would have wept.

Maman kept coming to visit for several months (even over Christmas, while her father stayed home due to his fear of flying) to counsel her only daughter, to look after her and even cook for her a bit. Normally Jeanne always went to restaurants, because she hated cooking.

Maman admitted that she spoiled her daughter, but she herself was already past her mid-thirties when she had had Jeanne, and she loved her only child. "Why did she have to move so far away from us?"

Her in-laws berated her mother when she stayed on for months, insisting that she pay for her own groceries. Jeanne's outrage at this knew no bounds.

She couldn't sleep at all anymore, she worked at her computer through the night, sought refuge yet again in training programs, new degree programs, language courses. Foreign languages, foreign countries – she lapped it all up like mother's milk. Learning represented the one activity that she could perform to her satisfaction.

Her mother paid up, setting aside money from her tiny pension.

She made phone calls every day between Italy and Canada. Without her mother she was incapable of dealing with life, incapable of dealing with conflict. She couldn't handle all the difficulties piled up in her life by herself. So she fled for the third time, this time to Hamburg, with a handful of antidepressants, sleeping pills, and painkillers in her bag.

She stared contemplatively at her reflection, lost in the middle of the throng of people in the huge shopping center.

All her wits screamed for an immediate divorce, but Italian law worked differently from Canadian; three years' separation was required, she knew that much. Unbearably long. The Italian family would never pay out any money to her.

"It's hopeless," she whispered to herself, in tears. "I don't want to any more. I give up." She lingered there, standing in front of the racks full of bottles with luridly colored labels.

"Hello, Jeanne Alien, where did you come from?" The friendly English greeting yanked her back out of the muddle of memories and perilous ideas swimming through her head. "We've met before!"

She could only muster up a vague memory of some company party last year. "When? Who are you?"

The young man had an open, cheerful air about him. "Do you need any help?"

His English saved her from being completely stranded in this German city. Meanwhile though, her own talent for languages bordered on genius. With Maman she spoke French and Spanish, English with her dad, Italian with her husband. She'd only need a few months in Germany to learn the language, just as she had mastered spoken Japanese after only six months there. Her genius hovered just shy of the line bordering madness.

Did she need underwear? He could go with her to pick some out; she was, after all, wandering around a completely foreign place and needed some help. Any sense of inhibition appeared not to bother him. He'd be happy to accompany her, seeing as how she seemed so lost. Readiness to help was his calling card.

The young man -- who introduced himself as "Felix Stern, like a star" -- had an easy light-heartedness about him that put a stop to her melancholy. He beamed at her like his own namesake, like a sign from heaven. It seemed someone up there didn't want her just yet.

Chapter 1

I'm thirsty."

Seventeen-year-old Felix sat waiting restlessly on a bench down in the shopping center's entryway. He'd met his mother here after school to help carry her shopping. He was looking rather pale.

"Did gym class make you sweat that much today?" Felix said nothing.

"Can we quick stop at the shoe department first, before we get something to drink?" Katharina was, as always, in a hurry.

Felix nodded mutely. He appeared not to have the strength to push his request for a drink. His mother noticed nothing. Together they pressed on through the crowd, who, like her, apparently also scrounged around the mall after work. The fragrant aroma of the perfume department wafted over to Katharina, luring her in. It would just be a quick detour on the way to the shoes. She didn't come here that often. The family lived in the country on the edge of Rostock, and her visits into the city center usually involved more than just one purchase. Katharina was always finding more things to decorate the house with, or little presents for family and friends. She hadn't broken that habit from the time before the reunification: always on the lookout for nice things, even if she didn't need them right away, just to stow away for special occasions.

Suddenly Felix stopped in his tracks.

"I'm really thirsty. I can't wait anymore." Surprised, Katharina looked at his face. He looked unusually serious. And he looked somewhat unwell. Her maternal instincts kicked in.

"That bad? Well come on, then. Right over here across from the mall – there are drinks in that little grocery shop, too." Felix shuffled along behind her, noticeably lagging, while she egged him on. "It's not far, come on, we're almost there."

She almost felt a bit annoyed that he couldn't wait until they got home. On the other hand, it must have been pretty urgent, considering her patient, even-tempered son let almost nothing ruffle him.

They filed into the small shop, where they were greeted by a little bell on the door. It smelled musty, like potato sacks and beverage crates and cabbage. The shop girl turned a friendly face towards her only customers and waited.

"How can I help you?"

Katharina didn't turn to look at Felix when she asked him if he wanted apple juice or a seltzer. In that moment there was a crash behind her, like a crate of drinks had been knocked over. Felix lay on the floor, not breathing. The shop girl bolted out from behind the counter in alarm. Katharina knelt down and shook him, her eyes wide. Fear gripped her. Had it only been a few seconds, or minutes already? Her heart seemed to have stopped beating.

"Is there a phone here?" she shouted at the shop girl, who was similarly fluttering about in a total panic.

Suddenly a very weak voice, trying desperately to drown out the two excited women, whispered. "Hey, what's wrong? I'm getting back up."

Felix slowly came to, though he didn't immediately understand why he was lying there. Katharina held out a bottle of water, which he sucked down greedily.

"Just stay there, we're calling a doctor."

"What for? I'm totally fine." The two of them pulled him up, and he tried to move with shaky knees. "Everything's fine. Yeah, of course I can make it to the car." Carefully Katharina shielded her son, and walked the endless five-hundred-meter stretch to the car with him.

Later, she could not recall the thoughts that had filled her head during the short drive back to the house. An insane fear had suddenly paralyzed her.

What exactly was she supposed to make of this? What did it mean?

January passed.

An indescribable panic propelled Katharina from doctor to doctor with her young son. MRI scans of all his internal organs. No result. No doctor could find an explanation. Perhaps school was overwhelming him. Maybe it was a psychological problem?

In February they got nothing but headshakes of surprise and

dismissal from internal specialists. "We'll do an MRI scan of his head just to make sure. – There's nothing to see there. – It'll go away on its own."

Spring came. The boy lost more weight; the dark circles under his eyes were becoming permanent fixtures. He needed to rest more, his graduation exams were weighing him down.

Katharina's agitation grew.

In spite of this, she followed up an opportunity to go on a six-week educational trip to America. One of her life's dreams suddenly had a chance of coming true. Was she supposed to stay home and take care of her son? Subconsciously she was tormented by guilt. Even in a nurturing family, no one – not a father, not an older brother, not the grandparents – could relieve her of the maternal responsibility weighing heavy on her shoulders.

Felix passed his driver's license test while she was gone, right after his eighteenth birthday. He didn't want to wait a single day longer. To him, cars were part of a new freedom associated with adolescence. They e-mailed each other every day of the American tour. For the first time, Katharina was trying out a completely new experience, traveling across huge distances.

"Mom, I'm doing better. Dr. Weise gave me some meds so I don't keep having to go to the bathroom all night. That way I can get some sleep again."

"What else did Dr. Weise say?"

"She's got a theory, but she doesn't want to discuss it yet."

Katharina's first impression after her trip was that he didn't look better, and he had lost even more weight.

The otherwise lively boy was very quiet in his classes. He couldn't focus anymore. An eye doctor declared his field of vision to be severely impaired. He could only see what was right in front of him. Nothing to the right, nothing to the left. Felix, spoiled by his own hitherto excellent grades, stopped concentrating on his exams. The poor results shocked his self-confidence deeply. He didn't understand. He was exhausted. Dr. Weise, an experienced internal specialist with 40 years of professional practice, was puzzled.

"This is really very unusual. All signs point to a tumor. But

I know there was nothing in the scans back in January. I don't understand this. We'll do another scan of the head."

For months Katharina felt the weight of an irrepressible and immovable mental pressure. It couldn't be a tumor wreaking havoc on his system; the Rostock doctors had ruled that out in January. Why so afraid, then? That she might lose her son? She pushed the thought away immediately. Never would she risk saying it out loud, lest the mere utterance degenerate into a self-fulfilling prophecy. Deep down inside her lurked a susceptibility to superstition.

What could she do? For him, it seemed, she could do nothing.

For herself? Long ago, as a ten-year-old, she wrote in a diary whenever she wanted to get out her worries and troubles. That helped. Every day, for ten years. Five thick volumes were born out of the worries of a young girl. Then she thought every problem in her life had been duly processed and resolved.

But now, twenty-seven years after her last diary entry full of pubertal uncertainty, she began to jot down her personal thoughts again. Writing forced her to analyze the facts and actively grapple with a situation that would otherwise doom her to helpless inactivity.

Sunday, September 1st, 1996

The last day before his operation – finally, an end to this debilitating uncertainty. They're going to open his head. Last week we received – against all expectations – the final awful results from the MRI: brain tumor. My hand is shaking as I write these simple words. Seven centimeters in size. The doctors didn't see it for months. Too long. A false diagnosis. Even though it should have been seen in the MRI scans back in January, Dr. Weise said. I can't believe something like this is happening to us. A brain tumor, all along. That sounds horrible. Like a death sentence.

We still have to find out whether it's benign or malignant. Does benign mean it's only half as bad?

I write this not knowing, his last day before the operation, although my fear doesn't feel any different. Meanwhile I think of how the enormous crown of our fruiting walnut tree juts out and casts the garden into shadow, so that the young plants lose the struggle for precious

*life-giving light. If I look out the window to the railroad embankment
across, I hear the savage racket of the freight train hammering angrily
along the tracks, as though it wants to take out me and my fear all
in one go. In contrast, I feel so far away from the time when the kids
and the walnut tree were still small and growing up in the sun in the
garden, and the train to Hamburg would rush past like a ray of hope
for our unspoiled world.*

*This morning Felix is painting the last bits of the new filling station
in his father's agriculture business.*

*Karl gives practical work to everyone who supposedly has nothing
sensible to do. He'd never understand that the students in my school
can get into mischief or even have mental problems. He thinks picking
up rocks will knock the nonsense out of their heads.*

Felix is noticeably happy that he's finally made it.

*From now on the couch is his again, just like every day for the past
eight months.*

*But in the afternoon Olaf persuades him to come back to the cow
barn at Daddy's business, to help out with coating and building. He
lets Olaf tell him what to do, since his brother is, after all, five years
older and more mature than he is. Felix needs the distraction.*

*He's barely even at home Sunday evening! He calls up all his friends,
seemingly without a care in the world, and goes to meet up with them
for an evening get-together. (What would he have done before the reunification, when we didn't have a phone? In the whole area there was
only one phone at the doctor's, one in the school, and one in the co-op.)*

Tomorrow morning it's supposed to get serious.

Katharina was part of the happy post-war generation, who never
personally had to witness a war.

For almost forty years of her existence she lived untroubled in
a country that the later generations might remember calling the
German Democratic Republic, or the GDR. There was no other
name for the country besides those three letters, making it easier to later disregard the traditional name Germany, to which it
no longer belonged after World War II, and moreover wanted to
distance itself from Germany's Nazi past.

She had been born only five years after this dreadful war,
which, responsible for more than fifty million deaths, had come

into its own as a symbol of human madness. If she'd asked questions as a child, she would have been able to learn more from the unsettling stories of her parents and grandparents, eyewitnesses with contradicting accounts. But she was still too young, and the stories with their terrible content barely grazed her consciousness. The grown-ups whispered, when they talked about it, how her grandparents, from what was then known as Liegnitz, had lost everything except for a single suitcase during the war and how the events of their escape from the East were seared horribly into them forever. The escapees recounted their unimaginable suffering often and over and over again.

So these accounts were part of Katharina's everyday childhood in much the same way as her makeshift playground of ruins, flattened debris cleaned up from the buildings in Leipzig that had been destroyed by bombs. Where before there had stood wonderful stately rows of houses from the Gründerzeit, there were now gaping holes everywhere by their house on Alfred-Kästner-Straße. For children, these were great places to play. She thought it was lovely.

On these playgrounds Katharina collected glittering glass fragments of all colors, pretty little gems that had once been part of a magnificent chandelier. She discovered the remains of colorful toys with long since faded colors, and searched eagerly for the pieces that went together. Then she tried to reassemble the treasures she'd found, feeling like a knowledge-thirsty explorer on an excavating adventure in Ancient Egypt.

The six-year-old had a particular love for the overgrown garden behind the remains of an old wall across from their house. No one chased her away from there, because no one owned it anymore. Wild bushes grew so high out above it that one could build their own little romantic hideaway there. Undisturbed by the eyes of adults, together with the wild hordes of neighborhood children, she created a safe and peaceful kingdom out of the excavated bits and pieces of the bombed playground.

As a young pupil she went on the peace education excursions to the concentration camp at Buchenwald. Here she even stood in front of the door behind which the great Ernst Thälmann had been shot. She strolled through the actual barracks, a cheerful and unconcerned child, and looked at the pictures of mountains of withered corpses and heaps of gold dental fillings that the Soviet army had gathered after the camp's liberation.

Very early on, Katharina was confronted with pictures and events that she simply was not capable of grasping. To her, the stories behind these pictures seemed just as inscrutable as the idea of millions of victims in World War II, which was what the speech was about. So she had long since grown accustomed to being faced with this sort of thing, and every time she nodded in understanding, but she hadn't understood a single thing.

Given the repetitive assault on Katharina's ignorance and innocence by the depressing memories of the adults, and the cautionary tales regarding phenomena from Fascist-era Germany, none of it really sank in anymore. Dangerous truths need only be diluted through regular repetition, the shock comes to be replaced by habit and indifference, and people stop asking unpleasant questions.

This was most apparent when it came to the war stories Katharina's father told. The way he told it, his time spent in France as an eighteen-year-old German radio operator had been nothing but a thrilling adventure. In June 1944, when the Allies were invading and his troops withdrawing, he was wounded and taken prisoner by the Americans. Together with his friend Ernst, he managed to escape the prisoner transport and spent three weeks wandering around Germany. Following a horrific odyssey through his war-torn country, where every moment his life was in danger, he managed to reunite with his mother In Lützen, after she escaped from the East in 1946.

Katharina heard this story at nearly every party. As soon as her father had had a bit of alcohol to loosen his tongue he hogged the spotlight, appointing himself solo entertainer for the evening whether his guests liked it or not. To Katharina, his words sounded funny, but she didn't understand what he was talking about, and she soon lost interest whenever he "talked about the war again."

By the time she was finally old enough to understand her father's experiences, he'd told the story so many times, using the same words over and over and over again, that she couldn't stand to listen anymore. So her ears remained closed to the unbearable wrongs committed, and she never had to face up to the gory excesses of human ingenuity that had risen out of ordinary human minds in the name of God, the people, and freedom.

Monday, September 2nd, 1996

I still have two hours of class left. Class can never be cancelled. A teacher always brings a smiling face into the classroom. Never show weakness. Especially as a teacher. Even when I feel like I'm choking on fear.

Felix comes in our red Passat and picks me up from school. His driver's license is still new; he took the test just a few days after his eighteenth birthday. How he did that in his condition is a mystery to me. Three months ago it would have seemed perfectly ordinary.

My father wants to drive with us to Greifswald. The anxiety for his grandchild won't let him wait placidly at home. He's on medication, which he absolutely needs in order to cope with the horrible depression that's haunted him for years. I've learned from him that there are illnesses that can alter a person to the core. It all starts in the head.

Felix will drive by himself. It takes more than two hours of driving through the country roads of Mecklenburg-Vorpommern from Rostock to Greifswald, with tons of little places in between. There's no fast route connecting the two university cities.

At the clinic on Sauerbruchstraße we're waiting on Professor Nahm, the principal of neurosurgery. He has a good reputation as a specialist. I immediately have full confidence in him. I want him, the expert, to perform the operation.

"Does your private insurance cover treatment by the chief physician?" asked the secretary. My heart dropped. No idea. I had never really paid attention to the details of my insurance before. "Otherwise the operation will cost 5000 DM more, to have the chief physician do it." I called Karl as though in a trance and counseled with Grandpa. We were in immediate agreement. Of course we would pay it, no matter what. We would figure something out.

Katharina lead the picturesque life of a woman born in the GDR. She started school at age six on World Peace Day, followed by eight years of polytechnic secondary school (or POS, as they called it), four years extended secondary school, passing the last-year exams with honors, four years earning her degree in English and German studies, with resulting qualifications of the highest possible score. Done.

"When I was twenty-two I had my teaching degree in the bag," she happily pointed out later, in contrast to the teacher trainees on internship, who, during the course of their years-long journey through academia, often grew right past the ideal teaching age before they'd even had a chance to start.

"Done," for Katharina, meant that at twenty-two years old she was available as a qualified teacher of English and German for all children between the ages of ten and eighteen, according to "where the state needed her." She'd had to agree to that in writing at the start of her teacher training. Exceptions possible in case of marriage.

So she married right before her deployment was to be decided, and landed at a small POS with just one class for each grade, in Pammerow near Rostock. She felt happy; newly married, pregnant, and full of idealism and illusions of being able to make the world a better place, if one started with the children. Heaven on earth.

With casualties, she learned how to live. First she was deprived of her husband for a year and a half when he deployed with the army. Second, she lost her child at the end of the first trimester, getting a gold medal in the long jump at a teachers' sports day. She kept her tears hidden. Through her work load, she was quickly able to numb the feeling of loneliness in this little village away from the familiar city. Her idealism and illusions would hold out for a while longer.

"You'll take over as English and German teacher for the seventh grade with thirty-six students, as well as all the English classes for every grade in the school," Principal Hollenkamp instructed her. "Up to now we haven't had a qualified teacher for English. Aside from that, we still need history, music, and biology. – Do you play an instrument?"

"Yes, the accordion."

"That'll do. Then you'll also take on all the music classes for grades 7 through 10." Katharina's breath caught. She'd heard of such unprofessional things from a colleague in the lower level, who had only started a few years before her at Pammerow. In fact, she successfully taught four grades, 1 through 4, which she had to teach all in one classroom in an old building down by the Warnow River, far removed from proper school buildings. The schools in Mecklenburg appeared to be remnants from the last vestiges of the middle ages. Though it was bewildering, she would never voice the thought out loud.

"But I never studied that at university," she objected timidly.

"Doesn't matter. At least you'll recognize the notes. We haven't had that here in ages."

"And how am I supposed to teach history and biology properly?"

"That's part of general education. For history you just need a class standpoint. You'll pick it up soon enough." And with that she was dismissed from the principal's room.

It didn't occur to Katharina to disagree, out of her complete trust that authority must always be right. Principal Hollenkamp enjoyed a special "expert" status in her eyes; surely he had already put some thought into his instructions. Her own upbringing as an obedient child living in this country led her to behave herself. No one ever really asked for her opinion.

She had to be thankful that, with her Saxon linguistic background, she hadn't also been offered to teach Low German. In these parts many of the older people spoke the traditional Low German, even her Karl, but it appeared to be decreasing in the younger population.

So she sat night after night preparing music lessons as well, which took even longer than her already enormous workloads for English and German, and struggled with her class standpoint through the history of the labor movement and the anatomy of the ringworm. As the only music teacher, she took over the after-school choir as well, every Thursday at 5 pm.

Her mother, far away in Leipzig, warned her: "If you want to raise your own kids soon, you're going to have to change your work schedule. Karl is in the army and we aren't going to be right there to help you."

"I know. I'll manage on my own."

Felix has his own phone by the bed in his room at the clinic. He doesn't want to be alone and is calling all his friends again. He invites them to visit him in Greifswald on the weekend. Free of concern and full of optimism. Why does it again strike me, that in 1990 we only had 8.3 telephone connections for every hundred residents?

There are two young men talking in the room, who are doing surprisingly well already following their tumor operation a couple days ago. Secretly I envy both of them their freshly bandaged white heads. They've already got it all behind them. Maybe.

I had no idea that I'd arranged such great health insurance – we got a call back on our inquiry today. I am indeed covered for chief physician treatment. Fantastic!

Felix goes with the other two patients to walk to the nearest ice cream parlor, without getting permission to leave. Then he smirks at the commotion in the clinic like a hero returning from an adventure. Is this another effect of our newfound freedom? I never would have dared do such a thing.

When baby Olaf was born later, she didn't change her work schedule. From the very first day, little Olaf was accustomed to going into his crib at 5 pm. The baby happily slept through the night, waking at 7 am. That saved her.

Why was it that this child radiated so much peace and contentment? Katharina amused herself with her own theory. "It's all down to class standpoint. As early as his own complicated birth, the little one wanted everyone to know his outlook on the world. While five doctors were hovering over me with a bunch of equipment, ready to start cutting away at any moment, the little one greets the whole little world of the GDR with his tiny butt first. 'Leck mi in Ors,' as they say in Low German. Kiss my butt. You can't blame him for it."

While Katharina felt elated after making it through the birth, the radio spent the whole day playing tragic melodies on every station. Walter Ulbricht, the first secretary of the Socialist Unity Party of Germany and chairman of the state council, had died. His hoarse Saxon voice would go down in world history – with the words that reached everyone in 1961: "Nobody has any intention of building a wall."

Olaf didn't disturb his mother's time consuming schedule of school and her classes. To take care of him during the day she had found Grandma Hanschke, a 72-year-old, white-haired, friendly old woman who never took off her grey-checked apron and would happily take care of little ones for a few extra Marks to add to her slim pension. A hard life with a violent alcoholic husband made her look older than she really was. Having had no children herself, she'd raised his four children during the harsh years of and immediately following the war, in which there was often little to eat and the garden behind the house was full of provisions, vegetables, fruit and potatoes, chickens and geese.

With Grandma Hanschke little Olaf was content. She took him with her into the garden and showed him the brown-speckled baby bunnies. She went walking with him, played with him, fed him the supplied puree out of a little cup, and cleaned his cloth diapers.

These diapers were made of woven cotton Katharina had to cook in a large preserving pan, but she could never manage to get the fresh white back again. Over months, despite Katharina's greatest efforts, they slowly turned yellow from the hard, chlorinated water, so that she didn't dare to hang them outside on the washing line anymore. The people in town might talk. She would be ashamed. There were model housewives there, whose lives consisted solely of daily cleaning and washing, and who refused to tolerate a single speck of dust anywhere, let alone raindrops on the window pane. She hung snow-white diapers on her line. It was an example of keeping up with the unwritten laws of the town, and Katharina's guilty conscience grew with every load of laundry.

While collecting the ingredients to make a cake for tomorrow's birthday party, Katharina discovered that she was almost out of sugar.

"Damn it, it's already after six, the co-op is closed by now. But I need the cake to be ready tomorrow right after school. I need to bake it tonight," Katharina thought out loud. She was getting into a panic. Maybe Maria could help?

Katharina hurried to ring at her neighbor Maria's, who also lived on the newly built block.

"Could you lend me some sugar?"

Maria, pleased by the unexpected company, immediately invited her in apologetically. "Katharina, you must excuse the mess in my household, I haven't gotten around to cleaning yet today. Come in." Katharina expected to see a slovenly, chaotic home, even though there weren't any children. But what she saw behind the kitchen door was completely sterile. She saw a lifeless room, where a few books in the wall shelves were ordered by size, a pair of green plants dutifully decorated the windows, and the sofa pillows had been plumped to perfection. That was the way they were, in the little world of Pammerow.

"The important thing is that you have sugar, or else I'll be up a creek tomorrow." Maria did. "I'll get it back to you day after tomorrow at the latest, when the birthday party is over and the co-op is back in stock. Bye!"

Katharina hurried back. Inadvertently she cast a critical eye around her house. She knew that she, too, would have excused the mess to an unexpected visitor. That was something she'd picked up. Her mother always told her, "Your living room should look like anyone could drop in at any time. Otherwise people might talk about you. And your underwear should be clean in case you have an accident and they have to undress you at the hospital." Potemkin villages were very important in this country. First priority was what you put up for others to see, then your own well-being came second. Katharina knew that. Worthless aluminum money wasn't part of it. Of cars as status symbols or the destructive influence of fashion on the mental health of children in school, Katharina knew absolutely nothing, completely unaware in her small little world.

But on the other end of Grandma Hanschke's garden was a gate out of this little world. Lead by her hand, little Olaf stood marveling by the wire grating, behind which clucking chickens laid their eggs, and by the hand-built rabbit hutch, where at Easter in the spring time the little Easter bunnies hopped around. The most interesting thing seemed to be the secrets beyond the gate, where another world rushed by. He marveled open-mouthed at the racketing monstrosity of a steam engine train that was practically thundering through the garden. Grandma Hanschke's house stood directly in front of the high railroad embankment, where the trains roared past on their way back to Leipzig, and the heavy freight trains made the tracks clatter. But some trains also bore metal signs, that were hard to read fast enough from the garden, and rattled past to the unfamiliar destination of Hamburg. Day after day. But it was still met with astonishment in the tiny world of Grandma Hanschke's narrow horizon.

In Katharina, however, it awoke a vague feeling of wanderlust. Hamburg, in another part of Germany, felt just as far away as the London from her English class she'd dreamed of, as though a closed door stood between her and where she longed to go. In both cases, it was a famous city and the capital of a country whose language, features, and traditions she had only studied for four years, without ever being able to go there, much less make contact with the inhabitants.

So Grandma Hanschke's garden also held a certain fascination for Katharina, with its gate to forbidden dreams. The glorious London in her imagination came solely from the pages and pictures of an English lesson book. She was missing the real connection to the people living there, and it brought her crashing back down to reality. She pictured in her mind's eye her idealized version of London, a bastion of magnificence. Aware that she would never be able to travel there, Katharina's longing developed into an obsession, and her unrealistic, dreamy imaginings twisted her perception – it was magical there, like heaven – with free, happy people, fine culture, always green grass, curiosities older than the dirt itself, proof of its noble history, and a contented royal palace, whose merry children wanted for nothing. This heavenly delusion culminated in imagining a rich city without borders, where many different races of people lived together in peace and harmony. She spun fantasies, dreaming of this other world, of heaven on earth.

Wednesday, September 4th, 1996

Felix has his operation today. The operation will take almost four hours. I'm leaving Rostock after the first hour of class, so I'll arrive at about 11. Grandpa will be coming with me again. I don't know who worries more, my father about me, or me about my father. His strong meds have curbed his depression for twenty years now. We're waiting on the first results from Professor Nahm.

This conversation opens up the blackest day in my life: malignant cancerous tissue in Felix's head, right on the hypophysis, the central gland of the whole human system. Total cessation of hormone production, loss of sight, and failure to regulate water balance. Impossible to treat without incurring severe damage, if at all.

What happened to me afterwards, I don't remember right now. Suddenly Karl and Grandma were standing there. They appeared to be beyond the point of anxiety. I also don't remember how I got back. Blackout.

Everything I've ever done in my life suddenly seems to be dissolving into meaninglessness. What really is the meaning in life?

One of the many short stories about meaning in life in the seventh grade lesson book was called "Der Fahrplanschuster," by Günter and Johanna Braun. For the second time Katharina found herself teaching the dubiously optimistic story of the Train Schedule Shoemaker, about a shoemaker who used to (i.e., before World War II) indulge in a curious hobby. The first time, it had been for a unit test on German in a seventh grade classroom, for her teaching degree at Humboldt University Berlin. It had been a success. So she never doubted being able to translate it perfectly into a classroom context, using her prepared questions and answers again word for word.

In the 1930's, the shoemaker fellow's favorite book was the train schedule for the German State Railroad. There, he found fine-sounding names of great cities of the world, like Amsterdam, Stockholm, New York, or Corpus Christi, Texas, but also tiny villages in Württemberg or Oderbayern. He could only dream of fulfilling his longing to travel, though, because the poor shoemaker didn't have the means. But he dwelled on his fantasy escapades all the more, traveling in his mind beyond the borders that in reality fenced him in. In this way he experienced the wide world, a passionate expert on worldly train connections from his timetable, his unsophisticated substitute for real travel.

The incredible art of reading a train schedule and piecing together the most ingenious travel itinerary in the world was equally as difficult as learning a foreign language that you needed in order to travel. And Heimerich the shoemaker perfected the dream of traveling in his fantasy world to the minutest detail, knowing there was no possibility of being able to apply it to the real world.

When the narrator happened to meet the old man again after the war, he told Heimerich that they were now a cooperative society, and when he asked him about train connections, just as he had before, the shoemaker said in surprise, "No idea." But he would have always known the schedule before, the narrator observed. "Yes, *befo-ore*," he said, dragging the word out. "Now I travel myself."

The eyes of the children in her seventh grade class were glued to her lips and there was absolute silence as she read them the story of Fahrplanschuster. Thirty-six pairs of eyes followed the narration attentively. Katharina encouraged the candor and gentleness of these children, who sat surprisingly politely at their tables, hands resting on the bench, materials stacked in a pile on the upper right corner of the tabletop. The experience with city children during her teacher training in Berlin had been completely different. In contrast to the insolent, feisty, disruptive, jumpy and unfocused students there, she felt like here, in the seventh decade of the twentieth century, she had gone back to paradise.

Katharina asked the questions from the reading book on page 94. Even though the questions sounded dry, the children responded eagerly. They raised their hands and waved them excitedly in the air, because they couldn't all talk at once. They seemed so bright!

"What do we learn about the Fahrplanschuster from the description of his appearance in the first part of the narrative?"

"He has had to work hard."

"Think about the way things were before – and the working conditions for the shoemaker and explain the reasons behind his hobby?"

"He was just the assistant in bleak old Winsleben, didn't own anything, and didn't have much money. He couldn't travel. He could imagine traveling really easy, just like you can imagine heaven even though no one's there."

"Why did the shoemaker give up his old hobby?"

"Because now he lived in a country where things were better for the working people and now he was free to travel to all the places that before he could only dream about."

It was that simple. Katharina worked through the questions and was pleased by her class's lively cooperation.

Without thinking about the enormity of the statement, she had lead the children to the incredible understanding that the freedom of unlimited travel was a symbol for happiness, and that the defining trait of socialism was traveling by oneself.

And thus she did the same over and over in her career as a German teacher. Every time, in the same way and fashion, according to plan from the centrally provided teaching aid in the reading book. Always the same pattern. The knowledge of the Train Schedule Shoemaker Heimerich was kept in one of the various drawers of her brain, which she pulled out when planning lessons. Her own inability to travel by herself to England stayed in a different drawer. Her subconscious didn't protest and she never discovered that there was a painful, unrecognized connection there.

Thursday, September 5th, 1996

I'm driving with Karl to Greifswald to the university clinic. He wants to see for himself how his son is doing.

Felix greets us cheerfully in the intensive care unit with tubes ripped out. He had answered the unit door when we rang, the nurse responsible being occupied elsewhere.

His memory is completely impaired; he talks only nonsense, but keeps up a lively stream of conversation. "Go into the living room, I'll be right there."

"Our black cat from Pammerow keeps coming in through the window, that's why I sleep against the wall."

"We got grass to eat today, because the lawnmower is here."

"I was in heaven before, but there was no one there. So I came back."

Mark Twain? Why in this moment does the memory of the story "The Mysterious Stranger" surface in me? – A person pleading to be made happy, the devil obliging by robbing him of his senses.

Karl says nothing, upset, and doesn't speak a single word on the way back home either.

"You are out of your mind! We can't just do something that's not in the education laws." Principal Hollenkamp tried to curb the enthusiasm of his young colleague. His easygoing nature sometimes left him floundering a bit, when it came to the balance between common sense and bureaucracy. It only became dangerous when it came down to his credibility regarding the politics of this state. In that area he would not deviate even the remotest degree from regulation, even if it was a matter of life and death.

She wanted to persuade Hollenkamp to let her seventh grade class take part in English classes for the first time in Pammerow.

"I know English classes are only optional, but that's dependent on there being enough qualified English teachers for the whole country. But I'm right here now. And why should only a few students ever have the chance to learn a foreign language?"

"Alright. On a trial basis. But if anyone complains, we're getting rid of it."

"Yes, yes, I know. English can't exactly be a compulsory class. No one needs it in the GDR," she teased. "And as the language of the political enemy, it's still just a barely tolerated step-child in comparison to Russian classes."

"Stop it." Hollenkamp fended her off angrily. "I will support your attempt. But with stuff like that you can very quickly get in a load of hot water."

"What a bunch of baloney," said Katharina, carelessly voicing her reaction out loud as always. She didn't know any other way.

It was almost revolutionary when, in 1972, for the first time, the television was integrated into her seventh grade class. Once a week she launched the new unit with twenty minutes of "English For You" with Daphne Lösau. She must have been the only native English speaker in the GDR, who could or would want to be used for that. As a young student she married a German professor. Love can convince people to leave their own home countries. For the GDR. The reverse situation would have been called treason.

The children watched and paid careful attention. Television in class! What an unbelievable privilege!

"Can we watch TV again first hour on Tuesday?" asked little Thomas.

"Yes, of course, learning from real native English speakers is the best way!"

"This would never happen in Pammerow!" his bench neighbor Gitti exulted.

"Well, then it really is high time! We don't want to let Mecklenburg sink a full hundred years behind the rest of the world."

"But I don't understand that," said Thomas. Since Katharina knew that these words had something to do with a historically glossed over Bismarck, she let the ironic little observation fizzle out. "And you don't need to," she consoled the young ones.

The anticipation of this Tuesday hour continued almost the whole school year. The corresponding questions to ask as a teacher were in the "teaching aid," which was officially sacred. If you didn't stick to that, you ran the risk of giving a "bad" lesson. Katharina would never dare deviate from that, in case someone sat in to observe her class. For years she asked the exact same questions, exactly as they were written. In these first years of her life as a teacher, she wrote out the expected answers verbatim in her lesson plan.

But she mustered up the courage to establish her English classes for all children without exception, opposing the privilege of Russian to be the only foreign language they learned. For the first time she felt within her the courage necessary to change a mistake made by bureaucratic blockheads.

Friday, September 6ᵗʰ, 1996

God grant me the serenity
to accept the things I cannot change,
the courage to change the things I can,
and the wisdom to know the difference.

(I brought this saying back from America with me. It helps. Serenity can heal the soul. But suddenly I'm doubting that I know what this much-vaunted difference is. Where all of a sudden is my conviction to make the world a better place through nurturing and educating other people's children?)

The school day is slowly driving me off the edge. My colleague Rollauf demands to know what we're going to do with Peter, who has already cheeked him for the third time. And Paul's parents want to complain because their son, who is forever skipping class, especially on Mondays and Fridays, has a bunch of unexcused absences on his report. They want me to erase all the absences of the past school year (really, ME), so they won't know which days he'd been absent. They have already invented a justifiable reason for their son after the fact and signed off on everything. These parents have really earned their dishonest son.

But in contrast to my son, he's healthy as a horse.

I'm freezing. I'm afraid of driving alone to Greifswald. Karl doesn't have the time. His business needs him. Who will come with me? Grandpa. My father always has time. I get in the car and drive with him without thinking – as though in a trance – significantly longer than two hours to Greifswald, because I need to get out of myself. I don't know where, but I'm finally arriving. Nowhere to park near the clinic. I'm standing somewhere.

Felix is still in the ICU, only one floor lower. His memory seems more logical than yesterday, but it's hard for me to fake a happy face for my son. He greets everyone who enters the room all over again, even if they were only gone a short time. He always recognizes me anew and is happy that I'm visiting him. There's a brochure about Greifswald lying in front of him. I'm trying to make a connection with that.

"Do you know where you are?" He smiles.

"Yes, why are you asking so weirdly?"

"Where are you?" He looks out the window a couple times.

"In Rostock."

"No, in Greifswald at the clinic," and I explain to him, what's happened in the last two days. He tries in vain to understand what has happened.

A minute later: "Yeah, I'm in Rostock."

We go together into the TV room, and he seems to recognize elements of the room, because he was here just a bit ago. When I pass on greetings from Ulrike, his dance partner in the Rostock dance circle, he suddenly starts to cry.

"What's wrong with me? Explain it to me." His maltreated brain is flaring up.

My parking near the clinic is going to be penalized. The parking ticket is for 40 DM. There is no excusing a panicked mother in despair *for an hour, the free parking places are for residents only. The law is the law. I should have planned out my parking earlier.*

Her life consisted of plans. Every day at her desk. It consisted of hundreds of pages of planning: for lesson material, for scheduling hours, for classwork, for material distribution, for parent visits, for class trips, for the teaching plan, for Pioneer and Free German Youth afternoons.

And there was also Katharina's life plan, which she had adapted to her work rhythm: change every four years. Four years of primary school, four years of POS, four years extended secondary school, four years earning her degree, four years in Pammerow with Karl and baby Olaf. Now a second child was due, because after four years it was high time. Katharina had been clever and intentionally planned a year longer for the sibling age differential. Her argument: she didn't want to abandon her class that she had taken over in the seventh grade before they graduated after tenth grade, as she had planned. The way she perceived herself, she held the school, classes, and her students in higher priority than everything in her private life. As a result she included a four year gap of staying at home with Olaf on her plan, i.e. she could start making the necessary attempts nine months before the tenth grade graduation.

Karl and Katharina started trying in vain. A man-made plan shows its inadequacy when it is made without the Lord in heaven, her grandfather said, at which she wept her heart out. The child didn't want to come. Month after month they were jolted by the outward signs of failure. They sought consultation. As if she hasn't already known all along measure basal temperature every morning, use the calendar, determine exactly when ovulation is occurring. Adjust love-making to this exact schedule. She had used these methods for years, though of course for the opposite reason, as a contraceptive. She didn't want to go on the pill, she didn't trust chemists. She could narrow her ovulation down to a precise two-hour window, and furthermore it hurt. Despite this, no results. The pure mechanical work, the feeling of concentrating on a designated two hours, nearly cost her her capacity for love. Karl didn't recognize that. Men are different.

After two years they were both tested by doctors for infertility. With no conclusive results. The doctor said to Karl, winking:

"There was a long time during your second deployment where you were exposed to high levels of radioactivity, but that's only decreased your ability to sire a child, not destroyed it. Be careful! It could happen really quickly with another woman." That reassured Karl.

Katharina would have probably taken that consolation badly, if her gynecologist hadn't given her the same theory: it could work with another man. Her uterus fluid was a bit too aggressive for Karl. Which was fine. But a bit embarrassing. Katharina's moralistic and prudish upbringing brought a red flush to her cheeks at the thought of such things. Although, or perhaps because, she had grown up with the nude beaches on the Baltic Sea and therefore connected no shame with the natural naked body, conversations on her sex life were not routine for her. So, for example, during her English studies she'd had to read D. H. Lawrence's "Lady Chatterley's Lover" in English as part of a compulsory lecture. Whether it was her poor English or her inexperience – only ten years later, when the novel was made into a film, did she realize at the cinema that it was about sex.

"You have one child," her mother soothed her. "It's not such a bad thing if you don't have any more. You were also an only child."

"Our family is big enough anyway. Karl's mother was a farm wife on Fischland and had six children," Katharina consoled herself.

His mother had actually read about contraception, in total amazement, in the sex education books by Siegfried Schnabl, whom Karl and Katharina kept on their bookshelves.

Out of the blue, Katharina stumbled across a new hope. The first fourteen days of her summer vacation, as always, were part of an exhausting trip with her incoming class. Exhausting not in part, because the children had been lively or even naughty, but because the active nights got in the way of her need for sleep after a full school year of hard work.

She was lodged in a school in the Erz mountains, and lay on

camp beds and air mattresses in the classrooms. As teacher she slept in the middle of her students, better off by the boys than by the girls, because they had more energy at night. At three in the morning the last one had to pee, some snored, some talked in their sleep. At five in the morning the first one had to go to the bathroom and stumbled with exaggerated care across a friend's camp bed. There was a crash. She held her breath. Nothing had happened. She felt knackered after these nights. But her normally punctual-to-the-day period was absent. Maybe it was just the excitement of the trip? The different climate, that she was reeling from? Often enough in the last three years she had mentally dismissed any delay in her biological cycle, so that she didn't get her hopes up only to come plummeting down. Despite this, there was always a secret wish burning in her subconscious that a miracle might happen. She cried to the heavens, although she had long since abandoned any sort of religious feeling.

"Give me a sign! Tell me if there's no one in heaven, then I'll accept reality and give up. Then I'll never believe in heaven or its happiness again," she whispered to herself. "But maybe there is someone there, who can make dreams come true and turn illusions into reality."

The secret prayer of an atheist in the summer wasn't exactly the bud of a spiritual conversion, but it did lead to the joyous birth of a healthy boy. Felix was double the birth weight of Olaf, his older brother by five years. And so without complication, he was able to present the world the brow of his thick head.

Saturday, September 7th, 1996
The guilt from neglecting my duties as principal compels me to spend all morning at my desk this weekend, to try and catch up what on what I just couldn't manage in the past week.

Afterwards I'll drive the long stretch to Greifswald again. With Grandpa and Grandma. Their grandchild is not allowed to be ill. My parents want to see and understand. Grandma's brought a cake with her. It's Felix's favorite cake, one she always makes, that only she can make.

He greets me effusively like it's the first time in ages. He knows that I'm Mom and that Grandma and Grandpa have come with me.

But today he cheerfully answers questions about where he is with "Wustrow, of course."

It occurs to me that he is always hungry and eats an amazing amount. The nurse in charge laughs about his seven bread rolls at breakfast today. No problem? Unusual, very unusual. But Grandma's cake reminds him of nothing. It tastes good, like he's tasting it for the first time.

With the gorgeous weather we try going for a walk outside. Felix recognizes a fellow patient from the ICU again.

But aside from that he's forgotten everything, even who's already visited him.

CHAPTER 2

She had the English lesson book "English for You" memorized line for line, due to having taught the same units, the same exercises, the same content year after year. There was only just this one book series for teaching English, in every school in the GDR.

Every single year, the children are newly excited to learn English with Katharina, but for her the material has become stale over time.

"The typical English family sits at the breakfast table with their children Tom and Peggy. And the father reads the Morning Star, the paper of the Communist Party of Great Britain." Katharina didn't question the content of the text. She just taught the material straight from the one teaching book. That was what was in it. The printed word had to be true, because it had been printed. Everywhere and always.

Katharina always looked forward to the last hour of class before vacation just as much as the children did. She didn't need as much time to prepare as usual, because she could spend the whole hour reading to them. Just simple reading out loud.

"Goody," exclaimed little Dorothea, clapping her hands gleefully. "We haven't had any real classes yet today at all!"

"Well, then," Katharina smiled. "What would you have instead?"

"Well, Frau Menschke let us write our own poems, and in the hour before that Herr Hollenkamp actually taught us a new song!"

From the ten-year-olds to the sixteen-year-olds, all the students in her various classes followed along eagerly with the stories she read out with great expression. Reading out loud counted as something special, or at least as something other than demanding schoolwork. It was good practice for their ability to concentrate. Even Phillip, the most jittery, restless boy in the eighth grade, and whom everyone called Fidgety Phillip after the ill-fated storybook character, paid attention. Much to everyone's entertainment, Katharina recalled the amusing stories of Lothar Kusche and Elizabeth Shaw. Kusche was part of the circle of authors who had been permitted to travel to London – for whatever reason – and he described his "outrageous" experiences with England's typical weirdness in a collection of humorous stories. A bit of contemporary England from outside the textbook served to fill the whole last hour before vacation. Every year, it never failed.

"Picture it, in English cinemas you're allowed to smoke, eat, and drink during the movie! Candy, nuts, tea, soda, and even ice cream are all sold in between the films! And right in the middle of the main feature the story usually gets interrupted by ads."

"How's that supposed to work?" asked little Dorothea. "That's really annoying! I wouldn't be able to concentrate at all."

Fidgety Phillip yelled in between them rudely, "I would rustle paper all the time and slurp really loud to annoy everyone around me!"

"But I don't think this is really something to laugh about," little Dorothea piped up again. "Then there would be garbage lying all over and everyone would have to traipse around on it."

"That's all typical English," Katharina shrugged her shoulders. "I 've never seen inside an English cinema, myself."

"Why not?" little Dorothea asked.

Katharina pretended she hadn't heard the naïve question.

Kusche's description of a cinema was a sensation for the children and proved to be a vivid, critical example for the demise of a culture in the Western world, just like what Principal Hollenkamp was always saying.

"But they're stupid," Fidgety Phillip blurted out in summation of the story, which was drowned out by the loud and cheerful laughter of the children.

Singing songs was also part of Katharina's repertoire that wouldn't count among her students as "real class," and would be greeted with great enthusiasm.

Every child in the school knew the simple folk song "My Bonnie Lies Over the Ocean," from her accordion. Everyone could also sing the peace song "Blowin' in the Wind." However, the class glossed over the fact that this song was sung by the American singer, Bob Dylan. Every now and then Katharina dared to do a little Pete Seeger with "We Shall Overcome" and "Little Boxes."

But in the four-year cycle of English lessons, comprised of eighty units, only two of those covered the US. They unfortunately weren't scheduled on the teaching aid until the very end of tenth grade, where the last unit before the math tests was often discarded as "unimportant." So the American artists hardly stood a chance.

But her first timid foray into the British Beatles (on whom she'd already tried, during her degree study, to publish a reading that could be used in classes, but the only native English speaker at the English language institute, Daphne Lösau, had thrown it out due to "capitalist philosophy") looked different. Katharina carelessly allowed the children to get excited over the English lyrics. The whole school building could hear them singing "Hello Goodbye" through the closed door, and the Socialist Unity Party secretary Georg Wagner took notice.

"Katharina, I understand that you like music, but this imperialist content simply doesn't belong in the classroom of a socialist school."

For the first time in her scholastic enthusiasm as a teacher, Katharina felt protest sprout up inside her. Only a little protest, but it was the tiny seed that would later blossom and flower into hopeful resistance and, in the spring of the reunification, push Katharina onto the road to Leipzig.

"What nonsense."

"It's not nonsense. You know what kind of damage this deviant culture can do to the youth. I would advise you to stop going off on your own like this. I don't wish to discuss it." Katharina only shook her head defiantly. But she said nothing.

The next time, she taught "Imagine" and "Give Peace a Chance" by John Lennon. All the same, it was with a mixture of protest and trepidation that she told the children these songs weren't allowed in their kind of school.

"I would ask you all please not to advertise publicly that we are covering English pop music in class," Katharina instructed her students, "or we won't be able to do them anymore."

For their listening assignment for "Imagine," she asked them to analyze the text and try to figure out what might have caused the song to be banned.

No one came up with anything. This lack of reaction surprised Katharina.

"Now, 'Imagine there's no countries' could very well be interpreted as an explicit attack on our borders," she prodded. The originator of the ban had written as much. The children were not provoked; there had always been countries and there always would be. But why the song had been forbidden, she would never understand, in her naïve world view, any more than the children of the GDR.

During the long recess, the lyrics to "Imagine" were still up on the board for the next hour. Wagner stormed into the room.

"I want to know right now what you're teaching in here. Is this in any way compatible with the teaching plan? Translate this for me at once."

Wagner was actually a clever person, even if a bit of a Philistine, like the politically small-minded character from Goethe's *Faust*. He lived with absolute belief in a black and white world. Socialism good – capitalism bad. In this school, the word of a party secretary was worth more than that of the principal. He taught history and civics, and knew the meaning of partisanship. He listened silently to the translation, and then said, "Well, it doesn't matter. It's got to be wiped off now anyway."

"What sort of tone is that, Georg?" Again Katharina was filled with a mixture of annoyance, aggrieved self-righteousness, and rising protest. They celebrated their shared birthday together every year with their families. Now who was he? "That's insane. These contemporary bits of Western culture are the only current, relevant things I can use!"

"Come on, now," Wagner muttered.

"Isn't it bad enough that as the English teacher, I can rattle off all the landmarks of England and London by heart without ever having seen them myself?"

"That all you need to do!" Wagner smiled.

"That for ten years I have taught the English language, without any contact with a native speaker?"

"Daphne Lösau," Wagner smirked.

"That my grasp on the sounds of the language comes solely from studying books and an outstanding theoretical class with my phonetics professor?"

Wagner said nothing.

"That I teach the geography, mores and customs, traditions, art and literature, and all the great places of interest, down to every last detail, without any chance of ever once being able to travel there?" She was working herself into a frenzy with her own arguments, even though this train of thought had never once occurred to her before this moment.

"Why is this forbidden? What did I do?" She felt like her emotions had spiraled out of control, and she was fighting the tears that threatened to spill over.

Wagner waved his hand. "We historians also couldn't be at the Thirty Years' War, and yet we manage to teach a good history class." He let Katharina stand.

"You should prepare a bit better for the next party ideology seminar. It will specifically deal with the history of the working class. Then perhaps you'll understand."

In 1978, that was the final shred of any interest she had in history.

Sunday, September 8ᵗʰ, 1996

Once again I find myself spending my Sunday hours behind the desk, before driving to Greifswald to see Felix. Drafting ideas for school, scheduling, doing programs, giving directions, supervising. I can't neglect school. None of it happens without me.

Do I still really believe that?

A short walk with Felix outside. He looks so very, very tired.

Professor Nahm says the problems with his malfunctioning short-term memory are worse than anticipated. It's all supposed to be coming back a lot more quickly – something isn't right. Does he even still have a long term memory? Which is more important: to be able to recall a memory of something in the past, or be able to organize life in the present? Or can one not be done without the other?

But the operation is now a closed case for the clinic.

And what now? And what ... now?

In recent years, Katharina had all but forgotten that her beloved English even existed in the world outside her class in Pammerow. Her passion for her subject carried over quickly to the children. But Hollenkamp warned her carefully every now and again.

"Make sure they aren't getting more excited about the optional English classes than they are about the mandatory Russian. It's a political thing."

So she could indeed help her colleagues organize the Russian language fest, as part of a Free German Youth afternoon, but for English in the 1970's that was absolutely out of the question.

"You can't celebrate the language of the enemy," warned Wagner.

So Katharina tried searching outside of Pammerow for the few cultural highlights in her subject, where she might find sympathizers. She became a member of the GDR's German Shakespeare Society and drove to the Shakespeare Fest Days in Weimar every year. Along with a dignified monument honoring the two great German playwrights, Goethe and Schiller, in front of the German National Theatre, the city had also erected a tribute to the famed English master of tragedy and comedy, William Shakespeare, in the middle of a glorious park. Every year Katharina and her old college friends were drawn again to the wonderful statue of his likeness, which lacked the usual stiff solemnity, instead looking coolly into the distance over the heads of his quizzical spectators. These days at the festival quenched a little of her thirst for authentic English culture.

She could experience *A Midsummer Night's Dream* or *Hamlet* in English in all their artistic glory on the stage of the German National Theater, even if the dramas were performed in the original Middle English of the sixteenth century and could barely be understood. But they heard the voices of "real" English people at the wreath-laying ceremony in front of the Shakespeare monument, and she even thought she spotted English people sitting at the breakfast table at their hotel ...

So the reality she was trying to teach her students about really did exist! And the wise Shakespeare cheerfully greeted her every time, from up on his pedestal. "And don't you forget it," he seemed to remind her, "or else all your efforts will simply be 'Much Ado ...'"

"About Nothing," Katharina finished with satisfaction.

She sat over lesson plans at her desk, the radio humming the latest hits in the background. She worked much more enthusiastically with music.

"A lovely melody. I've got to find a recording for my class," she said and absently warbled a line over again to herself. The bit stuck in her head drummed insistently on her subconscious. "Distant lands are not so far away. I don't know why we don't go ..."

Monday, September 9th, 1996

Felix is being relocated from the Greifswald clinic to the university psychiatric hospital in Rostock-Gehlsdorf. A two-hour ride in an ambulance for him. When I visit him in the afternoon in Rostock, he believes he is still in Greifswald. He seems a bit proud that he no longer answers the question "Do you know where you are?" with "Yes, in Rostock" like on the first day.

A doctor makes a routine screening, but has no idea what's going on. She examines everything all over again, even though everything is written down right there in front of her. She asks questions about his whole medical history again, without seeming to get anything out of it. Is this how doctors react to patients at this kind of clinic? My respect for authority is deeply shaken where doctors are concerned. What a strange woman. There's a potted baobab in the window of her examining room. The plant is barely recognizable as such; it hasn't seen water in about three months. The fleshy leaves have completely dried up into grey, brittle little curls, and the little tree has consumed every last bit of soil in a desperate bid to live. No one here spares a glance for a living thing on the brink of death. All a matter of routine. I remember the words of my grandfather from a very long time ago. "Never trust a doctor who's let the plants in their room dry up."

The year 1979 delivered a blow to Katharina's conditioned respect for authority, and for the first time, truly rattled her self-confidence as a citizen of the state known as the GDR.

"See here, Karl. You have a full program in the field again this summer, and I've got seven weeks off. You really won't need me around the whole time."

"Just do something with the kids again! Or what are you trying to say?"

"I've enrolled in an English course in Potsdam. I've been stewing in my own juices here in Pammerow for seven years now. Just once I'd like to do something for me."

"How much of your summer does this course take up?"

"A full three weeks, including weekends."

"Isn't that a bit much in the middle of summer vacation?"

"That's exactly why I have a chance to get into this course, only twenty English teachers out of the whole GDR can take it! No teacher's going to willingly sacrifice three weeks of vacation for professional development."

"Why's that?"

"Well, it basically eats up their whole vacation."

"Whole vacation?"

"They spend the last week of summer vacation already back getting ready for the new school year."

"Is that all that's left of the seven weeks?"

"Of course not. You know that. We have to spend the first two weeks as leaders for the students' trip."

"You call that work? You all just sit around with kids lazing on the beach, or go hiking." Karl loved provoking her. He had been married to a teacher for seven years, and of course he knew exactly what going on a trip with thirty-six kids from her class would look like.

"Oh, shut up. Anyway, it involves English and there's been nothing worthwhile on that front in Pammerow in years. Always just the same old Marxism and Leninism and a little mandatory pedagogy and psychology for everyone!"

"But your English is already good enough for this school."

Katharina looked at him reproachfully. "Do you know why this opportunity is so novel, and almost unbelievable for me?"

"Why?"

"There are dozens of real English citizens coming along! Not just ones who've lived in the GDR for years and have long since lost their original connection. Real ones from Great Britain!"

"Well, then. Hmm, okay. Then we'll just have to work something out between us for Olaf and Felix?"

"Grandma and Grandpa are fine with coming in from Leipzig,

or surely they could go stay with your parents at the farm in Wustrow."

"Of course."

That settled the topic where Karl was concerned.

Tuesday, September 10th, 1996

Felix is in a room with old Herr Gartner, who's suffering from Parkinson's Disease, but he takes no notice of him. Herr Gartner recounts how Felix went to eat eight bread rolls in the morning and stopped eating because there were so many of them, not because he felt full.

Felix doesn't remember anything from more than three minutes ago. While walking to the bathroom thirty feet down the hall, he forgot which room he belonged in and had to ask the nurses. He admired a purple rose outside the entrance, and forgot about it in the time it took to do a short lap around the flowerbed.

To Katharina's great surprise, the Socialist Unity party organized her summer course at the Potsdam teacher's college in cooperation with the Communist Party of Great Britain. "Your party is barely recognizable!" she cried to Karl, who had just come from the field with dirty boots.

In the world of the GDR, the Socialist Unity Party was officially known as The Party, because in the face of its claim to sole representation, the other so-called bloc parties were virtually meaningless. Katharina didn't find out until after many years that her then-principal belonged to a bloc party, and many scenes from the party ideology seminars became clear. Its members also faced open disapproval in the field of education, and were wary of voicing aloud that they had only joined in a form of protest against having to be a member of The Party.

"What makes you say that?" asked Karl, who had sat down to have a quick supper on kitchen duty, before he went back out to join his workmates in the nice weather.

"In allowing this event, the comrades have forgotten that contact between teachers and the class enemy isn't allowed." Karl waved her off.

"Don't make such a big deal out of it. They'll make sure it's all properly safe." Karl poured himself a fresh cup of tea.

"Incidentally, Wagner nearly got Hollenkamp to deny my application."

"Wagner? Why?"

"Well, you know, he couldn't be at the Thirty Years' War either!" The hot tea almost burned Karl's tongue.

"Your party secretary seems to have a pretty strong influence over the school administration."

"Just like everywhere." Katharina was getting annoyed. "It's the party's main function."

The Party-CPGB connection gave teachers participating in the Potsdam event the comforting reassurance that they would be duly protected from any possibly influence of capitalist ideology.

The courses on England itself were taught by English people from various parts of the country. Even though the entire course revolved around party politics and its contents were strictly controlled by Party officials (the government would never have allowed such intensive contact between native speakers and GDR teachers under any other conditions), it still gave Katharina her first opportunity to talk face to face with genuine representatives of the mysterious Great Britain. To finally get to hear the true viewpoints of the English people from her textbook filled her with wonder. The GDR teachers debated animatedly all night long, extolling the virtues of socialism, to which the Brits were quite receptive, if a bit taken aback.

During the course of the class Katharina got to know Colin and Vicky Draper, a married teacher couple from London, and their two children, Mark and Jane. English spoken by a child! How unusual and cute it sounded!

"A nine-year-old child can speak better English than me," Katharina joked when she was home again. After three weeks her mother greeted her, with eighteen-month-old Felix in tow.

"We learned to walk," she effused, "on the village road, at Pammerow's old fire station."

The heated discussions from the three weeks in Potsdam were continued through an intense letter exchange in English, which was to Katharina, being an English teacher in the GDR, what his train schedule had been to the Train Schedule Shoemaker.

She studied the letters feverishly as though they were install-ments of an English serial, and learned new, modern vocabulary from them. All the details of daily life in England contributed to crucial updates for her English class. Karl fed her counter-argu-ments for every single interpretation of history made by Colin and Vicky. Sentence for sentence.

Katharina sucked down the contents of her first correspond-ence with "real English people" like a dry sponge. She had never before gotten to hear the thoughts of people who had fallen right out of her imagined paradise. These new friends, who had grown up in different conditions, with no border running through the middle of their own country, opened up a window for Katharina, allowing her to glimpse what life looked like outside the GDR. Something beyond the official propaganda of socialist utopia. The Drapers seemed to be GDR-friendly, which from her expe-rience with Wagner and his judgment of "the language of the enemy," didn't make much sense. So she threw out any letters that appeared to have extreme content. She meticulously studied the strange answers to her questions. For the most part she just didn't want to believe the stories that were offbeat to her.

Many of these letters had clearly already been opened. Kath-arina could tell by the ripples on the adhesive edge where it had probably been steamed. Who would be interested in these pri-vate letters? She wondered, but in her political naivete pacified herself with the thought that there were juicy tidbits in there that would interest anyone. Everything was controlled in this country.

"How surprised do you think the post office is, Karl, to see that our enemy England is just voicing friendly criticism of critical friends?" she said, gloating just a bit. "What do you think?" Karl had no answer.

In any case, she kept these letters in a shiny silver tin can, so they didn't get lost in the shuffle of all her many papers. To her, their contents were exciting beyond belief and worthy of saving.

Wednesday, September 11th,1996

Felix goes upstairs for the first time to see Dr. Schmidt, a psychologist. The results are not good and he is physically very weak after climbing the stairs. Her colleague feigns sincere astonishment. Allegedly she determined Felix's IQ to be 130 – I would like to know just how she claims to have found that out in such a short time – but his cognitive performance is appalling, which doesn't fit at all. What am I supposed to say to that?

Karl followed Katharina's excitement with attentive curiosity.

"Do you really think that Brits from London, a city of millions, would want to come visit the tiny village of Pammerow if we invited them?" he asked skeptically.

"Sure. They've indicated interest," Katharina speculated. "For them, our socialist way of life is unusual, almost unbelievable, they say."

"I can believe that. Their world is obviously completely different."

"Do you think it's better?"

"No, just different," Karl grumbled.

So they invited the Drapers to visit Pammerow for the first time. Karl hadn't had much interest in language when he was in school as a boy, and hadn't taken elective English. But he had his wife to translate. The nightlong discussions went round and round.

"Your socio-political achievements are crazy, terrific!" Vicky exclaimed.

"Does it pay off then?" Colin wanted to know.

"It doesn't always have to pay off; our focus is on humanity," Karl said pointedly.

The four kids got on splendidly. The GDR trip to Pammerow wasn't just an unforgettable experience for twelve-year-old Mark and nine-year-old Jane, but also for Olaf and Felix, who were respectively just six and two years old.

The children didn't seem to have any problems with communicating or language barriers. Felix in particular developed an unbridled affinity for the English language during these days, and a special kinship with those who spoke it.

With the promise to write again soon, the Pammerowians hugged the four cheerful Brits and waved fluttering handkerchiefs, as they drove away in their old Beetle.

A letter from Susi, a friend from his former class, brings a smile to Felix's face when I give it to him. He had already forgotten it by the time he read the end.

I skip the local council meeting, instead waiting on a promised phone call from Professor Nahm in Greifswald, who operated on Felix. "Urgent." That word from the mouth of a doctor makes the drama of the situation unbearable.

He calls at 10:30 at night.

The germinoma in Felix's head needs to be treated by the radiology clinic. The problem is that it's surrounded by healthy tissue, right behind the pituitary gland, the central organ responsible for all hormone production. It's not possible to aim radiation so precisely that the pituitary gland won't be affected. But what happens if the center of a person's glandular system gets destroyed by radiation?

Do I have to allow this?

Life or death?

THIS LIFE or death?

I wouldn't wish this on my worst enemy, having to make this kind of decision for my child.

Professor Nahm has communicated with the head of the clinic in Gehlsdorf, Professor Ruhe, and ordered the radiation treatment.

"Listen to what the Drapers have written," Katharina said happily, and reread the letter that had just arrived in German for Karl, as she had so often done, so she could hear what he thought and analyze the English opinions with him, which often were seldom what she expected. Her syllables tripped over themselves as she translated, making the words sound a bit choppy.

"London, August 31st 1979. We are all settled in at home again after the wonderful trip to Pammerow. Even the children were sad to have to leave.

It was very interesting for us to drive a couple hours from the GDR to Britain via West Germany. The most obvious difference between the GDR and the others is the pervasive promos and ads everywhere. The first city we came to in West Germany was packed with ads, generally in the most trivial and ridiculous ways. And of course every single shop window was glittering and gleaming full of colors that made GDR shops look very dull. They all compete with each other for space. And naturally there are more cars and better streets, both in West Germany and Britain. We got caught in a Western-style traffic jam in Hamburg and an hour-long one in London. We wished we were back in the quiet streets and public transit system in the GDR."

Karl smirked. "That's one way to look at it. It sounds like they had a really good time here. See, the GDR isn't all that bad!"

In the next letter, Colin seemed to concede Karl's point in responding to their questions.

"London, June 27th 1980. You asked about London, the perfect city? You know, today I went from Wembley to downtown and suddenly found myself in a very anti-capitalist, pro-GDR mood. Maybe because a couple of skinheads were loafing around the tube station at Tottenham Court Road. The platform was filthy. Litter all over the place and old newspapers just tossed around. Vandals had smashed both of the vending machines. The walls were smeared with obscene graffiti that you can't even laugh at – just the opposite. (The only good thing was something feminist. On the dirty wall there was a tattered poster of a naked woman, waving her finger. She was meant to look seductive – to sell cigars – but someone had scribbled the slogan "This degrades women!" over her face in blue ink.) Yes, I was beginning to long for the clean, wholesome GDR, in the middle of all this capitalist filth."

Katharina's naïve, idealistic visions of the idyllic and wonderful world on the other side of the wall were always put into perspective with these letters from the Drapers, even if not for long.

"London, February 8th 1981. John Lennon nostalgia is still sweeping the nation. Lennon's albums have been topping the chart since he was shot at the beginning of December. The whole country is still in mourning. Everyone's whispering on busses and trains about the big Yoko-John love affair. There are pictures everywhere of John and Yoko, and the stores are all re-selling all of his records. In just the past few weeks, four books about him have already been written, published, and hit the shelves. It doesn't matter to the media or the stores that Lennon was a radical leftist. They would sell Karl Marx on every street corner if they could turn a profit from it."

"That pretty much sums it up," said Karl.

"London, September 11th 1980. Can you not believe the Solidarnosc strikes in a socialist country like Poland?

For example, let's look at the head of Polish radio and television, Maciej Szczepanski – the strikers demanded that he be dismissed from his post. One reason they wanted him fired was because he refused to broadcast their grievances on air. But the other reason was his 'socialist' lifestyle. According to the official labor union (not the strikers), the case of Maciej Szczepanski is now being looked into by a special committee of the Polish United Workers' Party. It's accepted that he owns seven cars for himself and four for his secretaries. Besides that he has two aircrafts he uses for official business, a helicopter, and a two million dollar yacht for his own personal use. The discharged Szczepanski also reputedly owns a sheep farm near the Soviet border, a villa in the Zakopane mountain resort, and hunting grounds near Kenya's capital, Nairobi, where he spends his winter vacation. It's even said that Szczepanski employs 31 servants in his villa and farm. Of course this all has to be proven – but he's been let go and the official labor union has made these accusations public. Thus it's very probably that it's all true.

The other problem with Poland, of course, is that they don't have an elected government. In East Germany, Czechoslovakia, and Bulgaria there's a form of majority for socialism (the Social Democratic and Communist parties in East Germany); but in Poland the farmers' party was elected, Stalin threw their leader in jail, and brought the PUWP to power in their place. As a result, there's never been support for the communists in Poland, which is also made clear by the fact that more than 90% of the population go to church on Sundays."

"Where on earth is Colin getting all this information? You've got to be careful about believing this sensational media stuff," said Karl.

"London, June 26th 1981. No, we don't have a teachers' day in Britain like you do to acknowledge our teachers' accomplishments. We wouldn't dare! It seems like a wonderful tradition to me, if bouquets of flowers are filling up the schools and class-rooms. There's no recognition for teachers in Britain or the US, especially not in the larger cities. Of course, I wouldn't want to give you the wrong impression there. You have to understand, there's little recognition for any arbitrary job in our culture. It's fairly normal to openly detest your own job and all the others. The public officials are the most hated, e.g., politicians, judges, attorneys, and public servants. Teachers are more appreciated than them, at least.

By the way, if there was a shortage of teachers here, qualified teachers wouldn't be deployed. The GDR did that in 1949 too, when the pro-Nazi teachers were fired. So it's not impossible."

"It must be damned hard to work as a teacher when your authority over brats is openly undermined and respect for cooperation is going down the tubes. Being a teacher is more than just a paid profession, isn't it?" said Karl.

"London, October 16th 1983. You're drowning in plans and preparations for your class, and you're unhappy when the students don't succeed at their assignments? In England we have people who are specially in charge of sorting out paperwork and organization details. There's a principal, who doesn't teach any classes and just handles paperwork. Then there's also a deputy principal, who only teaches four or five hours. And aside from them there are still others who teach nine or ten hours. No, the individual teachers don't plan much. We have our lesson plans approved years in advance, and all we have to do is enter the students' grades into a register. Everyone who gets 45% for the whole school year passes. Everyone with less than that fails. Where's the problem? If they're working properly or would rather spend their time in clubs, that's their own business and they get let go. "The expected performance after a year"? There is no expected performance. Every student in a class can fail, or everyone can pass. That depends on them, not on me. I do my best as teacher. I don't try to be God. It seems to me that the GDR education system is trying to play God."

Karl raised his eyebrows and looked at Katharina questioningly. She just shrugged her shoulders.

After the first round of radiation with Dr. Libernicht in the radiology clinic, Felix is allowed to spend the weekend at home.

Old friends come to visit him. He is very unsteady on account of his memory, but he recognizes all of his old friends without a problem.

Today Karl drives Felix back to Gehlsdorf and does some intensive practice with him on remembering the room number 7, so he can find his way back to his room after going to the bathroom. His recall only lasts less than three minutes. Any longer, and the number 7 is already wiped from his memory.

A second letter from Susi came, this one with photos. He's pleased, and he seems to remember who Susi was. Is she already in his long-term memory? It's the same as with the first letter. He's already forgotten the beginning of it before he reads to the end. Where does his short-term memory end, at three minutes? No one can live like that. At least not independently.

On May 24th, 1982, a curious letter was stuck in Katharina's mailbox. She never received anonymous personal letters. She opened it in surprise and tried to wade through the text, messily typed by a typewriter. Was the first sentence supposed to be English? Unintelligible. If it was supposed to be English, the first sentence was full of typos that rendered it completely unreadable:

"'Prust the withal goiath plie together and the god well bigt the way!' These words will bring you good luck! The original is in the Netherlands. It has gone around the world five times. Now the luck has come your way! Nine days after receiving this letter you will have good luck, provided you copy out this letter twenty times and send it on. This is not a joke, good luck will come to you through the mail. Send this letter to people who you think could use some luck. Don't keep this letter!!! You have to make twenty copies and wait and see what happens. This dare was written down by a missionary from Venezuela. I'm sending it to you so that the dare goes around the world. Send it to your friends and family. After a couple days you will get a surprise. This is true, even if you don't believe it. A farmer in the Alps didn't send the letter on, a couple days later he and his livestock were dead. An office clerk passed it on and won two million in the lottery. His son Fandit threw this letter away, a couple days later he was dead. There is no reason in the world why you should break this chain. Don't forget!!! Don't send any money!"

Katharina felt something like annoyance and unbidden inward fear rise up in her. She believed her English was quite good, but she couldn't make any sense at all out of the first sentence. Even the crude German left something to be desired. Aside from that this letter contained an extortive death threat – superstition wasn't at all part of her general mindset, but what was she supposed to make of this? The Erika model typewriter with blue paper would barely hammer out three copies clearly. How on earth was she supposed to reproduce this nonsensical letter twenty times? What was really behind it? The writer couldn't possibly believe this story themselves! Was it just for fun? Why was this kind of letter coming to her in Pammerow, of all places? Because of the muddled English sentence? An extract from an English bible? Maybe it was from her students? But they would never make such idiotic English mistakes. She read through the letter again. Damn it, she swore silently. This could have maybe been heard through a telephone and written down without knowing any English. Mucked up beyond recognition, which was aggravating.

Katharina hated superstitious claptrap. She folded the letter back up emphatically. She wasn't going to respond to it, but she could feel guilt rising. Should she rip the letter up or just throw it away instead?

"What a piece of shit," Karl laughed. "Just chuck the thing out!"

She hesitated. She had learned bible verses in her religion class as a child. There she'd heard about Satan's devices. They brought misery and misfortune through unexplained magical forces. Would it be better to follow the advice of the mysterious letter writer? What were they trying to tell her and the many other potential recipients? Was someone tangibly benefitting from this? The post office? But there wasn't even a stamp. A spiritual message for her?

"Oh, what garbage." Uncertainly she stuck the letter into her English dictionary. Maybe she'd at least have to chance to figure out the English sentence.

The psychologist Dr. Schmidt is starting with tests (computer, etc.). Felix always seems to be teased again and smiles deprecatingly at the "rude" questions, but forgets them much too quickly. He shows alarmingly low memory retention.

We go for another walk in the park. The flowerbed with the purple rose and three benches from before still isn't in his memory.

Grandpa actually comes here on his bicycle to see his grandson. It's about nine miles to Gehlsdorf, and he's seventy-two years old and has been an invalid for the past twenty years due to severe depression. Now he's exhausted, of course. He's used all his strength just to make it to Felix. He's struggling. I would have picked him up in the car. But Grandpa doesn't want to bother anyone with his wants or needs, preserving his autonomy by any means necessary, never depending on anyone, he would rather risk his own health. This generation has the experience of a World War behind them.

Needless to say I bundle Grandpa together with his bike into the car.

Wednesday, September 18th 1996

Today I drive with my mother to see Felix. Grandma: " Grandpa was completely knackered last night." Felix: "Well, he came here on his bike." – What a ray of hope! Felix remembered, even though Grandpa's bike expedition was almost twenty hours ago!

I'm very anxious for today's tests. We have to find out if his tumor has spread to his spinal cord. The doctor with the dried up baobab has to try to tap into Felix's spinal cord to determine this. I say "try," because she's started three times and it was a catastrophe. Felix screamed in pain. I had to hear it from outside with Grandma.

After the attempted puncture he'd lost all the memory capabilities we'd painstakingly built up over the last few days. He dissolved into tears and was even afraid of his wheelchair.

Towards evening I sense that along with the slow oblivion, the puncture has also brought him an inner peace.

Flustered, I call Olaf, who had the same experience in Gehlsdorf years ago. He confirms my distressed reaction. "Don't let them tap him again." Naturally I feel uncertain. My whole life I've always been sure that experts and politicians inherently know what's best for me. After all they're cleverer than I am. So I thought. It's always been easy to unnerve and intimidate me. And life is just easier, when someone makes the decisions for you and you don't have to do it yourself. So I thought. But that was a long time ago.

I go up to the smiling doctor and, without explaining myself, but very firmly and angrily, revoke my written permission for the spinal tap.

CHAPTER 3

"Guess what, Duncan, for my teacher training I got assigned to a little school out in the country." Reni Meyer was looking forward to finally getting to properly work with children in a school setting. She had a tall, slender figure, and her long, wavy, light blond hair was pulled back into a simple ponytail that bobbed saucily from side to side with every step. She blinked her huge blue-green eyes directly into the sunshine, where her boyfriend stood.

"Good for you. It's really cozy out in the country. The world has yet to be spoiled there. Where exactly have you been assigned, then?" He stared at her fixedly, as though searching for something more in her gaze than her words could convey.

"Pammerow, is what my university advisor told me. I'll be in good hands there. She rolled her eyes weirdly when she said that. She thinks I'll have a lot of problems, because of you."

The University of Rostock was always abuzz with student activity. In particular, much attention was lavished on the superior posts assigned to teachers receiving their training. In Pammerow, Katharina was always pleased when these 22-year-old student teachers, with their youthful verve and fresh ideals, completed their three months of teacher training with her at the end of their program. And it had worked out again this year. This time, she would be mentoring a student of both her subjects, English and German.

During the long recess, Katharina walked out of the faculty lounge over to the school secretary in the building next door. She was expecting a call from Potsdam. Her friend Angelika wanted to sign up for a visit at Pentecost. She would have preferred to write a letter, because telephones were hit or miss for Katharina. She didn't have one at home, almost no one did in Pammerow. She was allowed to use the secretary's phone, if the need arose, and so Angelika was able to call her friend through the secretary.

"Everything is set for your Pentecost visit to Pammerow," Katharina said crisply into the gray plastic phone receiver, still out of breath. "I'm looking forward to the days off. Somehow I'm once again in desperate need of a vacation, even though my student teacher has been a huge support for me."

"What? You're mentoring another student teacher again? Why are you always saddling yourself with so much extra work? Practical teacher training always ends up being an insane project for you. Every hour preparing together, observing, and analyzing every little thing bit by bit, hammering out methods with hours of demonstrative teaching. And every single minute of the hour has to be elaborately planned out."

"But I enjoy it. Why are you so upset?"

"I've already done it myself plenty of times. You spend whole afternoons discussing practical application of dry methodology theory that no student teacher remembers from college. And there's almost no time to spend with your family," her friend complained. "No one's paying you for this time. You sit restlessly at the back during her lessons, because she's too inexperienced to be able to handle class discipline. The brats won't take her seriously, because she's 'just a student and not a teacher and isn't the boss of us.'" Angelika mimicked the high, snotty tone of her pubescent eighth grade students.

"They're all the more delighted when you go back to teaching your own class again – they didn't even appreciate it at all anymore," Katharina chimed in, laughing softly, and with one sentence swept the problem off the table.

"And if she isn't any good, you and your lesson plan go into a tailspin and then you end up taking all the blame, too," Angelika persisted, "and you won't even get a thank you. By the end of the school year you'll be worn down to your last nerve."

"Nee, nee, I won't, icke doch nich." Katharina briefly slid back into the laid-back inflection typical of Berlin that she had adopted to conceal her old Saxon accent during her four years at Humboldt University, with Angelika. In Berlin, being a Saxon meant you were doomed beyond all hope. There was a good deal of prejudice leftover from old stories or even from the recent past. The building of the Berlin Wall had, after all, been denied with a Saxon accent.

"There's still a little idealism left in people. This country needs good teachers." Suddenly the line crackled. "And if it sounds trite and preachy, our kids are the most important thing we have in life. If we lose them and they just slip away until one day they're not there anymore, then we are poorer than we can imagine. And who's supposed to do it, if not us?" Now she was on a roll, wanting to defend the blond Miss Meyer. "This student is good. Someone should really make something out of her. You know, I'm convinced that good teachers aren't just good sports, but they're actually capable of moving this unforgiving world."

"My God, I'd love to have your idealism. You aren't allowed to do anything on your own, you're always being controlled. What are we, as teachers? The doormat of the nation."

"Nonsense. Good teachers can affect a lot, as long as no one takes away their independent thought and their reputation doesn't get destroyed by overt cynicism. Good teachers aren't just made through studying books. Good teachers live out their lives as good role models. You learned all of this in your own training! And besides, it's fun for me."

The principal's secretary silently looked up from her work with raised eyebrows. Then she deftly laid a blue bow between two pages and tightened as precisely as possible between the rolls in the typewriter.

"From your lips to God's ears!" said Angelika. "Just think of how in spite of all that, overzealous, overworked teachers end up getting sick and depressed. And then they can't put all that idealism of yours to use. Make sure you yourself don't fall flat on your face with your precious idealism ..." Again there was an annoying sound over the line. "Others call the shots in this state. You can't just train the teachers based on your own ideas!"

Katharina chuckled into the receiver. "I've got to get off now. There's someone waiting behind me. Recess is over, I have to get back to class, to Miss Meyer. I'll see you at Pentecost, in Pammerow. Give my best to your family."

"Then we can philosophize some more. All the best. Ditto."

The attentive secretary appeared uninterested and continued to type with exaggerated enthusiasm at her typewriter.

"Something's wrong with this old phone. It keeps making weird sounds. As if someone's listening in on the other end," Katharina quipped, before leaving the office.

Felix is getting a different room, and after all the days spent train-ing him to remember Room 7, now we have to switch it to Room 11. It seems hopeless again today – he stills answers "seven" when we ask him his room number. He can't even find the new 11 coming back from the bathroom, because it's the other direction. He has a new neigh-bor in the next bed over (blood clot in the brain, was driving the car, didn't come home for four days, family called the police to help look for him, two kids – 25 and 23 years old). Felix can't remember his new roommate's name – nor does he understand why the room number 7 is wrong now – it's now inhabited by a patient who broke his spine bungee jumping. It's all madness here.

I'm anxiously seeking advice from outside observers. The brother of one of my colleagues is a professor of brain surgery. She puts me through to him on the phone tonight. He suggests calming down. Tap-ping is meant to be done as a precaution. I'm torn. You get stuck in the middle of this madness and can't fight back. You have to do everything as a precaution. Shit.

The small faculty lounge at the school in Pammerow barely measured six and a half feet across. But it was a little more than sixteen feet lengthwise, so that the teachers had to spend their recesses wedged tightly into a long row of chairs together, eat-ing their breakfast rolls with a freshly brewed pot of coffee. It faced a long, light brown wall of cupboards, as was common in GDR living rooms, with attendance registers and a worn Ger-man dictionary on the bottom shelf. Higher up, under a thick layer of dust, was a red six-volume edition of the Selected Works of Lenin, next to the twelve blue volumes of the Selected Works of Marx and Engels. Every so often Katharina reflected on the magnitude of the collection, which, if it had been up to her, would have been left out. Further to the right was a soccer tro-phy that had been won long ago, and still further over were a couple of forgotten copies of "History of the German Labor Movement." The long table with its colorful tablecloth com-pleted the ensemble, making for an overall unintentionally funny picture. In spite of this, the atmosphere was companion-ably cozy, where they could talk to one another as friends, and just had to share their little triumphs and tribulations. There were no secrets in this staff lounge.

"Norbert didn't bring his homework today for the second time, and tried to tell me that he doesn't understand anything in my class anymore. Just mine." – "Yeah, yeah, he tried to tell me that too and I almost bought it. And then on top of that, he completely wreaked havoc on Miss Meyer's last hour! But if you say..." – "Well great," interrupted Ingrid, who was Norbert's class teacher. "His mom swore up and down to me at the last parent-teacher conference that she would talk to him about it. I'm going to go right back into my class when we're done here and resolve this."

The individual teachers' problems were often nipped in the bud, because being able to confide in each other meant that no one was left alone to deal with whatever misadventures were carried on behind the classroom door. Ill-behaved children had no chance of playing the teachers off one another and annoying them. They did their best to be consistent and instinctively support each other, like one big happy family. Any chain is only as strong as its weakest link. The little group of Pammerow teachers took this notion to heart when it came to their business: the children needed to be accepted by everyone, and to have a set of guidelines for coexisting at school, consistently enforced by one and all, which allowed them to learn undisturbed and perform to their appropriate level. One teacher couldn't just yell "gee" and the other one "haw." That went for everyone who worked with children. Even parents, even families, even media.

And so Reni Meyer wound up in this harmonious, open group of colleagues, with the heavy burden of a secret weighing on her that she felt she might be able to rid herself of in this teachers' room that inspired so much confidence, but her previous experiences at the university had made her cautious.

Due to the closeness of the small room, the school's teachers mostly spent their free periods working at home, when they could indulge themselves in some distance. Almost everyone lived in Pammerow or in the immediate vicinity. And so it happened that Katharina asked her student teacher – two minutes away, around the corner – to her little house right next to the railroad, so that they could discuss lesson plans in peace.

Professor Ruhe, the head of the clinic, is stepping in now. Together with Olaf, I go have a talk with him, since I refused a repeat of the spinal tap. He's very persuasive for both of us, but discerns that after our experience with the doctor with the dying baobab, treatment will need to be with the head physician. He wants to perform the next tap personally. Reluctantly I give in.

It was supposed to be a weekend break at home. Felix was already home, then his doctor called; the sodium content in his blood is too high (180), and he has to go back into the clinic for an IV drip. He gets four more liters of glucose today, and six by Sunday. I must say it's 'lucky' he forgets everything, so I'm the only one depressed because I have to drive back.

Felix got an acceptance letter to a computer science program in the mail last week, so this morning I officially signed him up at Rostock University – it's only a couple weeks away and his memory problem still needs to subside before then! I'm trying to be optimistic.

"Oh no, the freight train really drowns everything out here, Mrs. Stern," Miss Meyer noted, as she came through the squeaky garden gate for the first time. "How do you stand it?"

"I don't," Katharina realized with some irritation. "At the time we were happy to buy Grandma Hanschke's house when she got too frail to take care of a house by herself. Luckily we knew her very well, because she'd looked after our son Olaf for two years as a toddler. She trusted us enough to sell to us seven years ago, when it was basically gold dust during the housing shortage. Since then I've tried to sleep in every room in this house at least once, to try and escape the racket from the train," Katharina explained. "I'll never really be used to it."

As soon as they stepped into the study, where a window had been left open to air out, Reni Meyer's attention was fixed on the next train.

"Does it go to Hamburg? That's what it says on the sign whizzing past. You'd just need it to stop once and then jump on!"

"Ah, you seem to have an interesting sense of humor. We're just going to completely ignore this train. Hamburg, the door to the world? That's nothing to do with us."

Reni was quiet. So this was Pammerow. Simple Pammerow. Here she would be in good hands. This was what Duncan had meant, when he said the world was unspoiled here.

"Coffee?"

"Yes, please."

"Where should we start? The next English hour?"

"I'd rather go over the last hour of German first, when you weren't there. I have a couple of questions." The eager student let her worries all spill out chaotically.

"I never could have predicted Norbert's behavior in my first German hour without you. The whole thing was completely thrown off because of him. He just doesn't have any interest, I don't think he has the mindset for learning. He was actually really cheeky to me. Said my lesson was boring." Katharina leaned back with a smile and crossed her arms.

"And I didn't have a thing to say to him. Even his mother would have said that. I just wanted to throw him out of the room, but I'm not supposed to do that."

"No," Katharina agreed.

"So I confess, the objective for the hour wasn't achieved. It took four hours to prepare and write down every question ahead of time. Everything down to the letter, based on the teaching aid. I memorized the whole procedure by heart, barely slept the night before – and all for nothing. What disciplinary measures can I use to make sure it doesn't happen again? Punishments are part of house rules; that way everyone knows what they're not allowed to do."

Katharina listened quietly to her student's bitter description of events. "Didn't the other students pay attention to the lesson?"

"No, they did actually. But you know it just takes one to throw off the whole team."

"Well, in this instance you'd better let me deal with Norbert. That's the advantage of your teacher training. I'm always here at the ready as your mentor; they're ultimately my classes."

"But discipline has to apply to everyone. And if it's not working, you have to expand your disciplinary measures."

"Well, you know, discipline by itself isn't enough. It's much more important that the majority of children – easygoing, mature children – don't feel oppressed by a system of rules that was only put in place to regulate the small minority. It's always a question of what is appropriate to the situation."

"But it really hurt me. It used to be that if students didn't want to learn and behave themselves, you just put them in the detention room for a couple hours."

"You can't be serious! Did your great grandfather tell you that? Believe me, our work as teachers is also to set aside our own feelings, and prioritize the feelings of the children, even if it's difficult sometimes. You obviously can't take any of it personally. There are many reasons why children don't behave the way we'd like them to. And that is not the fault of the school."

"I've got to correct you there, though. You can check in every newspaper, school plays a crucial role in child development. I would always blame myself if something went wrong in class."

"Commendable." Katharina's voice carried a hint of derision. "If I were to tell you right now what you should do, you would run the risk of never being able to handle your own problems. But I'll give you a small tip: excitement is contagious. If you understand what I mean by that. You have to carry across your own enthusiasm somehow. It's self-evident that a school environment where people feel smart and good while they're working is more effective in the long run. In this respect, a classroom is like a theatre stage. We are here, as professionally trained experts, to play a role. Because there are times and situations where we just have to keep going in spite of the difficulties."

Reni nodded, and Katharina continued.

"And stop clinging so desperately to a dry lesson plan when you're working with real live people. Plans don't account for human weaknesses. Children aren't always predictable. They have tempers sometimes, or they panic out of nowhere or get scared. They follow the herd mentality, and they can be lethargic, or frivolous, or defiant. That's not even mentioning their hormonal urges. They're just people."

"But you still need a basic education plan. Not everyone can just do whatever they want."

"Plans are only very tenuously related to what you actually do here. Teaching requires genuine intellectual energy and communication. It's an illusion that lesson plans or a whole school environment can be completely planned out and arbitrated from above. Yes, we need the basic education plan, but at the end of the day behind every classroom door is a teacher standing alone, adjusting this plan based on their own strengths. Even you! Dictation of pure theory is no substitute for the quality of your convictions, your ideas, or your creativity."

Monday, September 23rd 1996

The weekend ended up being organized around the infusions. Karl and I went to visit Felix every day and helped him with memory training. Yesterday he actually remembered walking through the flowerbed for the first time!

The dreaded spinal tap with Professor Ruhe proceeded with no pain, no problems.

We take shifts watching him to make sure he stays in bed. 9:30 to 12:30 me, 12:30 to 3:30 Olaf, then Karl starts at about 4.

By evening, Felix is too tired. He doesn't remember anything anymore, not even the spinal tap with Professor Ruhe. On that front, it's good for Felix that his dysfunctional short-term memory erases any traumatic experiences, and so he can't be depressed by them.

Tuesday, September 24th 1996

Grandpa's heart attack was later recognized as being the third one he's had in his life!

Felix brought Grandpa back to the bus stop today after just a short visit, because he wasn't feeling well. The problems with Felix overshadow everything – the old man would do anything to be with his grandchild. And he always pulls himself together again. He is still needed.

Felix's friends come to visit and give him a cup with the inscription 'we love chaos, therefore we need you.' As if they've caught the double meaning of the situation? Young people get to view the world through rose-colored glasses!

Felix looks noticeably bloated. Water retention. Six months ago, when his body wouldn't retain any water because of his undetected tumor, we used Minirin to reduce urination. But apparently it was too much? Even the doctors are relatively helpless when it comes to fluid retention. There are too many of them involved in treating him, and the left hand often doesn't know what the right one is doing. Every new doctor who comes in has to read all the records anew, ask all the questions over again, can't quite connect the dots. Sometimes I think I'm the only one who knows what's wrong with him. But no one believes me ...

Reni Meyer spent the entire time scooting back and forth on her chair, restless and obviously a bit anxious. She still desperately wanted to ask something private, even if she found her mentor's philosophy shocking. At last she screwed up her courage and interrupted the conversation.

"I also have another problem, Mrs. Stern. I can't come to class on Thursday and Friday next week. I have to take a long weekend off." It was the first time that she had even come near to alluding to her secret.

"What, just because? We don't have vacation time. What's happening then?" Katharina asked.

Reni squirmed around at first, but then she looked her straight in the eye. "My boyfriend is coming to visit."

"But ... " Katharina was momentarily at a loss for words. "You boyfriend visiting is no reason to stay home for two days in the middle of your traineeship. Every day counts. Couldn't you get together another weekend, like maybe Pentecost?"

"No, that wouldn't work."

"Why wouldn't it work?" Katharina felt uncomfortable at the thought that she might have to straight up say no here. But the young woman hadn't even asked permission, she had just issued an announcement.

"Because my boyfriend lives in America and can only be here during a specific week. Duncan is a professor of American history at the University of Providence and he just comes in occasionally as a guest lecturer at Rostock University."

Katharina was speechless. The state was allergic to this sort of fraternization and exceedingly vigilant. Even the act of holding hands was seen as akin to fleeing the GDR. Her thoughts were in a jumble. Was this why Reni Meyer's university docent had asked her so sanctimoniously what she thought of her new student teacher? The question had sounded almost sarcastic, as if she already assumed the student must be horrible. Had anyone there already come under pressure because of this liaison? She knew that Rostock University employed native speakers as guest professors, and that an American was among them. But he must have been well into his mid-forties. Was that him?

In fact, in a manner of speaking, the girl was actually very lucky, thought Katharina. Only twenty-two years old and she was already learning authentic English quickly. Katharina suddenly realized she'd have to watch out for Reni Meyer's deep nasally American accent, since she was supposed to be teaching British English and didn't want to confuse the children.

Katharina didn't try to pretend not to be surprised by this information. There had been just a few seconds of silence while Reni waited for her answer, but now she shrugged her shoulders helplessly.

"Well, if you feel that you absolutely need to take these days off ... ?" Reni Meyer's face relaxed.

"He's already offered to come into one of my classes as a native speaker and teach the kids about American traditions and typical American games." Her eyes were lit with enthusiasm. And Katharina found herself being swept up all at once. This was clearly a wonderful chance to teach with a native speaker who used the language every day! He was teaching at Rostock University anyway, wasn't he? And he was friendly with Miss Meyer, surely he wouldn't demand any compensation for doing this too!

"That sounds really good! We just have to work out which part of the syllabus he'd fit into!"

"You've said yourself that it's okay to deviate from the syllabus, if circumstances call for it. I think in these circumstances we could shove regional studies of America somewhere in there."

"You're right. Maybe he'd even be willing to organize something outside of class for us? We have to come up with a Free German Youth event every two weeks anyway, that could easily be sports."

"Baseball is a typical American sport. He would certainly have fun with that. I even know the rules."

"But I don't," Katharina pointed out.

"We can take care of that. Then it will be a real lesson, for students and teachers alike."

In no time at all, the mentor-student conversation had turned into a professional dialogue of questions about the class that would teach American way of life, both of them excitedly buzzing with ideas.

Thursday, September 26th 1996

After an hour and a half long walk through the park, we come across Professor Ruhe, who sits with us on the bench by the infamous flowerbed. He expresses concern about a possible "accident" during the operation. Perhaps a memory nerve has been damaged? He wants to do another MRI scan to look for any possible trauma.

Felix's sodium content is back to normal today. But through the infusions and the water retention connected to that, Felix is very heavily bloated. He's weighing in at 187 pounds (as opposed to 145 before the operation). Professor Ruhe gives him permission for his first weekend break today.

Reni Meyer had gotten permission for the vacation days for Duncan from Katharina, and agreed to teach two hours more on other days to make up for it. She neglected to submit a written request to the foreign language department. Such bureaucracy would have only meant a lot of unnecessary commotion and paperwork, since it was an exception to the rule.

When her unusual boyfriend – and he was unusual in this part of the world for various reasons – was in Rostock, he walked with her everywhere, when his schedule permitted it. Love had struck here, in all its powerful, intoxicating glory, even though the man was twice the age of the young student. As the two of them sat with Katharina in her study, to prepare for the sports session, her besotted gaze went inconspicuously here and there and their fingers touched furtively behind their seats. Katharina pretended she saw none of this. She felt awkward, not being one to show her feelings on the outside. All of a sudden she realized was an outsider observer with the view of Shakespeare with the feuding families of Romeo and Juliet, but it was none of her business.

Duncan Miller was nothing like the German idea of a serious

American professor. Lean and athletic, with a roguish grin, he wore a knitted brown wool sweater, casually thrown on over a checked shirt with its blue collar gaping wide open at the top. His rugged blue jeans boasted the washed out streaks of pants that have been worn at every possible opportunity.

"The title isn't that big a deal for us," he said, waving off Katharina's question about himself. "If I'm not going to have any fun working at a university, I might as well go be a waiter in Providence." Katharina gave him a skeptical look. He smirked again. "And I wouldn't have any problem with it."

"So now that we're trying to be gym teachers and baseball coaches for the first time," Reni interrupted, "where can we get equipment for the kids?"

"There are American students in my study group too. I know they brought bats and balls with them. They'll help us out."

"Alright. Then we can head out now. – Where did we park the car?"

"At the front of the main street, hopefully not in a no-parking zone."

The car was not in a no-parking zone. But the foreign license plate number proved highly interesting to certain sets of eyes.

Friday, September 27th 1996

Felix wakes up every two hours in the night, disoriented. There's just a thin cardboard wall separating his little room from our bedroom. We leave the door open, and luckily I can hear every movement, since I'm such a light sleeper, and can steer him back into bed and comfort him. By morning it feels like I haven't gotten any sleep either.

We have to go to a localization appointment in the radiology depart ment at Rostock's Südstadt clinic. The only radiology expert available right now is Dr. Libernicht. He's in touch with Tübingen (University of Heidelberg?), where a few special cases like ours are being researched and the findings are being shared and discussed. The team of Professor Baumberger and Dr. Becher – no idea what it means!

He decides to treat the spinal cord with radiation. Twenty doses, 1.5 Gy.

Supposedly Felix's brain tumor has a high rate of recovery, even if the shape is atypical for its age. It's not unheard of among children. In any case, the histology is going to be examined one more time.

My subconscious is wildly excited. This sounds like a new sliver of hope.

Felix has lost four pounds since his Minirin dosage was lowered to once per day.

Saturday, September 28th 1996

In spite of the weekend at home, Karl is driving Felix to the Gehlsdorf clinic to check his blood levels. Hopefully they're fine!

No, they're actually keeping him there again because his sodium content is 157, which is apparently life-threatening. He's getting a liter of glucose infusion which was supposed to take six hours. So I'm driving there six hours later, feeling rather sour and dejected. But the doctor with the dying baobab has left instructions for Felix not to go home, the one day wouldn't be worth it. I protest and simply take Felix with me. Sometimes it's worth it to ignore inhumane bureaucracy. It's good for mental health. Sometimes the authorities struggle. But even authorities are just people.

At home, phone call from the locum physician, seems to be an embarrassing situation. Whatever.

Sunday, September 29th 1996

We're at home. Felix sleeps up through 10 o'clock. Today I'm struck by his rampant appetite.

Lunch: a whole roast chicken, no salt

Coffee time: half a cherry cake from Grandma

Supper: three eggs, half a roast chicken, cheese, sausage, bread

And he still weighs four pounds less than yesterday!

(That damned water in his body as remedy again sodium is gone today.)

From then on, Duncan Miller accompanied Reni with increasing frequency. He also brought along an American student from his Rostock seminar every so often, so that they could demonstrate realistic speaking situations in English class. Together with the students they sang "We Shall Overcome" and "Wimboway," with Reni accompanying on guitar. The students were flushed with joy. Their liking for Miss Meyer and her fun, lively language class improved the young ones' learning efficiency by leaps and bounds.

Out on the playing field, the seventh grade class attempted to learn the game of baseball with great enthusiasm. Even Felix Stern played with them and raved about this method of learning English. "I was standing there, not even knowing how to properly hit a baseball, and then took off running like crazy when everyone else started shouting. But we were yelling and speaking in English, like at home when the Drapers visited us from London. It was amazing!"

No one in the school, not even the school or party leaders – who weren't witness to what went on in practical lessons behind the closed doors of the classroom – was aware that contact with Americans at this school could disturb anyone in the village.

"Reni, I've got a huge favor to ask you," said Katharina. By now she addressed her active, hardworking student as an equal.

"What's that?"

"You know that I'm the specialist advisor for all the English teachers in the district. Part of that involves being on a committee with seven creative people, who meet regularly to develop new solutions for better English classes and test them out. We also try and have our own self-improvement meetings so we can keep our professional abilities in shape. In most of our rural schools there's just one lonely English teacher stewing in their own juices."

"Do you want me to come along and collaborate?"

"I wouldn't have anything against it, but you only have a few days of your teacher training left here. And once you're out of reach, Duncan will be, too. But when we played those interesting baseball games together, I thought that would definitely be something for next year's committee program. Can you imagine what it would be like for our English teachers to have a native speaker at the meeting? None of them ever have a chance to use their English skills on site or socialize with anyone from England or America. Next week we're meeting to discuss the annual work program, and I could just bring it up with them then?"

"Yeah, if there's no senior office that has anything against it? I'll ask him. I know he's coming back to Rostock in the spring semester of next year. Then it would work perfectly. Why would he say no?" With a wink she added, "And that also gives me a reason to see you again."

Katharina was pleased.

Of course Professor Duncan Miller would agree.

Monday, September 30th 1996

I've found my savior: Professor Mann from the Rostock University clinic, head of the endocrinology department (expert in endocrine disorders).

He is the first one to listen thoughtfully and attentively to my observations and complaints, and put them together with the medication.

Felix is going to go in for a CAT scan at the university clinic at 3 o'clock. They'll take an x-ray from all angles, and put it into 3-D form. Great technology. Though it'll involve a fair amount of radiation too. We have no choice. An ambulance is taking him there.

After work my maternal instincts urge me to drive to Schillingallee, just in case. And sure enough, Felix is still sitting there, waiting for something that he doesn't remember anymore. No one knew he needed to go back to the psychiatric hospital in Gehlsdorf. Once again, there seems to be a recurring problem getting the left hand and the right to work in tandem!

So I drive him back to the clinic, in the middle of the horrible mid-day traffic. We welcome his new roommate, who is from Güstrow, 31 years old. Ticks have gotten to the neural cells in his spinal cord. Felix barely takes any notice, he is just too tired.

In the TV room there's a patient sitting in a wheelchair and smoking like a chimney, a huge hazard for cancer patients.

Next appointment for new MRI: tomorrow morning at 8:30, Schillingallee. He has to lie still in the tube for forty-five minutes. If he can remember where he is for that long. The pictures will be more exact, luckily it's not the X-ray again.

The members of the English teaching committee met to evaluate their work for the 1984/'85 schoolyear at Café Meerschaum, a cozy little café on Kröpeliner-Straße, a stately pedestrian street in Rostock that was steeped in tradition. Outside the five-gable house, over the café, was an impressive, newly installed glockenspiel that had been crafted by Peter Schilling, the master belleter. The little troop of teachers listened to the captivating chimes in surprise. It seemed as though the perfectly pitched bells wanted to draw their audience's attention to the hour that was being struck. From there, Katharina could make out the university square with its statue of Field Marshal von Blücher, who'd had to fight so many battles in the name of freedom, and she saw the frisky, controversially cosmopolitan sculptures of the Brunnen der Lebensfreude, by Reinhard Dietrich and Jo Jastram, which for five years had invited tourists to pause and reflect. She herself never stopped here and accordingly contemplated the sinking sun, or the long shadows it cast over not just radical sculptures or battle-fighting field marshals, but also over extraordinary events.

Their usual dull meeting room in the 'House of Teachers' on Blücherstraße was lacking in atmosphere, something the by-now well-acquainted circle of teachers insisted upon for their last meeting of the school year. It was nice to sit and enjoy a cup of coffee and some cake, and share their personal experiences with the new teaching ideas as part of a casual conversation. Worries and hardships didn't come into it. The warm friendliness amongst them grew out of an occupational loneliness that was an inevitable part of teaching English in their district. As with all the schools, they were decidedly lacking in male colleagues, despite the official legal guarantee of equality. Looking closely, one might notice that those few male teachers more frequently occupied managerial positions. They didn't have to be absent as much, for biological reasons. On the other hand, it should have been a mark of good leadership that everything still ran smoothly in one's absence. That was Katharina's opinion.

Most of the teachers on the English committee shared her fate. A single teacher was sufficient for all the elective English periods at each school. Without this contact with each other, every individual teacher ran the risk of getting tired of the habitual rut of daily life and losing their once vivid creativity.

Today they were going to hash out the work plan for the coming year, and Katharina asked Heide Schmidt from the school in Weisertorf to write the minutes, which the committee would need to turn in as proof of their work. Heide always worked very neatly and never left any mistakes.

Then Katharina brought up her momentous encounter with the American professor and the game of baseball.

"My student teacher is acquainted with a professor from Providence, New England. She was able to persuade him to visit her class in Pammerow. You know, it was really spectacular and refreshing, to liven up the class with a real American."

"An American? Did she get permission for that? Guests have to be registered, we can't just let any old person into a school," Heide said skeptically. Katharina laughed easily. "I gave her permission myself. Why even bother with all that bureaucratic red tape? The classes went great with him as a guest."

"Isn't it really difficult for you with American English?" asked Dörthe Pagel, from the school in Sonnenhagen. She admired Katharina for her self-confidence. She always doubted the quality of her own classes, although her zeal, studiousness, and the length of time she spent preparing for lessons bordered on self-destructive. "Don't you teach British English? Were your students even able to understand any of it?"

"I admit, even I had to listen closely to understand his accent. But the children thought it was so exciting, they could barely work up the guts to ask him questions or join the conversation. I just want to know what else I can try to get the kids to talk more freely."

"That's not what we want," Dörthe murmured in her timid way.

"What do you mean?"

"Why do you write down the answers you expect to your questions when you're writing lesson plans? So that nothing else happens in the room besides what you planned! The children aren't looking for their own answers, they're looking for the answer you want!"

Katharina detected an unusually sharp ton Dörthe's to criticism, which she didn't want to agree with.

"And with Professor Miller we don't have these expectations. They would rather ask themselves something, instead of being quizzed. But instead of that, they've practiced asking their neighbors "where do you come from" even though they already know. Nothing that you would ask in real life."

"Yeah, yeah. Life-relevant classes – that's what the theoretical postulation is called in the new methodology textbooks. With the slogan "create real-life situations for English classes, unless of course they're situated in capitalist countries?" scoffed Elke Winter, from the school in Heidesande, and the youngest in the circle at 23 years old. "How did we learn English? By applying it in practical situations?"

Ulrike Möwe waved dismissively. She hated abstract discussions about things that couldn't be changed anyway. She had been teaching for fifteen years at the school in Wiesenborn, where nothing like this had ever been discussed. "We're not teaching English so they can talk to people from England and America, that never even happens."

"No," Elke objected sharply. "The best real-life situation is in the teaching aid: "Imagine you're in Prague at Wenceslas Square, and suddenly someone asks you for directions in English. What would you say?"

Everyone smirked knowingly.

"It also works with the Red Square in Moscow," Dörthe added, and was surprised when no one laughed at her contribution. Only Elke made a dubious face. After all, she also taught Russian.

"Well, whatever! I think a meeting like that would be an enormous benefit for us, linguistically," Katharina said. "I heard of a colleague who just did a course in Potsdam where they conduct English seminars. She said it was incredibly fun and reinvigorated her spoken language skills."

"Of course, being taught by a native speaker is surely the most intensive form of learning a language. First hand is always more authentic," noted Clockshagen's teacher, Eva Zauder, who had made herself comfortable in the back corner of the wooden bench that framed the round table. "But aside from development for Russian teachers, no one's aware of that here, or else it would be mandatory for English teachers to do their teacher training in England."

"Now don't start yammering. Katharina knows from her colleague Wagner that the history teachers also couldn't be at the Peasants' War, and they still manage to teach a good lesson anyway. You don't have to have gone to England to be an English teacher. 70,000 English teachers in the GDR are proof of that," Elke teased somewhat bitterly. She had long since felt undervalued in her little village of Heidesande. Katharina corrected her. "It was the Thirty Year's War, not the Peasants' War."

"It doesn't matter anyway." Elke always got right to the point. She had both feet on the ground and hated beating around the bush. "In any event, we should use the opportunity. Let's get down to specifics. Who? What? Where? When? Why?"

Tuesday, October 1st 1996

At 2 o'clock I drive back with growing mistrust to Schillingallee first, rather than Gehlsdorf. And sure enough, after the MRI Felix has been sitting for five (!) hours in the waiting room. He had already forgotten why he was sitting here, though seems contended nonetheless. I must suppress my thoughts, or I'll wind up with my father's depression. Forgetting is not the same thing as suppressing, on both a small and large scale; a damaged brain unconsciously struggles with the sickening incredibilities of human failure. If I could do it the way I wanted, I would simply disappear with him and go search for help myself. But I can't just do that. So we move again through the traffic to Gehlsdorf. Felix suddenly says he doesn't know how to get there. He is 'glad' that he doesn't 'have to' drive the car.

On his eighteenth birthday in March he successfully passed his driver's license test and since then has chauffeured us all everywhere with increasing enthusiasm. He got his very good sense of location and direction from his father. Just good. There's a detour in my brain where the synapses for sense of direction are supposed to connect.

Surprise in Gehlsdorf – Professor Mann from endocrinology, the expert in hormones, was there in person because of Felix and has settled a few changes in treatment with Professor Ruhe:

- *Adjustment of medication (like I myself had suggested, experience corroborates science)*
- *Eye exam (even before the operation, his field of vision had shrunk to only a third of what it should be)*
- *Private TV for Felix as device for memory therapy (every time he watches a film he's already forgotten the plot by the middle of it)*
- *The competent Dr. Engel instead of the dying baobab doctor*
- *"Cherry tree" as the first word to get him to remember*

Isn't it crazy that by now the damaged short-term memory nerve, which was just a tiny surgeon's mistake, is now a bigger problem for Felix than his missing hormones?

Without memory, without ideas, without thoughts, the hormones don't matter to personal happiness.

Katharina jumped right in. "Does anyone here know the rules of American baseball?"

"No, why?" came the surprised chorus from the other side of the table.

"Cultural studies. Part of that. We could learn to play baseball in English with the professor, and he might be able to bring a couple of his American students with him who are taking his spring semester course in Rostock. Real-life application of the language. But there aren't enough of us, so we could invite all the English teachers in the county."

"Good idea." Ulrike perked up – finally something concrete. She hated weighty discussions about things she couldn't impact. "But I think if we're bringing in foreigners specially, the event needs some firm ground to stand on. Just playing baseball with people who don't know anything about sports, isn't that a bit weak?"

After thinking a moment, Eva spoke up from back in her corner. "What would you all think if we invited the gym teachers too? You've got such great colleagues at your school, Katharina. And I guarantee there'd be interest at my school, too. They may not speak any English, but we could create a real-life language situation out of it: interpreting back and forth!"

General agreement.

"Great. I'll ask the new gym adviser, Herbert Just. He'll be pleased, because he hasn't finished his work plan for next year either. This would be something different," Katharina thought out loud.

"And where are we going to get a decent playing field for this? We don't want to make fools of ourselves. Something like this would be a strike back at the GDR," said Elke, this time not joking, her face serious.

"You're right. In Pammerow, our crappy gymnasium is down on the Warnow, where there aren't even decent toilets. Not exactly showing off," Katharina said. "The best and nicest gymnasium in the county is actually in Clockshagen, it was just built a few years ago at Wilhelm-Pieck school. Doesn't the gym adviser live there, too?"

Eva, who taught English and gym there, didn't necessarily want to be at the forefront of this project. It meant extra work, preparing. She didn't respond right away.

"Sonnenhagen, Hanitz, and Blankenhagen also have a lot to offer," Dörthe said. Then she spoke directly to Eva.

"Eva, what do you think? Could we do this at your school? We just need to know if the gym is free for the date we want."

"Well, I'd have to ask my principal. Why not?"

Months later, they would all look back on this tentative agreement from the back corner of the bench with regret and horrible discomfort.

Dörthe slurped her coffee, which had already gone cold. "And after that, we could all finish off with a cup of coffee. Hospitality demands it." Slowly their excitement grew at planning an solid event.

"And we can each bake a cake – from a German recipe, I've heard American cakes aren't very tasty," said Heide, who feared that Weisertorf would be chosen as the venue. Her principal didn't hold much with new ideas.

"Does Wilhelm-Pieck school in Clockshagen have suitable room with a good atmosphere? We can fix it up ourselves with tablecloths and decorate it a little," she continued.

Eva stuck out her bottom lip and thought a moment. "Yeah, there is."

Dörthe's excitement was aroused. "And then everyone who's interested and has time can come together for a nice little chit chat. And if even the gym teachers want to stay, translating is such good training for us."

Before the small group dissolved again, to return back to their respective villages, Heide, in her order-loving way, asked what to put in her notes.

"What should we call the event in the yearly work program to turn in to the educational county board?"

"Baseball as a popular sport in the USA."

"And when exactly?"

"April 3rd 1986, 2:30 pm."

Wednesday, October 2nd 1996

Intensive eye exams, and the first piece of good news for our stressed minds: Felix's eyes are back to normal!

How is that possible? I don't believe it!

Second piece of good news: the MRI showed that the first ten radiation treatments have significantly shrunk the remnants of tumor.

Hope? I dare not believe it. The part of my brain that releases joy reacted as though paralyzed. Not a bit.

Felix isn't allowed any salt. His sodium level is at 150, weight 81 kg.

After the first round of modified radiation (still on the spinal cord, as a precaution, but only 1.5 Gy), Felix looks drained.

He remembered the word "cherry tree" and seems to remember the room number 11. He even remembered that on Monday his Wustrow grandma went to Stralsund to have an operation on her knee. A small glimmer of hope is sparking back up inside. The wish is father of the thought. I hope I'm not counting my chickens before they're hatched. Sometimes that happens.

Professor Duncan Miller came with Reni Meyer to Katharina's house in Pammerow on March 2nd, to arrange the details for the event. Now the car with the foreign plates was parked at the front of the main street again. The village was too small for this to go unnoticed.

Duncan was looking forward to the two-hour event they'd planned.

"I can bring a couple American students from my class who love baseball."

Thursday, October 3rd 1996

It's a holiday for the new Germany, Felix is allowed to come stay at home. Why was this day in October chosen as a holiday? Is there some historical reason?

His medication dosage has fallen to me, naturally, as he doesn't have the capacity for it yet.

- *Half a dose of Cortison (15 mg morning, 10 mg at night)*
- *Tablets taken with water twice a day (Torem)*
- ¾ tablet thyroid hormones
- *Effervescent calcium tablet twice a day*

I'm not even sure if I have the capacity.

We watch Felix while he spends an hour reading a copy of a news magazine called 'Der Spielball', as though he's discovering a whole new world. 'How safe are computers?' it asks. They're talking about massive data theft! He reads to me that the world of computers and the data net are a paradise for spies of all kinds, that intelligence agencies control the international traffic of data and even infiltrate security systems and that even the super secure bank networks can be tapped by professionals.

"Unbelievable. Now the robbers are smarter than the inventors. This can't be taught at school," Felix says. "Teachers don't know how to do it. How do people even get these criminal ideas – that would never even occur to me! But my biology teacher talked about these archaic suppressed urges that can't just be wished away."

There is more to the world than lying in a sickbed, doctors and clinics. His long-term memory at least appears to be functioning.

He takes note of today's holiday, aware of the day of the week and the date for the first time. Olaf and his girlfriend Stefanie play skat with him, to work on his memory and attentiveness. But by evening, he suddenly can't concentrate on the movie he was watching.

The gym adviser Herbert Just had accepted the invitation of the "English ladies" right away, putting it into his work program. In gym class they played "burning ball," which was supposed to be similar to baseball, so the offer appealed greatly to his gym teachers. Katharina called all of 'her' schools in the county and invited any English teachers who were interested. They had gotten official permission; the advisers' superior, Marianne Zauschke, had nodded generously and also wanted to inform the school inspector. The school principal agreed "since the bosses don't have anything against it."

So more than thirty participants met in the early afternoon in Clockshagen. To Katharina's surprise and joy, Duncan Miller brought eight more American students with him.

"I had no idea that so many of you were studying in Rostock! It's really lucky, this way we can play and interpret in a bunch of small groups."

The gymnasium was a fine specimen of a sports facility, gleaming with cleanliness and furnished with brand new, modern equipment. This would really impress the foreign guests.

The eight young students from across the Atlantic peered around this fabulous gym, still somewhat reserved, not quite believing their eyes. None of them said anything, because they didn't want to blatantly slip up. They had expected something different. But what?

The rules of baseball were quickly explained, even if the non-professionals had some trouble translating them. Reni helped to the best of her ability to distinguish the batter from the pitcher and the catcher from the runner. At first the balls flew helter skelter through the gym, to general amusement, and Ulrike and Dörthe ran erratically around the diamond. A few of the athletes were greatly amused. Katharina, who had played the game a few times now, confessed that she was still learning. After ninety minutes of intense play, Professor Miller blew the final whistle and everyone marched in their sports gear into the main building, to round out the afternoon of sports with a cup of coffee.

In her usual hectic way, Eva had whirled away an hour ahead, so that she, as the hostess with the nicest rooms in her school, could get the Pioneer room ready for their large group of people. The table was laden with matching white cutlery that the teachers had brought in from home. The coffee machine, also brought from home, was ready and waiting so everyone could have coffee right after their baseball game. The silver packet of coffee mix, produced by the GDR, was 40% coffee substitute. Since Americans were said to have no idea about proper coffee cake, today they would be shown that GDR products tasted good. Six appetizing, delicious-smelling cakes and cookies, baked by a few of the members of the English teaching committee themselves, were arranged in a circle on the table. Dörthe had even brought candles and colorful paper napkins. And so the table emerged looking quite festively decorated. On the wall was a picture of the first president of the GDR, Wilhelm Pieck, who looked down on the table in a friendly, benevolent sort of way.

"Ah, how nice! How beautiful! What a wonderful school!" With astonished faces, visibly surprised, the American students entered the room. Before they could do anything else Reni began to order them about, in her easy, boisterous way, so that they would mix with the teachers and not all just huddle in one place talking to each other. "Every American should pair up with a gym teacher, plus at least one English teacher to translate. That should just about work out!"

What a German tradition, thought the American students, coffee and cake at 4 in the afternoon. The one side, exchanging meaningful looks with each other, recognized this as a typical German activity from American guidebooks. The other side saw it as an obvious part of everyday life, particularly when there were guests. Who was really learning from whom, at this event designated for the development of GDR English teachers?

"This coffee tastes wonderful, and very different, ours is either much thinner and in a bigger cup – or too strong in a teeny tiny cup."

The homemade cakes were a delicacy. "This tastes so much better than the ones we have at home, we get cakes from the grocery store and they're so sweet that they stick in the mouth."

The ice had been broken. The Americans thought their cakes were great. Surely in the country of unlimited possibilities something as trivial as a simple cake – a homemade one, at that, and therefore cheaper – wouldn't be worth mentioning. And their boring old coffee mix? Better not to say anything. After all, they wanted their guests to have a good impression of the GDR.

Although the conversations and their translations started out timid and quiet, the small groups gradually grew louder and livelier. Insouciant laughter and incredulous questions filled the room. The young Americans described their huge, wide country, which even they hadn't explored completely. There wouldn't be any time or, more importantly, any money to travel to other countries. They talked about their problems with financing further education, of tuition and student jobs. Of drug problems. Controversial opinions on socio-political situations in both countries were boldly flying around, such as the significance of the Berlin Wall, which no one could imagine living without. And many of the large group of teachers praised the GDR, with its many advantages for the ordinary people, more than they normally did in the course of everyday life. The warm, friendly, open atmosphere didn't quite match up with the way Katharina pictured America, based on what she had learned. She couldn't stop herself from declaring her thoughts out loud.

"You are all such a great group. If you only knew what we've heard about you on the other side of the Atlantic!" She wasn't expecting the guests to answer her proclamation. But the students reacted quite unexpectedly with the same observation, almost in a whisper, so embarrassed were they at their own preconceptions. "If you knew … you can't imagine what we're told about you at home, when we were preparing to study abroad in the GDR! – But none of it is even remote true!"

Naturally, their hosts wanted to know more. "Like what, for example?"

"Well, for example, that everyone is being controlled by the Stasi – state security, that they had all the rooms bugged and at least one of them always sat in on meetings like this at schools." Everyone laughed.

"I heard that almost everyone here only speaks Russian, and hardly any English. But you all speak English!" Even a couple of the athletes nodded.

"Or that you're all really naïve and aren't allowed to talk to us. We heard you're supposed to be totally oppressed and can't express your own opinions!" Again everyone laughed, because everyone in this circle did indeed have opinions.

"And that the buildings and schools are all gray and run-down. But just look at this school, and the terrific gym!" Everyone smiled at Eva, whose ears had gone red with embarrassment.

"We heard there's no good food or commercial products. They should all try your cake!" More loud laughter, though a bit more subdued.

"We thought you all walk around like the Vietnamese, in blue smocks." At this sentence Ulrike Möwe snickered quietly. "I really have to ask who is more naïve here, you or us," she murmured to herself under her breath.

Everyone was free to go after the coffee-and-cake meeting, if they had things they needed to deal with at home, or were otherwise pressed for time. But no one left. Most unusual, after two hours of educational development. No one left.

The half hour set aside for coffee and cake became one hour, two hours, three hours.

No one left.

Dörthe was the first to rise. "I'm afraid I've got to go get my daughter, Kindergarten is almost over."

Both the English and the gym committees agreed that it had been a successful event. They even felt something like pride that they had managed to shift the young people's perception of the GDR a bit, and rouse their sympathy for this country. The young people from the United States of America had finally gotten to witness it with their own eyes.

As they bid farewell, a small American student with smart black horn-rimmed glasses expressed interest in the German language. "What's the difference between 'sehen' and 'gucken'?" Eva thought a moment. "There isn't any."

"Well then, auf wiedergucken! See you later!"

Eva only realized the difference between 'gucken' and 'sehen' a few days later, when saying 'auf wiedersehen' was banned.

Monday, October 7th 1996

The weekend brought a mixed bag of new discoveries. David Watts from Australia published the medical history of his brain tumor on the internet. He describes being aware of every process he went through. When I read it, I realized that it's actually a blessing that Felix has already forgotten everything from yesterday.

But why doesn't the Australian have any problems with his short-term memory? Does Felix have lateral damage unrelated to the tumor? Then again, Felix is aware that he doesn't want to forget everything. Together with his friends he begins to write down what happens to him. And then he reads his own descriptions the next day like the story of a stranger who happens to be named Felix.

Yesterday he began to keep a proper diary. Felix realizes that his own life is rushing by, without being able to remember any of the days.

Ten years ago today, we celebrated the birthday of a different republic. I remember the holiday. I wrote a greeting card to Reni Meyer in Providence. The card was never received. She still lives there today, but her (or his?) love changed to a more simple friendship. She never found out why we weren't allowed to say 'auf wiedergucken.'

'The best and most interesting development meeting I've ever been to,' must have been heard throughout every staff room in the county the next morning. Later no one could say whether the English teachers or the athletes had raved more. Only that their glowing reviews had caught everyone's attention. The best? And most interesting? There had to be some mistake. With Americans? In Clockshagen?

"What idiot gave their permission for this?" demanded the district school inspector, her voice booming portentously down the line on the county school inspector's phone.

That morning Katharina received a phone call from Marianne Zauschke, from the educational county board.

"Katharina, I think we might have made a mistake. We have to go see the district inspector today. Along with everyone who helped put this together. I don't know why the department is going crazy. But don't worry! It was a really good afternoon! I heard that from all sides."

Who could think the meeting had been inappropriate? Why should Katharina worry? Nothing could be blamed on her. To the contrary, she had organized an exemplary publicity event for the GDR's image.

Tuesday, October 8th 1996

Today Felix has to get up early to be on time for his radiation at 7:30. He recalls right away that it's Tuesday, that he's been home for a few days, and to some extent even recalls everything that's happened.

When I come to Gehlsdorf to see him in the afternoon, he remembers the TV show he's been watching for two hours, but nothing about lunch.

Professor Ruhe says he met with the doctor who operated on Felix, Professor Nahm in Greifswald. During the operation he must have hit (metastasis around the pineal gland) and damaged the hippocampus. That's what's responsible for transferring memory from short-term to long-term. It's not clear whether there's a mechanical injury there or it's just irritated. The last MRI wasn't able to verify.

We hope the damage is reparable. Professor Ruhe keeps talking about chemotherapy to follow up the radiation treatment, while Dr. Libernicht agrees with the hypothesis posited by the Heidelberg University team in Tübing that this tumor can eventually be killed with radiation. I would be so happy if there was an alternative to chemotherapy. Who knows what other parts of his brain would be destroyed by the side effects?

Felix has to stay under supervision in Gehlsdorf, even though I'm on fall vacation – I feel depressed, and a touch of the old fear flickering up inside.

The education department of the county council was a depressing gray building, with numerous tiny windows that barely let any light into the room. It was located on Rosa-Luxemburg-Straße, just over three hundred feet from the district council with its swanky estate and stone gate. It was ruled with an iron fist by the district superintendent Lola Harms, whose voice made the county board shiver.

(Katharina heard long ago of their proverbial devotion to Margot Honecker, the unimpeachable Minister of Education – her title had been given the German masculine form on every written ministerial directive, as opposed to the feminine *Ministerin*.)

She was capable of spreading fear. When she came to inspect a school, she checked with her index finger to see if there was any dust on the classroom cupboard of the teacher whose class she was sitting in on. If so, this hour of lessons was off to a very bad start. Katharina had heard of this, but not believed it, the same way she disbelieved (or rather, suppressed) any description of abuse of power or injustice in her country.

The supposedly competent county board scurried from that very building, alarmed and upset, back into their cramped dark offices with hundreds of files full of dry regulations. Not a single green plant thrived in their windows. They had no place for blossoming flowers or ideas.

The superintendent wore a precisely tailored gray suit with the party symbol conspicuous on his left jacket lapel. His white handkerchief was stiffly starched and freshly ironed. He wore a bright red necktie that seemed to have a little too much personality to suit him. Slim, attractive, ambitious, and not yet forty, the young man owed his fast-tracked career to his zealousness as well as his cunning intelligence. He wasn't about to let his advancement be debased by a couple of English teachers supposedly gone wild, and immediately demanded that the heads of the educational county board responsible and Mrs. Stern and her English committee report to him.

Katharina settled herself curiously into the circle of colleagues, and gave the superintendent a friendly, expectant look. He deliberated, wanting to thunder exactly just as effectively as his superior, and settled for starting with a menacing silence, while his thoughts wheeled transparently around the problem.

"Mrs. Stern, how dare you organize an educational development event for English teachers on your own?" The rhetorical question didn't require an answer, but in the pause following the accusation, an astonished Katharina burst out without hesitating. "I am the subject adviser and it is part of my responsibilities."

"Shut your mouth, or think about what you're saying! Do you even know what's going on here?"

"No, not yet, but you're just about to tell me."

"Why did you put together a language training event for English teachers with Americans, of all things?"

"They speak very good English." She shrugged, surprised by his ignorance. The superintendent gradually sharpened the tone of his questions.

"Do we need our teachers to acquire skills from Americans, from our enemies?"

"What do you mean by 'need' in this instance? In Potsdam, English teachers are successfully trained by native speakers. It's a very effective language program. If the college of education does it, we'll do it too."

The superintendent stared at her aggressively, with narrowed eyes. "We'll do it too? Just who do you think you are? We can't have every non-entity around here doing whatever they want." Katharina sat right down.

"In case by 'every non-entity' you mean me, I would like to point out the fact that I have taught at a socialist school for sixteen years and know very well what I'm doing." Katharina felt discomfort creeping up over her. What did he want from her? She looked at him, into his pinched face with ice-blue eyes. Suddenly she was reminded that he had never been able to hold on to a woman for long. He was far too pretty for that. How had he set himself up that way? Private affairs were no one's business. But the thought of his personal weaknesses put the supposed seriousness of the situation into perspective for Katharina, and was not devoid of a certain humor. Her imagination took the vicious edge off of any assailant, and let her smile inwardly and say nothing. She always did that when, in her eyes, someone was taking themselves too seriously in a discussion. It helped her inner poise. She herself would never react in a loud, aggressive manner.

Marianne Zauschke felt the pressing urge to butt in and nip the impending escalation in the bud. "I have to confirm this. Colleague Stern, who has been a mentor for thirteen years to student teachers at Rostock University, has already published two substantial educational readings with us, and conducted many other educational events for English teachers and academic studies. I value her work highly."

This well-meaning show of support hurt Katharina's pride. That made it sound as though she lacked self-awareness. But she tried in vain to take up the reigns of the conversation. "For a start, can you please tell us what exactly happened? I don't understand the reason for this unusual tone."

"You will understand very quickly! You met up with the people who bombed Lebanon! You cooperated with the enemy of this country and very possibly enabled them to spy on us!"

Katharina and all the other attendees were speechless. "We what?"

"Are you really that politically naïve, or do you just act like it? You illegally met with an ideological enemy of the GDR, Professor Miller, and knowingly did so near a secret military facility of the GDR!"

"That's not true." Katharina was gobsmacked.

"Of course it is. We know from reliable sources that the Professor's car was parked near your house on February 16th and March 2nd. You met secretly in Pammerow. The car was sighted multiple times as far back as a year ago. What did he want with you?"

Katharina took a deep breath. "What's that supposed to mean? Secret? We planned the educational development event and talked about the details. And besides, I was with my student as a mentor ..."

"... This Miller has already been a suspect for quite a while, due to his flirtation with a young GDR citizen," the school inspector interrupted her, not remotely interested in her argument. "And you organize a platform for the guy. In doing so, you have damaged the GDR. Do you know what kind of consequences that entails for you?" The superintendent's threatening tone began to take effect. Katharina's was changing from bright red to pale white, and she felt vague sense of confusion unfurling, which drove unwanted tears of helpless fury into her eyes.

"I assure you that our meeting was organized with the best intentions, and was ultimately a very worthwhile meeting that was anything but damaging to the GDR."

"Don't give me that! This Miller didn't come alone, he brought a whole pack of American students with him. That doesn't seem to have been made clear to you. Why did you arrange to have the whole thing take place in Clockshagen, when you know perfectly well that there's a secret military facility stationed there? And by complete coincidence," and here he stretched the second syllable of 'complete' slightly too long, so that no one would miss out on the intended irony, "by complete coincidence, one of the English teachers is also an officer's wife, Eva Zauder. What if she had told the Americans everything? She can be certain that her husband won't be allowed under any circumstances to study in Moscow! And then, under the pretext of baseball, you recruited the gym teachers to help perpetrate the crime with you!"

Katharina swallowed hard, struck dumb with shock.

"First of all, I hereby order you to record in writing every word, I repeat, every word that was spoken there. I want to be able to read every sentence that was spoken aloud there and by whom! With names and addresses!"

"That's not possible, with thirty participants," Marianne Zauschke dared to object.

"Shut your mouth," the superintendent bellowed at her and the other party members. By now he had found his form. Even though the distinguishably graying, highly intelligent woman was the same age as his mother, he screamed at her like she was a stupid child. "You were the one who allowed it, even though you were just standing in for Comrade Rutzlaff. We'll discuss the consequences for you as a member of the Party separately. In any case, by tomorrow everything should be written down on my desk. And I advise you all here not to forget a single word! From you, Comrade Rutzlaff, as head of the educational county board, I demand a statement by morning, even if you weren't there yourself! And as for you, Colleague Stern, we will let you know whether your position as a teacher at a socialist school is still tenable."

With this information, Katharina and all the other participants went back into their schools.

The shock spread like a wild fire through all the schools in the county, because the English and gym staff everywhere had been keen eyewitnesses at the 'inglorious episode' in Clockshagen, and knew the truth. An unwitting fear was spreading around. Some of them began to suspect that this grotesque political pressure meant the end of any idealized naiveté of teachers in this last "Land of the blind," as George Orwell described it. In that country, any person who was able to see the colorful world around them was described as an enemy of the truth by those who were born blind. This idea crept up even on Katharina.

Wednesday, October 9th 1996

Every day Felix is visited by friends and classmates, who touchingly look after him. They are all very cheerful, and claim earnestly that he has grown – is that the hormone tablets at work?

Today I pick up Felix from radiation at the Südstadt clinic, and we drive straight home, since he's too exhausted for anything else. We tape off the markings on his body so he can shower. It's shocking, the first clumps of hair are falling off his head in bushels. I think it would be better if we gave up on the shower. Felix seems to be having more difficulties with his memory today, a negative side effect of the radiation. He grows more serious, reflecting on his situation. We're going to get him a baseball cap so his self-image won't be shattered when he looks in the mirror.

Excerpt from a statement by Comrade Rutzlaff to his superior:

"The English committee's work plan for the school year 1985/86, approved by me, accounted for such items as meetings for regional studies of Great Britain, the visit to Shakespeare Day in Weimar, work with the English broadcasting course, the development of handouts for working with the teaching aid, and a gathering of the whole committee as well as all the teachers in their field in March 1986, on the theme of 'Baseball as popular sport in America.'

This event was supposed to serve as a joint practical activity for utilizing and expanding the English teachers' language skills. The connection between spoken foreign language communication and athletic activity was meant to serve as collective development for the committee.

The suggestion for this event was put forth by Colleague Katharina Stern, secretary of the English committee. In her occupation as mentor and author of essays on education and contributions to other academic works, Colleague Stern has contact to the foreign language department staff of Wilhelm-Pieck University in Rostock.

In January of this year, Colleague Stern informed Colleague Zauschke, who acted as my deputy during my course of treatment, of the intention to involve one or two American students studying in Rostock in the aforementioned event. As justification, she raised the possibility of direct communication with native speakers. In compliance with the requirement for authorization she made her intentions known, and willingly explained herself to Comrade County Superintendent during her request for said authorization. Based on her information regarding myself, she submitted a verbal request for authorization, and was issued verbal authorization to carry out her meeting. The written permission form was waived.

Later it transpired that on April 3rd, 1986, at the secondary school in Clockshagen, a meeting on the aforementioned theme took place; the participants included the English committee, several American students, and gym teachers from our county. Colleague Stern herself, per her testimony, was surprised that more American students than expected and gym teachers from different schools came to this meeting. It remains to be made

clear how gym teachers came to participate in a meeting designated for the English department.

Colleague Stern shared with me the contents of the meeting,
and that the formal political discussion that took place proved
to be worthwhile."

Thursday, October 10th 1996

*In the last four weeks Felix has grown nearly an entire inch. Is this a
side effect of the radiation? Growth hormones come from the pituitary
gland – I'm secretly hoping again. Can this doctor be trusted?*

*The ray they aim at the malignant tissue can also destroy part of the
healthy tissue, if it's in the hands of zealous, overambitious amateurs.
And then the whole system collapses. That wouldn't be the first experience of this kind in my life.*

Marianne Zauschke spent the night after the discussion feeling
anxious. She tossed and turned, agitated. Vivid dreams haunted
her. Thoughts and questions tumbled over one another. At 57
years old, she was part of the generation of the Socialist Unity
Party that, following their bitter experience during the war, had
built a more just society, founded on the strength of their convictions. She wanted a better world and she believed in the ideals of
the GDR, pressing back against the enemies of simple folks from
the old world. She lived in a superior part of the world. But the
sturdy columns of her old ideals had begun to buckle ever more
in the last few years.

Her own comrades wouldn't listen to her doubts. She tolerated
them with increasing frequency, and when the party leaders'
debate on how best to protect themselves from the enemies of
socialism no longer aligned with her own common sense, she
revolted inwardly. But meanwhile, she stopped putting herself
out there. She didn't even say anything to Willi Rutzlaff, whom
she with worked every day. Thus her rebellion remained within
the realm of fantasy.

Tonight she dreamed that she was sitting at her desk, working
on an accountability report for the next party leader conference,
when Willi Rutzlaff opened the door. He hadn't even set foot in
his office yet and already he was blustering about.

"You must be out of your mind to try and openly side with Stern at that kind of discussion."

Her response was straightforward. "Oh, cut it out, we're alone here, you don't have to explain about class standpoint to me again! I can't listen to your stories about the evilness of our enemies anymore!"

"Why are we even having a party leader conference if you don't want to grasp that our people have put all their trust and devotion into our party's work?"

She laughed out loud. "Hah! Don't make me laugh."

"The party is the embodiment of progress, success, and certainty of the future ..."

"Everyone's sick of hearing that!" Her attempts to interrupt were as futile as any action in a dream.

"I hold private conversations every day, and I hear just how deeply the comrades long for peace. How they'll do anything for peace."

Again, she tried to give words to her weak protests. "But weren't you talking about 'the silent ones' just yesterday?"

"We have to get them to declare if they're for or against peace."

"We do?" Her voice was getting hoarse.

"Of course."

"What sort of statement is that, Willi! As if there are no problems in this country other than world peace?"

You know perfectly well that there is nothing more important than world peace. That is the work of the party, that we as comrades must account for."

She talked on bravely in her dream. "Account for what, the fact that everyone is only allowed to praise the party, and no one dares to criticize? Is this our way of evading the real political problems in our work?"

"What's that supposed to mean?"

Her voice grew distinctly sharper. "Or are we unconsciously admitting that there is no party work to account for?"

"That's ridiculous."

"Or is the core of the party work to just repeat these stereotypes over and over until there's no room to think anything else?"

"Your doubts are disturbing, Marianne. All I get from you is trouble."

Her dream-self became clearer. "I understand. The doubters and denouncers would just be bothersome know-it-alls. They interfere with regulations, truly interfere, because the others would have to take sides, waste time, and get their butts off the sofa and try to convert valuable time in the party meetings into fruitful work, and nothing would ever come of it."

"Oh, Marianne. Just be happy that I'm able to have the conversation the superintendent demand here alone with you, without witnesses." Rutzlaff remained free of emotion. "That'll be all for now."

"Great."

"Now we have to formulate our standpoint for Lola Harms. Please type out these exact words."

The corners of her mouth turned down in discontent, she sourly pulled the report she'd started out from the roll on the ERIKA typewriter.

Rutzlaff dictated, without having to pause for reflection. Formulating these statements was part of his daily routine.

"First. Within our sphere of responsibility, a meeting of educators of our country and citizens of the US took place that we didn't plan and didn't intend, but for the reasons of insufficient prior knowledge and content-related examination on our side, did manage to materialize."

She looked up at him to interrupt. "So we're donning the sackcloth and ashes, even though we gave permission from the council?"

Without reacting to her argument, Rutzlaff continued.

"Second. Even if we consider the verbal permission of the comrades county board to a meeting of this ilk, there are clear political shortcomings in the treatment and execution of such a process."

Vaguely she heard her dream-self say, "Do I really have to write that meaningless sentence? It's amazing that these people pulled this meeting off by themselves! What's supposed to be wrong with that?"

He reacted defensively. "Now you're getting on my nerves. Keep typing."

"Third. We see the cause in the lack of control of preparing such meetings, regarding both content and organization."

She searched for a famous cliché. "Trust is good. Control is better. Aha."

"Just write, I want to go home sometime today."

"Fourth. Even if we wanted to believe the participants in their claim that they managed to lead a discussion on questions of peace, the worth of socialism, the socialist lifestyle and the crises of the imperialist systems, all from their viewpoints as socialist educators ..."

Her dream-self shook its head. "Oh god, oh god. What a glorious meeting."

"... We must nevertheless establish, though it burdens us, that we enabled a meeting that went directly against the requirements of our inner order."

"It burdens us? And what do we do now?" she asked immediately.

"Fifth. We must work with our associates, advisors, and secretaries of the committee with the imperative that the guidelines of our socialist order be fully known, understood, and wielded in a politically responsible way by all."

"You mean the way you want it wielded?" she thought.

"Uppercase A with round bracket. I ensure that the content and concepts of the meetings and overall work of the committee will be carefully recorded in cooperation with the appropriate principal through the faculty advisor, and that the common guidelines in question will be more correctly adhered to."

In her dream she shook her head, not understanding, but typed stupidly on.

"And do you actually want to do this personally? Katharina Stern hates reports and unproductive paperwork."

"Uppercase B with round bracket. The activities of the English committee will be made a significant part of my leadership duties, effective immediately."

She had to vent her misgivings. "You don't even speak English. It's inevitable that these teachers are going to seek out contact with people who can help them improve their teaching ability. That's what happens in Weimar. You can't hold everyone's hand."

"Uppercase C with round bracket. The trip that the committee planned to the Shakespeare Fest Days in Weimar was only permitted under the sanction that no one have contact with foreigners."

"You don't even believe that yourself!" her dream-self dared to argue.

"Uppercase D with round bracket. The comrade educational county board will be more thoroughly and accurately informed about the intentions of the committe and the other areas of our activity. Should it be necessary to come into contact with foreign citizens, it is ensured that this will be in adherence with all applicable laws."

"Always plugging state security ..." She heard the derision in her voice.

"Contain your sarcasm. This is more serious than you think."

"Uppercase E with round bracket. It must be investigated, whether Colleague Stern can continue to teach at a socialist school."

Silence. Her dream-self simply remained quiet.

"Uppercase F with round bracket. A message concerning the machinations of the student Meyer will be sent to the heads of the foreign language department at Wilhelm-Pieck University."

Silence.

"Uppercase G with round bracket. Those responsible at the university must take greater measures to control Professor Miller and his students."

Silence.

"And following clarification of the whole state of affairs – uppercase H with round bracket – don't forget, by now you've most likely grasped the inner logic of the entire thing – a further detailed evaluation will be arranged for the whole county. That needs to be underlined in the text for emphasis. Hey, why aren't you saying anything?"

The next day, Marianne Zauschke told Katharina about her vivid, worrisome dream from the night before.

"I was so preoccupied by that discussion with the superintendent," she said crossly.

The funny thing about a dream is that you strain to walk, but don't even move forward, you want to say many things, but you don't have the air to draw breath. This is what Katharina thought.

The staff at the school in Pammerow was shaken by this news; the threat to Katharina that she might not to be allowed to teach at a socialist school anymore, and that Reni might be pilloried, had the little group of teachers in the staff room banding together fiercely in solidarity.

"Rutzlaff convened another meeting of the English committee and demanded that we apologize openly for the incident and repent," Katharina explained.

"How do we do that?"

"He said, if we denounce our meeting in our written statement as 'working with hostiles,' then he would champion us. And if we don't, then something really bad will happen."

"And what did you do?"

"Refused. I tried to explain to him that we set up a fantastic meeting to get the GDR back on its feet. For the sake of tolerance and peace, in fact. That made him explode."

"This is all insanity." Heidrun Meschke gestured; when she was excited, her temper tended to take over. "I'll talk to Rutzlaff, I went to school with him. He's not really that narrow-minded."

"If they fire Katharina, we're all going on strike," fumed the gym teacher Ingrid Binsauer, who like everyone else had come back excited from the meeting with Professor Miller. She read a lot, and knew that striking, a distinct feature of hostile capitalist society, was unthinkable in socialism. "At least for the party leaders, the party group and the school leaders it would be risky, because they would have failed in their political relationship to the staff, and made themselves accountable."

Heidrun was getting worked up about the problem in her impulsive way. "Man, it's not just Hollenkamp as principal and Wagner as party secretary they have wrapped around their finger. Even Rutzlaff, and the school inspector too."

"What do you mean?"

"Well, because then something isn't right with the performance of their leadership duties! They failed in their political relationship to socialist convictions! What do you think, they'd be out of their positions too, if they went on strike as leaders. They would come up with something quick though, if we called to strike."

Very quietly and seriously, Ingrid said, "I'm for it. We can't put up with this anymore as teachers. We'll threaten a strike now." The other teachers nodded with serious faces, almost resolute.

Katharina felt queasy as she proudly nodded in solidarity with her small staff. The six attendees in the teachers' room were unified. They had already managed one strike against the microbe of human bigotry on their little island of Pammerow – and won.

Before the end of April, Rutzlaff popped up three more times in Pammerow.

"What's got you all up in arms," he said soothingly to Heidrun, who spontaneously made a distinct finger gesture on her head at her old school friend. "Heidrun, you don't seem to be aware what a bad situation this is," grumbled Rutzlaff, visibly riled, and he added pompously: "I've already averted that Mrs. Stern's reassignment to a different location. And keep your mouths shut that you let the Americans play baseball with students, that's just what I need. Then I'd have to change my report." Heidrun smirked contemptuously.

"How deep are you sunk in this? You used to have so much more common sense. It's shocking what sort of ideology can come out of thinking people. And here you're threatening a colleague with 'reassignment'? What's supposed to happen then?" She became somewhat more quiet at the table in the cafeteria. "Surely not ..."

Rutzlaff interrupted her. "Calm down – nothing has happened to you."

Had something happened?

Katharina Stern was not dismissed. It was a very delicate situation. A strike at the school in Pammerow would have, as Heidrun Meschke predicted, meant disqualification from the party for higher-ups on the county board. So Rutzlaff received a directive to pacify each and every local village, no matter what the cost. Instead of being dismissed, Katharina Stern was made into a vivid example of political ignorance and audacity in a teacher,

her name soon well known by all the faculty advisers – as well as the principals, student representatives, and even parents.

The district superintendent, Lola Harms, ordered that her record include an admonition for adverse contact with foreigners. So Katharina was indeed stripped of the title of head teacher and her higher salary bracket, and having been tagged as an activist, several of her previous awards were made null. She couldn't be a mentor anymore and was forbidden from coming into contact with any foreigners, and on account of all of this she had unwillingly become famous throughout the whole country.

Other than that, nothing had happened, as Rutzlaff said.

Nothing happened? The man appeared to have no idea. You always meet people twice in life. Then the truth strikes, Katharina philosophized.

CHAPTER 4

Katharina recalled the last *Parteilehrjahr* meeting. Principal Hollenkamp and Wagner, as party secretary, regularly invited all the teachers in the school to this meeting, which was a mandatory monthly conference designated for clarifying the unified standpoint that would serve as the fulcrum for all their lessons, whether they belonged to the Socialist Unity Party or not.

"I really can't listen to this boring drivel anymore," Katharina whispered to her neighbor Heidrun, while Principal Hollenkamp delivered his lecture to them straight off the piece of paper he'd prepared. Even she could have taken over his history classes, and she'd only been qualified for German and Russian.

"It's always the exact same thing. For seventeen years at this school. I just can't listen anymore."

Heidrun grinned. "You don't even need to. I'm working on my lesson plans for tomorrow."

"But what if he calls on you to answer a question, won't you have to come up with something clever?"

"You think? Not worth it."

"I don't see how. We have to answer."

"Better to ask him a question right back, get his dander up, at least it'll be funny. You should see how he scrambles to get himself out of it."

Hollenkamp's nervous voice rang out. He had become accustomed to addressing them as comrades, rather than teachers under his employ. "Colleague Stern, if you have something to say, could you say it out loud and not disturb the rest of us with your gossiping? Now, why does the socialist command economy respresent the safest method for an effective economy?" Katharina spluttered in surprise. Yes, why, or why not? The safest method? "Safe" in the sense of "no danger"? In the silence of her reaction, Hollenkamp offered her a big hint. "Think of the objective laws of history that Marx identified."

"Yeeees," Katharina drawled from her corner, as she shot a quick look at Heidrun. "The socialist command economy truly represents the safest form of economy today, because it has neither grown nor expanded in the last ten years, and so it poses no risk of causing an abundance of new technologies."

Heidrun woke up at this provocative remark on security and cut in. "Furthermore, the socialist command economy is safe because there's no danger of developing a materialistic society, where people have nervous breakdowns and do drugs because they're so bored with all their cars and new appliances."

Katharina couldn't stop herself from one-upping that ironic comment. "It's a really easy question, isn't it? Are all the questions today going to be as simple and direct as this one?"

She turned a friendly face forward and didn't let her frustration show. The nervous principal's reaction was surprisingly calm. He had been looking through his notes the whole time. Apparently not finding anything relevant to read at them, he merely said, "Thank you very much, Colleague Stern, for your contribution."

Katharina simply shut down. Almost dozing and from very far away, she heard the Friedrich Engels's connection of order with the natural laws of history as Hollenkamp read it aloud. "Freedom does not consist in any dreamt-of independence from natural laws, but in the knowledge of these laws, and in the possibility this gives of systematically making them work towards definite ends. Engels said that and it is also applicable to the laws of history."

Ingrid Binsauer, who out of frustration hadn't said anything else at the ideology meeting, as it was a waste of time for her, and the situation seemed hopeless, said that afternoon to Katharina, "Don't let these unpleasant Philistines with their small-mindedness and unbelievably lazy thoughts get you down. Yesterday on TV they showed how the Hungarians got rid of their borders so that everyone can go through to the West if they want. Today in an English paper it said that a representative of the Soviet government talked about the unification of a military neutral Germany, which obviously can't be true. And Stalinism has been, anyway. Forget it."

"What do you mean, 'forget it,'" Katharina retorted angrily. "What are you saying about Stalinism, the concept isn't even relevant here. Even Wagner said so. I've really had it up to here with all the Marxist-Leninist 'objective laws of history' that are objective because they operate on their own, outside and independent of our consciousness. Justified by science. You can't do anything about it. What's the point of talking about it?"

"You know, Marx and Engels didn't even come up with the 'laws of history,' I heard," said Ingrid, who was occupying herself with the history questions on the syllabus out of personal interest. "But in the second half of the nineteenth century there was all this infighting amongst socialist and non-socialist writers. The early Marx of the 40's had never once talked about 'laws of history' or scientific determination, but instead demanded that people stand up to the economic laws, which was a much more clever approach."

"Oh, get off your soapbox," Katharina cut in. "What does that have to do with us?"

"Well, everything. What Stalinism tries to do is relinquish all moral and individual responsibility. 'Laws of history' persuade people to shirk their duties, except of course for those concerning the state, which is the only institution that's allowed to decide what the 'Laws of history' mean. That's how it was with the ancient priests who consulted the oracle. Everything is manipulated. And that has something to do with us."

"Maybe you're right." Katharina waved dismissively. "But maybe you're not."

A letter from the Drapers in London was in her mailbox. As had so often happened over the last several years. Once again, Katharina shook her head at the envelope's appearance. "I'm amazed they don't just rip off the pretty stamps, if they're going to steam open the sticky flap anyway," she muttered resentfully to herself, and began to read the response to her last letter to England.

"This will interest you, Karl," she said.

"London, March 3rd 1988. East Germany isn't getting very good headlines here. The fact that people are being arrested for demonstrating for Rosa Luxemburg and Gorbachev doesn't help the labor or communist parties create a positive image of the GDR. There's even two anti-Stalinist films that've come out in London, both from the USSR. We saw one of them – *Repentance*.

These films are getting a lot of attention because apparently they've been banned from cinemas in East Germany. That's the only reason anyone cares. Soviet news isn't published in the GDR, although you can get it in Moscow, London, and Bonn. Clearly the whole thing is a giant propaganda gift to West Germany, which is now showing Soviet films on TV that aren't allowed in the east! Doubtless the information we're getting here is exaggerated and distorted by the capitalist press, but my East German contacts tell me that some of it is true, if not all of it. If you look at it, it's very contradictory; someone high up in East Germany told Vicky that they've been easing up on visits to the west in the past six months. They told Vicky that even people with close friends in the west can accept invitations now. Should we invite you?! It seems like pure irony that people with connections to the GDR like you, who would definitely come back, aren't allowed to leave, while unreliable people can go travel to the west.

You say there aren't any dogmatists at your school? It's been the opposite for us. The problem with dogmatists is that every last one of them thinks even the smallest criticism means someone's your enemy. I found out that 'Marxism Today' is actually persuading English readers to sympathize with East European countries, whereas no one believes the 'Morning Star.' No one here will buy that East Europe is perfect. That's just bad psychology, if not something completely different."

"Maybe Colin is right. They shouldn't have banned the 'Sputnik.' That magazine's finally interesting now. I never read it before," said Karl.

Friday, October 11th 1996

When I try to pick Felix up today for the weekend, he's hooked up to an IV again. His sodium levels had climbed up to 161 (140 is normal). His medication is changing again: no more Torem (which flushes out water), potassium three times a day, Minirin once in the evening (retains water), and keeping the Euthyrox (thyroid hormones).

The doctors are all wandering around the jungle of medical experience, hunting for the tree of knowledge. And in Felix's case, they're stumbling over one vine after another.

Why is all this happening? What's wrong with his pituitary gland, this gland that controls a person's whole hormone system? Apparently Felix's symptoms make him one of only seven in the whole world, and with help from the internet, he only ends up becoming the focus of other studies, instead of being able to find help for himself from others' experiences.

Today the patient next door (the one with the tick problem) is being released from his room – his condition has been diagnosed as incurable, and he has to live with it now. Is our array of medical knowledge really that impotent in so many fields today?

The head physician still radiates confidence, he answers all our questions about the future with unflagging optimism. My doubts on the truth are growing.

Katharina set the letter aside. As always, it left her feeling conflicted inside. In her head, she formulated an argument against every criticism her English friends had launched against the GDR.

But like the biblical serpent in the Garden of Eden, her doubts slowly snaked their way into her mind, urging her to pluck the apple from the tree of knowledge.

Maybe the socialist lifestyle wasn't exactly heaven on earth, the way she'd always painted it in every conversation in and about the GDR, at least in front of students. But it was good for everyone! There was no crime, no unemployment, and there were no drugs. Katharina was full of praise for her country. There was Kindergarten for everyone, tuition-free education, free milk at school, free health care, low housing costs, and a right to work. She didn't even need to do anything; someone planned for her, someone thought for her, someone decided for her. The party conference announced everything. One could rely on the political experts. They knew what they were doing. Or so Katharina thought.

She skimmed the letter again. Colin and Vicky had it pretty good, getting to live in such a great city of the world. They had some cushy advantages over the GDR. Every day, they could pick out millions of pieces of information from their media. Even from far away, they supposedly knew everything better than she did. The world was open to them and their children. Unlimited access to culture and knowledge. There was nothing that wasn't theirs for the taking. How did it work?

With her passion for the English language, why wasn't she allowed to travel there, even just once? To see the city she so longed to visit, and talk to its inhabitants? It would be a dream come true!

Any doubts her subconscious held about England had not yet pressed their way into her conscious mind. Just simple English words and phrases, like "happy" and "living happily together."

But like a bolt from the blue, an old memory struck her. " ... goath pli together ..."

Could "pli" mean "happily"? She thought uneasily of the strange letter, full of mistakes, that had arrived with a threat and no clue as to the sender, and which she'd never sent on.

Superstition.

But it had worked. Hesitantly she stood at her desk, and stared at the shiny silver tin can at the very bottom of her enormous bookcase, which one of her former students had made for her in the first year of his apprenticeship as a carpenter. The spruce wood was already bent under the weight of the books and the space between the shelves wasn't quite right, but the irregularities made it unique. It had provided refuge to some banned books, not just George Orwell's 1984. That was where she also kept the box with the letters that had been opened by the Stasi, but that had still made it to her. In this large metal box she collected all the pieces of writing that were important to her. Old obituaries of relatives cut out from the newspaper, rare silver coins from the 1920's, special photos from the past, funny postcards, old letters.

Katharina also kept many of the Drapers' letters in this box, the ones that fueled her idyllic fantasies of London. She could have thrown them away a long time ago. She didn't read any of them anymore.

Had she even understood the English contents correctly? The question came to her abruptly. With suspicion and unease growing in her stomach, she rifled through the large collection of letters, coming to the ones from the 1980's.

... "Kids are doing splendid" ... "they're still raving about our trip to East Germany" ... "Mark's problems at school are piling up" ... "He's dropping out at 17 without taking the final exams" ... "Seems to be having a nervous breakdown" ... "He's walking in his sleep but doesn't want to go to the doctor" ... "He's working as a window cleaner" ... "Wednesday he left the house at midnight and came back drunk three hours later" ... "He doesn't want to work this summer" ... "We're afraid his character is changing, as so often happens with unemployed young people" ... "His application to work at Tesco fell through because there were six thousand other applicants" ... "Got rejected, saying he's 'overqualified'" ... "Or underqualified" ... "He's taking a room of his own" ... "Now that he's got this newfound freedom, he's hanging around the types of criminals who wash windows for a living" ... "Jane is going to start at university" ... "Mark needs to come home so he can get out from under the influence of his criminal friends" ...

The thoughts tumbled over one another in Katharina's head. In the GDR, this never would have happened. Everything she didn't want to imagine in reality must be so dreadful for parents.

"What are they writing about Mark?" Karl asked. "If he's not graduating or getting any job training, can't they make him live at home?" Katharina translated.

"London, April 21st 1988. Mark is still cleaning windows and has been promoted to a consultant. He gets paid 180 pounds a week now. I think he's going to end up being the millionaire of the family."

"Cleaning windows can be a decent trade. But not without the right training. Pretty unlikely," said Karl.

"London, May 13th 1989. You asked if there's anything new to report about Mark? The last piece of news we heard about our son was that he quit his job at the Brownet Cross shopping centre, where he was on security staff. After that, he spent about a week here at home with us, then disappeared again. Back to Cardiff, in Wales, where Jane is incidentally studying. Luckily. He has a good relationship with his sister. He tells her more than he tells us. As far as we know, he's even found a girlfriend there. That might help.

We thought he liked living in London with us. It was such a relief to have him here! He even cleaned the whole house once, without being asked! But in Cardiff he's doing much better than before. He's happier than he was six months ago, and much happier than two years ago. But he still doesn't have any interests, any hobbies, or any motivation. He's like a drifting raft that made it through a shipwreck in the most madly competitive decade Britain's seen since 1945. So of course we parents are worrying, pondering, and hoping. Currently he's working in a dairy factory and having a lot of fun going to parties and discos. We're keeping our fingers crossed!"

"I don't know," said Karl. "That doesn't sound good."

Saturday, October 12th 1996

Sodium levels are at 156, Felix gets another half-liter infusion as a precaution before we can take him home for the weekend.

A lot of his friends pop up in the evening. Thomas, Olaf, Marcel, Maria, Martin, Robert, or whatever they're all called. They play 'The Game of Life' (which is similar to Monopoly) up until midnight. I'm not familiar with the game, I just watch from a distance and note the coincidental symbolism. Playing this game touches Felix profoundly, and he's memorized the rules by heart in spite of the trouble with his memory.

Where does his long-term memory start? I have to ask him what he remembers from this year. Final year exams? His driver's license test? Or do we have to go a couple years back? The trip through Great Britain? The reunification?

Every day over a ten-minute breakfast, before Katharina had to leave for school school, she skimmed the newspaper 'Neues Deutschland.' There was information about other countries in there too, so she thought she was learning enough. It seemed to be sufficient for school anyway. The two TV channels in the GDR both broadcast daily evening news, but after her strenuously exhausting day at school, they bored her and she only tuned in out of a professional obligation. After all, a teacher in a socialist school had to be properly informed. And 'proper' seemed to mean GDR TV. She'd been able to get western channels for a few years, but for the purposes of school they had the slight flaw of not being allowed. Katharina had listened to the arguments being aired with interest, but never seriously addressed them in school. So although she could get the western news in Pammerow, it swept right over her head, like so many things that she just didn't believe. She wasn't paying as much attention where it needed to be paid.

When the border in Hungary was opened in the summer of 1989, and so many young people fled to the German Embassy there, she found herself sitting breathlessly in front of the TV every night, scarcely able to believe her eyes.

"Have they all gone crazy? Treating their lives and their little children like a game? What reason could these people possibly have? Everything is good for them here, they're safe."

Karl nodded in agreement. "Over there they're expecting instability, unemployment, violence, drug use, lack of equality, and unpayable housing costs ..."

She wasn't even listening to his tally. "Is it because of freedom?"

"What is freedom?" said Karl. "Recognition of necessity."

"You know, when Grandpa visited his cousin in the wealthy west, he told me they had special parking spots for women in the parking lots, especially by the exit."

"What for?"

"Because women are in danger of being killed in a parking lot, if there's no way for them to escape."

"There's your freedom for you. Comes with a high rate of crime, begging, and homelessness."

"Well, but they can get cars without having to order them years in advance," Katharina countered, and stared at the television screen again. "And bananas without rationing. And the chocolate tastes better and the coffee ..."

"And there's piles of smutty newspapers in the supermarket!" She made a face at Karl's provoking. "And a big selection of washing powder to bleach dirty laundry white again."

"I don't really think that's funny," Katharina muttered.

"Seriously though. Look at that, they're risking life and limb to practically throw their kids over the embassy wall!" Karl shook his head.

"You think they're taking a deadly risk just to be able to buy bananas, chocolate, and real coffee?" Katharina's serpent of doubt darted out. "You know, Karl, someone tried to tell me recently that the captain of the GDR cruise ship 'Völkerfreundschaft' had similar strange experiences. As they were sailing through Bosporus, fourteen vacationers suddenly jumped off the sun deck. Turkish boats had been waiting for them underneath."

"Who would do a thing like that?"

"Maybe people with a lot of money, doctors, engineers, artists."

"Eh, I don't believe it."

The images from the TV of the fence climbers and those sneaking over the border touched Katharina deeply. Furthermore, the news awoke a faint echo inside her. The party secretary of the school was certainly seething. Not exactly because the country was starting to bleed out, but because he hadn't gotten any illuminating arguments from his superiors for the political discussion at the *Parteilehrjahr*. The guard of old men around Erich Honecker was laying low. Partly because they didn't want to believe what was happening on the screen, brush it off as slick propaganda and Western lies, and partly because their control on the situation seemed to be slipping, and they were becoming impotent in their consternation.

On October 18th, 1989, Karl and his wife – like almost every fall vacation – took their children to Leipzig to see Katharina's parents. Karl sat relaxed at the wheel, casually steering with just his left hand. Katharina intently studied the road map and kept trying to figure out the order of the rest stops on the Autobahn between Rostock and Leipzig. Olaf and Felix languidly paged through a couple of magazines they'd brought with them. The car radio was playing music. The Autobahn exit for Leipzig-Schkeuditz was steadily getting closer, and the voice of the news announcer spoke under the hum of the motor. " ... Comrade Honecker has resigned for health reasons ..."

Karl accidentally stamped on the brakes. The kids jumped forward in their seats and shouted over each other. "Wait, what? What was that? Did we hear that right?" Katharina and Karl looked at each other wide-eyed. "It can't be true." Katharina jumped to turn the knob up so they could hear more. She heard something about Australian Aborigines, who had finally been given the right to govern themselves after one hundred years of oppression. But the breaking news was already over.

"It's over," she lamented.

"And so are we," Karl noted laconically, as he had passed their exit in the excitement. "I'm dying here," shrieked sixteen-year-old Olaf into the din of the engine. Felix, who was five years younger, bounced up and down in his seat with excitement. He couldn't really understand the significance of the news. He only got the idea that something extraordinary must be happening when his father missed their exit in the commotion.

The children told their grandparents all about their shocked father's driving mishap, with great relish.

"It's still a surprise," said Grandpa, "but here in Leipzig all hell's been loose for the past two weeks – I'd imagine there's more reason for Honecker's resignation than just his health."

Grandma agreed. "Didn't you hear on TV about the demonstrations on Monday? People were protesting against the conditions here, and I see where they're coming from. There's no progress. You have to line up to get a single banana. Our hallway at home hasn't been painted since before the war. You can only get nice things under the table or by having connections to good friends in retail. Without money from the west, we're second-class citizens. The party bigwigs are getting on our nerves with their claims that everything is fine. The young people just skedaddle off, because it's better in the west than in the socialist state."

"Now Grandma," Karl interrupted her. "It's probably not as simple as that. You've never even been to the West."

"Neither have you," she retorted. "In any case, if it weren't so dangerous, I would have gone to Monday's demonstration too and given the comrades a piece of my mind."

Olaf smiled, because that was his grandma. Impulsive, bold, emotional, and honest. "I would have gone too. But we're here for a long weekend, up through next Monday," he said.

"Now, now," his grandpa stopped his grandson. "That's completely out of the question for you kids. What do you think went on here last time!"

"What's that?" Felix asked.

"I saw on TV how they ripped the banner away from peaceful protestors and hit them with police clubs," Olaf butted in.

"Why did they do that?" Felix inquired.

"They said those were the enemies of our people. They want a different socialism and demand freedom of expression. We have to protect ourselves and the people from these counter-revolutionaries, is what my principal said at school."

Felix thought a moment and then asked, "Who are they then, if we're the people?"

"I heard 55 people were arrested in September," said Grandpa, jumping back into the conversation. "A few weeks ago there were eight thousand police officers and combat troopers at the ready to get there ahead of the demonstrators."

"They even asked army soldiers to step in, just imagine such a thing," Grandma complained. "We're happy the whole damned situation is behind us. They should have done something smart instead, like make more consumer goods. Then at least we all would have gotten something out of it."

"Do the demonstrators fight back?" Felix asked his father worriedly.

"No, it's just a peaceful silent march on Mondays, people coming out of church from praying," Karl answered.

"From the Church of St. Nicholas," Grandpa finished. "But don't get the wrong idea – they're not praying to God in the traditional sense. They're not all believers. The church just offers a sanctuary where even different-minded people can gather without being attacked by the Stasi."

"Normally they'd never deploy such threatening forces around the Church of St. Nicholas!" Grandma continued to complain. "I heard from my friend Emma – her daughter works at the hospital – that they've stocked up on stored blood there! Her daughter has been on standby all day and isn't allowed to leave."

"What's that supposed to mean?" Felix asked, with the natural naiveté of a child.

Grandma continued. "It's not just a couple people who are standing up and might get hurt. Day before yesterday 120,000 demonstrators were said to have been on their way to the protests."

Felix gaped. "There are a hundred twenty thousand people in Leipzig alone who aren't part of our people?! They must need a huge load of blood!"

Karl put an end to the discussion. "It probably won't come to that."

"I'd like to go too!" Katharina threw in.

"What for? Willingly go to a demonstration? You don't even want to go to the demonstration on May 1st!"

Katharina ignored his sarcasm. "We can use the long weekend on Monday and go before we drive home on Tuesday?"

"Fine, if you really want to." Karl let himself be persuaded.

Katharina's parents were not at all excited about this idea. "But be careful! And the children are staying here, no matter what!"

The downtown appeared to be dead as Karl and Katharina strolled through Petersstraße in the late afternoon so they could get to St. Nicholas Church on time at 5 pm.

"This is really strange," Katharina wondered to herself. "It's already a quarter to five, but there's no sign of the demonstrators. Or maybe we got it wrong?"

"Let's just nonchalantly walk over to St. Nicholas Church, see if anything is going on there," Karl suggested. "Or we can just head home."

Scattered couples were loitering around near the church, just like them. They appeared to be looking in shop windows. Shortly before five, Katharina suddenly nudged Karl in the side. "There are a couple more people coming out of the side road, heading our way."

"Not just over there," Karl whispered. "Look to the left and right!" Several young people, for all intents and purposes on a casual walk, were going in the same direction. Out of nowhere, within a few minutes, a mob of people had formed.

"Where are they all coming from so suddenly? There was no one around earlier."

In a flash, the scene in front of the St. Nicholas Church changed. At once, all the surrounding rows of houses and romantic little side streets of downtown Leipzig seemed to spit out people. The plaza in front of the church was filled in a heartbeat.

"Look up there, there's a little platform rotating with a man on it, the one I saw before with a video camera."

"Where?"

"Up there, over our heads."

"Better turn your face away, or else the police might come after us later!"

"Oh, rubbish. I assume it's journalists from the western media – so sneaky, the way they slipped into the crowd here!"

The door of the church was open. Streaming out came men and women of all ages who had been praying for peace at the service. Their faces carried earnest expressions. They lit candles in front of the church – hundreds of tea lights, large and small altar candles, red grave candles – the symbol of remembrance and warning. Not a word came from the surging mass in front of the church. Slowly and silently, the caravan set itself in motion. As though they were being led by a hand, the tide found its way to the direction of the opera house, carrying Karl and Katharina Stern. From her childhood and youth in Leipzig, Katharina knew the path the demonstrators took every year on May 1st, when all the schools gathered together with the workers to sing the praises of the Party, with no one having particularly strong emotions, but the logistics perfectly planned out. This time it was different. Katharina could feel the sizzle in the voices of the marchers.

"Join to-ge-ther!" came a murmur, growing steadily stronger as it was carried by the chorus of voices. "Join to-ge-ther!"

Both of the Sterns observed that the train of silent people swelled to make way for new streams of gatherers.

"We are the peo-ple!"

Katharina's heart pounded, as the rising mass passed the Karl-Marx plaza in the ring road by the new city hall. Alright, she thought, these certainly aren't counter-revolutionaries or Western enemies of our people.

"We stay here!" By now, many people had illegally escaped to the west, at risk of their own lives.

"Tra-vel free-dom." A political joke reinterpreted the German initials of the state – *Deutsche Demokratische Republik* – to stand for "Der Dumme Rest – the Dumb Remains." Katharina had heard this a while ago. Was this group here the dumb remains?

"We stay here!"

"There must be over a hundred thousand people here," Karl whispered.

"Yeah, I'd guess more than three hundred thousand," Katharina replied.

Walking near them in the row on Dittrich Ring was a young man with dark horn-rimmed glasses and a jean jacket, who nodded at them.

"We're always getting bigger. Looks like today's the biggest Monday demonstration we've had yet. Hopefully everything goes smoothly once we get to the rounded corner."

"The rounded corner?" Karl asked.

"That's the Stasi," Katharina explained. "The district administration building for state security." Karl was silent.

In the background, the subdued storm grumbled, restrained for the moment, then carried on ever more distinctly and sonorously.

"No vio-lence."

A dark chorus of the hundred thousand sounded in rhythm the closer they came to the rounded corner. "No vio-lence!"

From afar, Katharina could already see the shadows of figures surrounding the building, their weapons held at the ready. Her shock and fear of the Stasi on account of American Professor Miller flamed up in her briefly. The rhythmic staccato of the chant rattled her emotions.

"No vio-lence!"

The chorus cautioned the shadowy figures ahead, but above all it cautioned its own enraged people to keep their heads.

"No vio-lence!" Katharina was afraid. She clung tightly to Karl, who calmed her. "Nothing's going to happen here."

The Stasi building lay menacingly in the shadows of the treetops. Now, for the first time, Katharina could see exactly how the revolution could blow up. As long as no one lost their nerve! As long as the angry masses didn't break off anywhere! Yes, it was a revolution! When would the Russian tanks be arriving? How would this go down in German history? The voices of the masses grew tenser as they approached the rounded corner.

"We are the peo-ple."

It could be our fathers or children who are shot there. "We are the people."

And on and on, the rolling thunder of the crowd's rhythmic steps. "No vio-lence! No vio-lence!"

The dark figures stood motionless. Katharina's neighbor ground his teeth. As the demonstration caravan slowly made its way to the rounded corner, a bit of Katharina's tension siphoned off. The streetcars stood still. They reached the train station, where the giant courtyard area was black with people and Katharina called joyfully into the echoing cry: "Tra-vel free-dom! Tra-vel free-dom! Tra-vel free-dom!"

Monday, October 14th 1996

The new roommate is named Torsten. He has epilepsy and is taking tablets to try and improve his condition. Hopefully Felix is the right partner for him! If anything happened, he wouldn't know where to start. He's already forgotten all his other roommates and their impressive ailments.

Felix gets an unusual visitor in the form of Mrs. Huber, his former class teacher up until the final year exams. She seems very concerned. Her own child was on the verge of dying from herpes at the age of eighteen. She senses a lot of parallels, though she doesn't comment on them in front of Felix. She says today she's beginning to understand what had been happening with Felix all of a sudden in the weeks before the final exams. He sat in the back row of class, looking smaller and paler all the time, with dark rings under his eyes. Where before he had been lively and engaged in discussion, used to being the top in his class, he had now become completely quiet and fallen behind.

I remember that too. He couldn't understand what was happening to him. He constantly had to go to the bathroom. And not a night went by without two-hour long disturbances because of that. He felt weak and almost fell asleep in class.

I even remember that we, as his parents, didn't even make anything of all of that. We both had extremely time-consuming jobs, and our private lives were rushing by. What was the most important thing in our marriage? We never even asked ourselves this question.

We didn't notice anything. Not until the day he collapsed at the mall.

Katharina almost slept through the reunification. Even the press conference on Thursday night, the bombshell that moved the world on November 9th 1989, didn't make it into her consciousness, even though the program ran while she was sitting wearily in front of the TV, as was her habit. Even when Schabowski tiredly answered "IMMEDIATELY" to the journalists who asked when the new regulations for the open border would go into effect, she took this in with no particular feeling. Berlin was far away. One of many legal regulations from the last few years that didn't concern her. She didn't have relatives in the west that she could have visited. The next day at breakfast she was surprised to hear there was more on the radio. Her oldest son Olaf came home beaming that day from his last day of tenth grade in Moscow.

"Mom, you know where I've just come from? From West Berlin! We heard on the plane that the Berlin Wall was being opened, and after we landed in Berlin we just crossed right over the border, to see how it felt. And came back after twenty minutes, because we had to catch the train home. A real adventure, huh? Look at my passport, there's a stamp in there!"

Unbelievable! Oh god, what a risk!

From then on, she didn't get her daily news from the TV anymore. Incomprehensible! Opening the border! Didn't that also mean she could travel to England now? The wonderful city of her dreams? That really woke her up.

Karl observed it all placidly. Alright then. Four days later, she applied for passes for the both of them, because the passport that would get them to West Germany wasn't enough for Great Britain.

"It takes six weeks to process a passport of the German Democratic Republic," a woman at the bureau told her. "That is, it could take up to Christmas."

What a Christmas gift! As soon as Santa had come and gone, and they'd finished their Christmas dinner of goose and stollen, the traditional German Christmas cake, Katharina and Karl set off the day after.

Friday, October 18th 1996

Why am I remembering Aunt Charlotte today, my mother's sister? I was nineteen when she died of cancer at age 48. None of it really hit me much. She just suddenly wasn't there anymore. That was the year I met Karl. We didn't have any troubles.

Today would have been her 75th birthday.

I pick Felix up at 2 pm, and this time all his levels appear to be fine, for the first time we don't make an appointment for the weekend. His hair loss is progressing rapidly. He's ashamed to go in public with his bald head and wears a baseball cap. "The girls all run away from me," he says helplessly.

The doctor with the dying baobab tells me, while I'm waiting in the hall and she happens across me, "His hair will never grow back. And he will never be able to show interest in females again."

Why did she have to say it like that? She wasn't even responsible for Felix anymore. Suddenly my last hopes come crashing down. He will never have children in his life.

But right now that doesn't matter. As long as he survives!

Where did the night train come from, that stopped in East Berlin on Boxing Day in 1989 to pick up a couple of travelers like Katharina and Karl Stern? Katharina only knew that it would be passing exclusive destinations beyond the border, which had been open for six weeks. West Berlin, Hannover, Brussels, Ostend.

The train rushed through the night towards its destination on the Atlantic coast, more quiet than the Sterns were used to hearing. Part surprised, part disbelieving, Karl listened carefully to the hum of the train, but all he could make out was an extremely low whooshing. In spite of their great excitement, they both managed to get a little sleep here and there. Outside they couldn't see much, it was too dark. At the port in Ostend, where they boarded the ferry to England, the bright sun emerged and showed them a little of the bustling activity of another world, which they eagerly feasted their eyes on with great curiosity.

The white outcroppings of chalk in Dover streamed from the distance as they drove off the coast. What a picturesque image! Crossing the border into England was Katharina's dream come true. Everything around her was right off the pages of an English textbook. She recognized every page in living color, there in front of her eyes.

Karl felt more comfortable when he heard the train rattling

on the tracks in Dover. He leaned back contentedly on the seat, which was upholstered in a plush blue pattern.

"It sounds like we're home in the GDR again. It makes me feel more sympathetic to England. I can barely make out anything past the dirty windows."

He loved taking shots at his wife's over-romanticized enthusiasm and pulling her back down to earth, in spite of his own excitement and anticipation. Although December was almost over, vibrant green meadows and pastures were flying past their eyes.

"So these are the renowned English lawns? The English green meadows are really different from ours, aren't they?" Katharina tried to pique Karl's apparently measured interest in the details of the English landscape by tailoring her questions to his agricultural interests.

"I couldn't say," he muttered.

"Look at the gorgeous hedges everywhere, they're still green!"

"In the middle of the field! Smaller crop production. They're only bogging themselves down, probably just a little family operation. I'd really like to talk to an English farmer. These conditions must be squalid."

Katharina ignored his arguments.

"Look, from here you can see the chimneys on every house, which are very English. They're so rustic, with those three long tubes, that these children could imagine Santa coming down into the living room through the chimney. They've probably hung gorgeous stockings down below for him to leave presents in!"

"Loads of dark gray row houses with black fumes piping up out of the chimneys. From here on the train you can see the dirty little backyards, where even the laundry is hanging out the window. Think they'll stay white? Not this close to the train! And there's nothing to block out the din of the train for the sake of people's health, like with us. It wouldn't surprise me if, like in Pammerow, the uncovered freight trains carrying apatite fly by the little gardens and send a white coat of mineral dust over all that magical green and in through the window cracks of those old houses."

"Oh stop it! Just sit back and enjoy the fact that we could take such a lovely trip! We're already in the suburbs of London!"

The train rolled into Liverpool Street Station with a delay of a few minutes, which Karl again noted with a smirk was similar to their grievances at home. He was pleased that the GDR really wasn't so bad in international comparison, like the media had been making out for the past few weeks.

On the train platform a large crowd of people was swarming, hurrying with colorful plastic shopping bags in various directions. Katharina only had her own handmade canvas bag that she carried as a hold-all for anything she needed. These colorful bags, which sported English words as advertisements, sparked her interest as she got in line to exit. "Everyone's carrying such neat plastic bags, not just one but a whole bunch of them, even though some of them aren't full."

"Yeah, yeah," said Karl. "And the big bins over there are full of heaps of plastic garbage." Karl always observed things differently than Katharina. Selective awareness. Everyone will see right away what they want to see.

Outside, two familiar faces were waiting, happily waving a red towel so that the Sterns might spot them more easily. The slightly grayed high school teacher Colin Draper, always a bit slumped forward, was of a height complementary to his shorter wife Vicky, being well over six feet tall and a head taller than her. He stood out distinctly from the crowd of people on the platform. Karl had already spotted him from the train. To Karl, they both looked the spitting image of the typical English citizen; very slim and haggard, with pale complexions and unobtrusive clothing. For an English couple, they had married and had children very young. Early 20's, just like Karl and Katharina. Now their two grown children, Mark and Jane, were waiting at home to greet their guests from Germany.

Since the Potsdam course in 1979, Katharina had been keeping up a letter exchange with the Drapers. The families sometimes met over summer vacation, or more often on New Year's Eve, though until today the visits had only gone in one direction. From London to Pammerow. Never the reverse. Several plans for Katharina to visit to Drapers in London had gone amiss. Somewhere, there was always someone who caused the application to vanish unanswered. Was it the person who was always rustling in the background on her phone calls? Or the person who steamed open her letters and glued them back up without a trace? Or the person who popped up at her home with a bouquet of flowers as her 'uncle from Berlin' to announce that the Drapers would not be allowed to visit Pammerow for New Year's? Or was it even someone suspected her of spying because of the American Professor Miller and Reni Meyer?

Until now, there had been no easy way for Katharina to visit her much-idealized dreamland. But now she got off the train and stood on the platform at Liverpool Street Station, and could hug her friends Colin and Vicky amid tears of joy. So simple. As if it was the most normal thing in the world. Colin, choked up with affection, couldn't manage a word besides 'hello.'

"You're here," said Vicky, brimming with emotion. "Just like that." Katharina wasn't sure how to translate this for Karl. But Vicky solved that herself by switching into German, saying "it's no trouble at all," as her German was perfect in contrast to Karl's grasp of English.

"Why on earth should I learn English when I've got my wife as an interpreter!" Katharina felt a bit uncomfortable with his open contempt towards the idea of learning a foreign language for himself. She thought his sense of reality could have served the devil as a slide in heaven, plummeting into a dreamless hell. Any minute now, Katharina feared, he would tell the joke about the two famous German fools, Tünnes and Schäl, and the uselessness of learning a foreign language:

Tünnes and Schäl are standing at the train station in Cologne.

A Japanese man comes up and asks in fluent German, "Where is the cathedral?" They shrug.

He repeats the question in fluent English. They shrug. The same thing in French. They shrug.

The Japanese man walks away in exasperation.

Then Tünnes says to Schäl, "He knew a lot of languages!"

Schäl says, "So what? Did it help him any?"

Instead, Karl yelled "Come over here quick, Kathi!" He pointed at a large television screen in the train station hall, which had suddenly drawn his attention. "Translate! What's happening there?" His presumptuousness was rewarded as Katharina began to interpret the words on the screen.

"In Romania. People are revolting. Nicolae Ceausescu and his wife Elena. They were attacked by soldiers while trying to escape. The trial only lasted ninety minutes. Verdict was given immediately. Execution by firing squad." Katharina stared open-mouthed at the couple lying in their own blood on the screen.

"As head of the country, he certainly didn't do anything different than Honecker? – Oh god, that could be really bad for Honecker and his wife, couldn't it?"

"Well, the situation looks a bit different in Romania! Are you worried?"

"Yes. We marched so peacefully through this world change. But people are still upset. When the mob strikes, our peaceful revolution will turn into war." It was right there in London, at that moment in October of 1989, that she was first struck by the seriousness of the situation.

Monday, October 21st 1996

Torsten had an epileptic attack today. Flustered, Felix recounts how he himself got a shock and went to get help when he saw Torsten lying in front of him, rigidly twitching. Felix said, "I will never forget that as long as I live." Well, we'll see.

Katharina seized her dream city London piece by piece, as if she'd emptied out her old textbook and the contents of the Drapers' letters of the last ten years about this city and set out to recreate the images branded into her mind, and match them up with reality.

"That little thing over there is supposed to represent the tremendous Tower of London, with its gory history?" Katharina had pictured the tower quite differently. Colin and Vicky, being born Londoners, and visiting the tower for the first time in their lives for the sake of their guests' curiosity, smiled in understanding.

"What do you mean, little thing?" Colin retorted. "There's thousands of tourists standing here in line for hours, just so they can get a look at the crown jewels. Opulence and thick defensive walls are what make this place great!"

In the inner courtyard, an excessive number of big black ravens with clipped wings were hopping around. They cawed loudly, peering at Katharina with sharply tilted heads.

"You're double the size of the ones in my textbook picture. As long as you don't fly away, Britain and the Crown will remain prosperous, or so I've heard."

"It's true." Colin grinned.

"That's why the Queen personally trimmed your wings, ravens," Karl said with his trademark ironic humor.

"What do you mean by that?" Vicky asked. As a typical Londoner, she thought very highly of her royal family and her traditions.

"The Queen and her whole entourage cost you a damned lot of money. If you got rid of them, you'd have enough money to get all the homeless beggars here off the streets."

"They're so well loved, and they make Great Britain so much more significant in the world."

This observation only provided more fuel for Karl.

"Only to the extent that the British Empire shrank while the royal family's popularity climbed."

"Now don't be so stubborn about the old traditions of the royal family!" Vicky's arguing spirit had flared up and she didn't stop to draw breath as she went on at Karl. "These traditions bring millions of tourists and their money into this country. The people need illusions of happy people, they want to celebrate with them or cry with them."

"What garbage."

"You should have seen how many people attended the magnificent wedding of Prince Charles and Diana Spencer in July 1981. Months in advance, they were selling cups, plates, tins, postcards, pens, and all kinds of great souvenirs with their faces on them."

"What can't people make money off of!" exclaimed Katharina.

"Apparently not through honest work! Trade rakes in the dough," said Karl.

"You know," Colin threw in, remembering an old time "we've brought you things like that as presents before!"

Vicky didn't let them interrupt.

"Well anyway, hundreds of thousands of people waving flags lined the streets. Spectators waited for 48 hours to get a good spot. It was a live affirmation of the people for the monarchy and the queen! The ceremony was broadcast all around the world! The festivities evoked passion in countries everywhere and made loads of money for our country. And that's why the ravens' wings will be clipped at the tower for a very long time!" Vicky laughed.

"Oh yes, even I watched the news on TV in 1981 when the wedding was being broadcast, even if it was more out of interest in England," Katharina remembered. "The couple was beaming with happiness. And people from all over the world were so envious of how in love they were, and were filled with admiration for the young bride's innocence and modesty."

"How can people watch this crap over and over again on TV," Karl muttered.

"What do you mean, over and over again?" Katharina protested. "I first watched the wedding of the Queen's second son Prince Andrew to Sarah Ferguson, and that was five years later on an English news channel. I needed material for current events in class."

"And?"

"I couldn't use it, for only one reason. Unlike Princess Diana, Sarah Ferguson insisted on using the old wording about the wife's obedience in her marriage vows."

"Which part is that?"

"She vowed to obey him all the days of her life."

"And therefore you couldn't use the scene in a lesson?" Colin asked skeptically.

"What century is that from? Or from what backward country?" Katharina's indignation at this flared up again, even after so many years.

Colin knew his history back and forth. "The old wording with 'obey' stems from the fact that one man has to make the decisions when it comes to matters of principle."

"Of course, one *man* – not one woman!"

Karl grinned. "There obviously wasn't any of that for my wife. At our wedding at the Gustav-Adolf Chapel in Lützen, she threatened to leave the room at once and disrupt the wedding if the vicar tried to use the old traditional wording in his sermon. And she would have done it, too."

"Naturally." Katharina made a disparaging face.

"It's a good thing we didn't have the Archbishop of Canterbury, like Sarah and Andrew. The pastor grudgingly accepted her terms, and she claims he was so annoyed with her that he purposely delivered a bad sermon."

"Even without that archaic phrase, his speech was horrible and completely contradictory to my values of love, respect, and tolerance."

"We had to leave the church straight after the wedding."

"And Karl joined the Party, despite my protests. That was almost a deal breaker at the time."

"Vicky was exactly the same way, in spite of her sympathies towards the royal family," Colin told them. "What can you do with such emancipated dames?" he joked, and conspicuously shot Karl a good-natured wink.

"Why haven't either of you ever been to the Tower of London, or into Madame Tussaud's?" Katharina asked.

"What're we supposed to do there?"

"Or into the Houses of Parliament, with Big Ben and Westminster Abbey, or Buckingham Palace, Tower Bridge, or St. Paul's Cathedral?" Katharina listed all the landmarks from her textbook. "Or to Greenwich to see the prime meridian and the Cutty Sark?"

Colin smiled. "We live here. We've always had the option to go whenever we want. We'd rather visit the amazing art museums. That makes a difference. Your excessive desire to see everything here grew out of the forbidden fruit of the paradise you imagined. When you have the freedom to choose, nothing is rushed. You don't have to scramble beyond what is in your reach, for the heaven of your dreams."

"Oh god, Colin always talks so refined," Karl thought to himself. "But it's true. I've never seen any of the tourist landmarks in Rostock, because I could go at any time. When we have visitors, luckily my wife is the one to show them around."

Katharina's camera was clicking constantly. She felt driven to capture all of London so she could take her impressions home with her. Every picture offered the chance of perfectly remembering what before had been unimaginable. If there were no pictures, it hadn't happened. She was frantic, for the day was too short. Her English friends thought the German sense for waking up early was barbaric. So every day they barely got started by 11 o'clock. Furthermore, the rainy weather and dark time of year forced Katharina to have taken all her important outside pictures by 2:30 in the afternoon. With no transition it very quickly began to get dusky, with not enough light to take radiant commemorative pictures.

Right after the ravens of the tower, she saw other birds at Trafalgar Square with the famed Lord Nelson. If a bit less legendary than the ravens, the rustling of the wings of thousands of pigeons was still crucially impressive to the tourists, who excitedly bought overpriced food from shrewd vendors so they could take pictures of themselves with the pesky birds covering their head, arms, and shoulders.

"Oh my goodness!" Karl stared at the incredible chaos surrounding the venerable statue of Lord Nelson. "Here you can get shit on in the truest sense of the word!" Colin nodded.

"There are so many pigeons here you can barely shield yourself from them and their droppings. I'm sure that German socialist pigeons would never do something so unseemly to a public landmark, it's too individualistic."

Vicky joked, "I even bet German socialist pigeons wouldn't walk on the grass without getting special permission from the central Party committee. Trafalgar Square pigeons are obscenely fat, since they're always getting fed by tourists all day long, and they waddle around – barely even able to fly."

Colin directed his gaze up above. "Look at the top of the statue! The aristocratic Lord Nelson is peering disgustedly down at this tacky white venue. The government tried shooting the pigeons, poisoning them, and even forbidding tourists from feeding them."

"Doesn't look like it worked though?"

"But there were always a bunch of protests and angry outbursts in all the papers – English people are so sentimental about animals, even these greedy, fat, poopy birds – that the politicians bowed to public pressure. That's democracy. The rights of the pigeons. Pigeon liberation."

Vicky confirmed Colin's story.

"In England, any politician who is unfriendly to animals will get voted out of their post at the next election. No one in England cared when the American president Lyndon B. Johnson leveled every city in Vietnam and contaminated their farms with napalm. But when he picked up two puppies by the ears in Texas in 1966 – that was the end of his reputation here! Our papers never forgave him."

"Really?"

"The Vietnam War had to be bad news when the guy who led it ran around and attacked little dogs! That was obvious, even to my grandmother. And that's why not even the Iron Lady, Margaret Thatcher, dared to have Trafalgar Square cleaned up."

They neared the first tangle of crosswalks, which wound around Trafalgar Square like a knotted ball of twine. In between, traffic lights and tips like LOOK LEFT and LOOK RIGHT tried to give the tourists on the ground a chance to master the roads as pedestrians, without having an accident. Karl waited at every green stoplight, but the endless chain of cars and busses didn't let him through. At the first red light there appeared to be a hole, but Karl didn't dare start there. Katharina stumbled along behind Colin and Vicky, without looking left or right, as they confidently crossed the road accident-free. Whether the light was green or red. Karl stood stubbornly in front of the red light, as Vicky gave him very pointed signs to start crossing. No good. He fell far behind them, and swore at the English lack of order.

"Why do you even have laws, if no one obeys them?" He grumbled, while Vicky clutched her stomach with laughter. "How German of you," she said, "you're the ones who break laws all the time!"

"Come off it!" (and again Katharina wasn't sure how she should translate that) "How can you compare this wild chaotic traffic with the German love of order?"

Now Colin's love of arguing had been provoked. "The English are very orderly and law-abiding! Germans are the ones who perpetually break their own laws."

"That's an unfounded accusation! You're getting it mixed up."

"I'm not mixing up anything. The English protest when someone breaks the law or wants to change it for no good reason. And what do you do, at least in the east? All you do is gripe, but not openly."

"What makes you say that?" Katharina asked.

"Don't you remember? During our all-night discussions in Pammerow, Karl and I determined that the West Germans have approximately three times as many bad car accidents on record as we do in England, and the East Germans at least twice as many. In England, we have fewer traffic laws, and they're all less strict than yours. For example, in England you can drink and drive."

"That's insane. You all must have a death wish. And you don't see anything wrong with that?"

"The reason is that we are usually smart, proper, law-abiding drivers and therefore don't need strict laws. Karl said himself that loads of German men go berserk when they get behind a wheel. Speeding is something typical of Germany. Stuff like that doesn't happen too often in England."

"But Americans, the French, and the Italians all have really strong laws!" Karl threw in.

"How would you even know? Have you ever been there?" Colin teased him.

"It was in our papers."

"Ah, right, in your papers that are always right? You know, I hadn't heard of Ottokar Domma before. Katharina just explained to me that he wrote about GDR problems from the viewpoint of a child. I'm sure I've read some of his articles in your party paper ..."

Karl made a face. Katharina grinned.

"The problem with Europeans and Americans, you understand, not just the Germans," Colin declared, sure of his argument, "is that they respect authority, like police, the army, judges, teachers, but NOT the law. If Europeans and Americans could change in that respect, one day they could be almost as good as the English."

"Come on," Vicky broke in to the squabble. "Let's go get a coffee and a beer over there in that pub. Then we can talk better."

"Oh, yes," Katharina agreed excitedly. "You can try a real English beer," she said enticingly to Karl.

Although the English beer didn't have enough foam for Karl

(which Colin claimed proved the barkeep's honesty, as Englishmen would never be cheated out of their beer with airy foam) and it was ice-cold from the fridge and shocked Karl's teeth, the slightly smoky pub had a comfortable atmosphere and the simple wooden table inspired a feeling of rustic warmth and coziness.

Colin jumped right back into their debate on order in society. "Maybe I should put it like this. We do actually have order in England, but it's different from the German order. It doesn't depend on bureaucracy, police, regulations, or formalities. We English see the Germans as lawless anarchists – oh, and the French and Italians, too. That's why they have to go through their bureaucrats to get every last little detail mandated."

Vicky finished with her own critical bluntness.

"You Germans have always had more prohibitions than freedoms, more rules and regulations than personal responsibility, and more demonization than enlightenment!"

Again, Karl pulled his face into a disparaging smile. But he waited to object until Colin had finished his arguments.

"We English actually have more order than other people. In England, everyone automatically lines up and behaves in an orderly way on his own. That's why we react so strongly to rules and regulations that aren't strictly necessary. If, for example, at night there happens to be a traffic light on red, but there's not a single car coming, a pedestrian's not going to stand there losing his mind until the bloody light changes. Here, we think of the traffic lights as being there for the people, and not the other way around. It's only proper that the Germans need so much discipline in the truest sense of the word, because they are fundamentally anarchic."

Tuesday, October 22nd 1996

At 5:30, I give up waiting for the doctor to come around so that we can escape the clinic just for an hour. But now no one can do anything. Felix reacts to this very mournfully. "Lying around all day ... I don't want to stay here anymore." As he grows more and more aware of his own misery, the atmosphere is sinking lower and lower.

I am feeling sour. Driving away depresses me more than usual this time. Luckily Torsten comes out of the city in a good mood (he cut out for a couple hours without the knowledge of the doctors) and leads Felix back from the parking lot.

In the silence on my drive home, I wonder about this strange young man, who seizes the right to decide his own personal happiness in his dead-end situation.

An old man at the next table over seems to have had a couple liters of beer too many and joins conversations at other tables – invited or not. He registered the Germans talking in the pub and swore colorfully at the European Community, including rude gestures.

It took all of Vicky's efforts to get rid of the troublesome guest.

"The people here don't seem to think very much of Germans? Or at least the socialist part of Germany?" Karl asked.

Colin sharply corrected the impression that the old Englishman had left behind.

"People in England don't think much of anti-socialism, except maybe the far right Tories. But they also fancy themselves anti-communist as well as anti-fascist. The great majority of English think of communism and fascism as the same thing."

"Hmm, well," Karl tried to interrupt him.

"The general opinion on Germany is that West Germany became democratic after the way, but East Germany stayed the way things were under Hitler."

"That's unbelievable," Karl ranted.

"I would just remind you that that's what the majority thinks. Hardly anyone in England sees the GDR as 'socialist.' They call it 'communist' and mean 'anti-socialist.' It's impossible to call the GDR a 'socialist country' in England without being laughed at."

"Crazy, isn't it?" Katharina looked at Karl with raised brows, and took a deep breath. "From your papers they only know what media propaganda has spun out of the truth."

"There's freedom of the press here!" Colin immediately countered. "Some serious papers manage to catch hold of the truth, even if they have to take a detour first."

"This topic might as well be closed for you now," Vicky chimed in. "The GDR probably doesn't exist anymore! Even though Margaret Thatcher is going to protest the reunification, based on her historical knowledge."

"Obviously it's not going to come to a reunification," said Karl. "That would never work. That would ruin our overall economy."

"It's already ruined!"

"No it's not. You can't combine the two political systems short-term. It would be an economic disaster. We'll have to keep the GDR for at least ten years, only as a democracy and with the freedom to travel."

Karl leaned back contentedly and looked out the window at the tall statue of Lord Nelson. Not just his head, but his whole body and the boots on his feet had been irreverently shat on by countless pigeons, who dived like vultures onto the chunks of food held out for them, he thought.

"The hundred-year-old Tower Bridge could have made a wonderful photo opportunity," Katharina lamented in the dimness of the late afternoon. In the gentle blue glow of numerous street lights, the steel cable suspension and cross bars of the bridge made for a fairy-tale like setting. "Both of the towers look like the filigree battlements on a castle out of a fairy tale, and you can even go in them. They've turned it into an interesting museum about the marvelous old lifting machinery and the history of the bridge."

"How do you know all this?" Colin wondered.

"I've taught it for years. In my fantasies I've been to London a hundred times, and I recognize so many details of the city now. The bridge is even greater and more gigantic than we imagined it – the opposite of the Tower of London."

Open-mouthed, Katharina stood before the enormous clock tower of the parliament building, which shone as though coated with pure gold. From beneath she saw the tremendous clock, whose famous "Big Ben" bell chime was known all over the world.

"In my opinion, the best photo spot in London is near Tower Bridge. It can't match up to the time-honored Westminster Abbey around the corner here, where the royal family traditionally observes their crowning ceremonies, weddings, and funerals."

"Now don't lay it on so thick," Karl said. "The whole parliament building with its 1200 rooms – yes, I know that from you – is a crazy building! Loads of officials gather there and can take apart your underdeveloped bureaucracy."

Colin smiled knowingly, but didn't respond to the tiny jab.

"Not just a crazy building, it has a crazy history too. November 5th – Bonfire Night. It's the second biggest occasion in England after Christmas. I'm sure you've heard of Guy Fawkes, who on November 5th 1605, almost succeeded in assassinating the English parliament by blowing up the Palace of Westminster. It's still celebrated today. He's known as the only man to get into parliament with honest intentions."

Karl smirked. "Black British humor. I can't even laugh at that."

As they let the unending masses of people sweep them along Oxford Street with its thousands of businesses and cozy little restaurants, Katharina stopped abruptly.

"Just look at these window displays, Karl! This one is called Anne Summers." Katharina excitedly shook Karl's arm and tugged him to the window with the barely clothed, tantalizing window mannequins and strange accessories that she had never seen before.

Karl followed her hesitantly and immediately looked away. "What the hell is that?" he growled in embarrassment.

"It's like an English Beate Uhse, you know."

"So what? I don't even know who Uhse is. Something to do with capitalist sex."

"Come on, we'll just go right in. We've never seen something like this!" Vicky laughed at Karl's stunned expression. "Well let's go, I'm coming too!" Colin decided he'd rather wait by the door.

Not three minutes later Karl was back outside. "You can't look at that stuff. You'd lose your appetite just looking at the filthy pictures in those magazines," he said apologetically to Colin. "What are the two womenfolk doing in there?"

Vicky moved nonchalantly through the dildos of various shapes and sizes. She looked impassively at the blown up sex doll with a strangely shaped round mouth. Katharina tried to pretend that this was all perfectly normal to her. But with a shamefaced sideways glance at the other patrons, she couldn't escape the feeling that everyone here was staring at her. After five minutes she couldn't take it anymore, and hurried back to the men waiting outside.

"Incredible, isn't it?"

"We don't need stuff like that," Karl said firmly. Katharina shrugged her shoulders and waited for Vicky, who was amused by her East German visitors when she came out of the store. "You guys aren't repressed at all, huh?"

"I've never seen that kind of thing before. You Brits must have the most extraordinary sex lives with these goods," Katharina teased. "I read in Lothar Kusche" (the book she'd always read to her students in the last class before vacation) "in his description of sex in England, that they don't have any, just hot water bottles." She turned to Karl, translating the last phrase for him.

"Even I would have understood that," Karl rebuked her. And with that the topic was closed for him. In the silence that followed, Katharina wondered idly where Vicky had learned the German word for 'repressed' – *verklemmt*. It wasn't really translatable. Oh, well. No matter.

The next day offered them new sights all over again, this time on a long walk through the city. Colin marched right across the carefully tended vibrant grass of Hyde Park.

"You can't just trample over the grass," Katharina called behind him, taking the longer path over the outer border of the grounds.

Karl shook his head. "They don't know the meaning of order here."

"Are you guys not allowed to walk on the grass?" Colin remembered. "When we were on the first course in Potsdam, we walked all over the green grass in Sanssouci to get to the park bench."

"Some kind of groundskeeper threatened us with his fist. It was a riot!" Vicky finished.

"As you can see, English grass is green in winter, even in our garden in Wembley. It all depends on the people walking on it, you understand? That keeps it nice, green and fresh." Colin's sharp humor captured international prejudices with disarming precision.

The Drapers played along with Katharina's adventurous game of finding all the things from her GDR textbook, as they themselves had many new things to discover. The Thames with its twenty-six bridges (were there really that many?), the underground tube network with its 250 tube stations (but there were more being built, even under the Thames), Oxford Street with thousands of glittering businesses and restaurants (43 km long, that couldn't possibly be true), St. Paul's Cathedral (250 years old, plus some for the age of the textbook), Greenwich (the prime meridian went somewhere through here), and the Cutty Sark with its Chinese tea, red double-decker busses (they somehow pulled up differently at the bus stops and always appeared to Karl to be coming from the opposite side), nostalgic-seeming red telephone booths (with broken phones, but Katharina loved them and shot twenty pictures of them), black taxi cabs with bullet-proof glass between the driver and the punters, the renowned Odeon cinema (which wasn't true at all, apparently every cinema here was called the Odeon), Piccadilly Circus (light up ads can be blinding), Leicester Square (too much culture for Karl) and Carneby Street (the Beatles had also been here), red dustbins with the heading LITTER (Karl almost threw the postcard for Grandma in one of these, he had learned in school that these said MAIL), Chinese restaurants with real Chinese food at reasonable prices (in Warnemünde, it cost Karl a month's salary to buy dinner for four at an exclusive Asian restaurant), Indian restaurants in Wembley (although the many Indians there didn't play soccer), wonderful examples of typical English pubs (one called the Horse House, which you weren't allowed to say out loud, Colin warned ominously) and so many souvenir shops (real treasures for Katharina's next lesson, so the students in Pammerow could touch an authentic bit of real England).

On December 31st, they were scheduled to have their first New Year's in England together, after the Drapers had celebrated three New Year's Eves with Karl and Katharina in Pammerow.

Karl and Katharina excitedly counted down to midnight with a couple friends and guests the Drapers had invited to meet their visitors from Germany. On the TV screen, Big Ben was chiming twelve for the last time in the world-changing year 1989! Their champagne glasses were already filled. "Cheers to the new year!"

Katharina and Karl hurried to pull on their coats and see London's New Year's fireworks, which were sure to be exceptional. Their first New Year in London! How fine that sounded. They ran outside. Darkness. They looked at each other. Nothing. No people on the streets. Not a single light in the windows of the neighbors. No fireworks, no explosions. Silence. Was this really happening? Was this New Year's Eve in London?

Vicky stood behind them in the warm glow of her open door. She laughed.

"I could have told you this would be the case. We're not in Germany. Most people here have already gone to bed."

Karl didn't want to believe it. "But on TV I've seen them do fireworks in London!"

"That was probably a broadcast from Trafalgar Square. In the middle of London, of course, there's always something happening. Here in Wembley all of the pubs are closed."

"All the bottles on the table are still half full! Pretty small amount of alcohol for such a night!" said Karl, who could even speak English with a rising blood alcohol level.

"Well, yeah, we aren't used to the boozing. The Scots are somewhat different than us in England."

"At our first New Year's celebration in Pammerow your friends poured the wine for us, we didn't do it ourselves. Schnapps in the fruit bowl and vodka in the Vita-Cola."

"Vicky felt so miserable that she didn't get out of bed at all on New Year's Day, thanks to her circulatory disorder." Colin snickered.

"After that I thought all Germans were heavy drinkers."

Curiously, Katharina stared at a couple of dirty figures who had lifelessly sought shelter from the grungy weather in the doorway to a house. An older woman even appeared to have gone to sleep in the dirt of the street, an old, ripped cover thrown over her. One of the figures tiredly lifted his hand to beg, and looked at Katharina with dull eyes and a toothless grin. "I've never seen something like that in real life," she whispered to Karl. "It's like in a movie." Karl turned to Colin. "Why doesn't anyone care about them – the thousands of people going past them every day like they don't see them? They belong in a protected shelter!"

"They don't have the money for that. Most start by being unemployed. Alcohol and drugs destroyed their decision-making ability over time. So they stay homeless and beg."

"They should be committed to a state-funded residence and a company should be obligated to take care of them. That's what we do, anyway. Everyone has to work. It's a matter of human dignity."

Colin smiled. "No, that's freedom. No one can be forced to do something, as long as they're not harming others. That would go against human dignity."

At home in Wembley, 22-year-old Mark sat flopped across the couch reading a thick Stephen King novel. Katharina didn't recognize the title. "Any good?" she asked him.

"Yeah, I love these wild stories about mysterious killings. You've got to read it! It explores the abyss between human feeling and thought, like you could never imagine in your wildest dreams of heaven and hell."

"That sort of book isn't available where we live, I think, they were on the banned books list."

"Could be. But that's what I love about our freedom, where everyone can do what they want. There's no barriers."

"But in school you need to have set boundaries and help," Katharina defended her own teaching ethos. "Teachers have to take special care of each individual student to make sure they do well, especially if personal problems come up."

"I would go crazy in a country like the GDR," Mark grumbled, unusually fierce. The teachers should just do their jobs, not take care of us. It's annoying. Get paid for the job and be done."

"But isn't it good when, for example, teachers take care of every student getting a good grade on the final exams and being able to secure a good job?"

"Hey, that's not the teacher's responsibility. It's just bloody coercion! In the GDR they even make people work who don't want to work!"

His sister Jane, who was still in the process of earning her degree and was only home for a couple days between semesters, sat next to him.

"I heard that too when I went to the GDR. You don't just legally have a right to work, which I think is pretty great, but you're actually mandated to work. That is actually against human dignity."

Katharina pouted, and simply said "We'll talk about it after dinner. And now, who has the obligation or the freedom to come with me into the kitchen?"

After five days, Katharina and Karl wearily decided to save the rest of their tourist activities for another time.

The last day of their first trip over the border into the city of her dreams came to an end after a week. Katharina traipsed around the souvenir shop on Oxford Street one last time so she could bring her students some perspective material for class. She was particularly fond of the English newspaper stand near the tube stop. So many different papers and colorful magazines in one place! She'd never seen the like before. And all in English! In the GDR she had clung to every current English newspaper and every English news article that the Drapers enclosed in their letters, to be able to take something from the original language into her lesson! Here everything was just lying about, even on the tubes, carelessly thrown away. She picked up one such tossed aside daily paper and lost herself hungrily into an article about the drug problem with youths, which wasn't something familiar to her at home.

"Translate it," said Karl.

"A survey showed that 97% of youths said they've tried marijuana, 40% amphetamines, 38% ecstasy, 33% LSD, 32% cocaine, 3% heroine, and 2% crack."

"What even is that?" Karl asked.

"Some drug." Katharina thought for a moment, but then translated further, if a bit roughly. "Over a third at raves, but those with higher education were even more than 50%. A reporter from TIME OUT said they believed that the sample of those surveyed represented one in every 500 25-year-olds in London, and was typical for the age group."

"One in every 500? But typical for 25-year-olds? How many of those are there in London?" Karl interrupted her translation. "At 11 million residents I would estimate ..."

"Oh, stop calculating in your head. Listen! RELEASE, the drug report agency, said last night that the survey showed how widespread the use of cannabis is. It's an argument for the decriminalization of drugs."

Insanity! Katharina hadn't believed the same article about England in a German paper – they just always wanted to make England look bad!

On the last evening, over flickering candlelight and a bottle of red wine, the four recalled their long discussion nights of the last ten years, when the Drapers came to visit Pammerow. What a feeling, to finally see the world on the other side of the border!

"Now what will become of your school system in the GDR?" asked Vicky, who a few years ago had analyzed the advantages of working in the academic profession in a social region.

"Hard to say," Katharina answered. "The old teachers will stay on." She thought of Ceausescu. "If not all of them. The principals will all be removed. Hollenkamp is gone already."

"In Leipzig all labor officials and party secretaries were let go from their school positions. Udo told us about it. You know, he was part of our group in the Potsdam course. He seems to be having a bit of trouble himself."

"In any case, there will be new school principals," said Karl.

"That will bring a lot of fuss," Katharina sighed. "A new school principal won't simply be appointed, like they used to be. It'll be more democratic, to be voted in in a democracy. All the teachers in the schools, all the students, all the parents have to vote on if they agree with the new candidates ..."

" ...or if they've got skeletons in their closets. Like working for the Stasi, for example," Karl threw in.

"And we won't call them directors anymore, they're 'school leaders' from now on."

"Sounds like it's an all-around new beginning for the GDR," Colin concluded.

Friday, October 25th 1996

These days, Felix often stays for dinner and spends the night with Grandma and Grandpa on Greifswald-Straße – that helps on both sides. My parents are getting to be very on top of things with Felix around.

The TV is playing a program on right extremism. They hide their political attitudes behind a fad, bald heads and black leather jackets. Felix stares impassively at their bald heads, which look so similar to his without their hair. Terminally ill, as the doctor with the dying baobab had pronounced.

"That's supposed to turn girls on? Or any young people, come to that?" Only his tolerance, which was still present, stopped him from protesting further. "It's not just that they don't turn me on. They turn me off."

CHAPTER 5

The architect had let his imagination run wild. As the sun climbed steadily higher over the Warnow Valley, the renovated school building's radiant yellow-orange walls threw its blazing light right back into the eyes of onlookers. The colorful campus buildings resembled nothing so much as toy blocks, tossed carelessly by a child and landed at the foot of a green hillside. In the winter, children went screaming down the snowy white slope on their sleds. But during the rest of the year there bloomed a diverse greenery, reflecting the hope for a thriving educational landscape in Pammerow. It was home to a forest of ten thousand trees, planted by the schoolchildren themselves twenty years previously, and what had been a flat muddy field was now a proud tribute to nature. In the time of reunification in the 90's, it was the bearer of a seed that symbolized a new life for society. What would sprout? Which plants would stay healthy and grow?

When Katharina came out of her tenth grade class and back into her principal's office, there was a lot of mail on her desk. She skimmed the various letters, determining her work priorities for the day. Here was another grease-stained and carelessly ripped open note from Mrs. Hass, apologizing for all the days her son had played hooky – a trifling gesture on Mrs. Hass's part. A class teacher's petition for the reprimand of another teacher who had made offensive statements and threats, this accompanied by a pile of letters from students – all wanting to complain to Mrs. Stern. A parent's warning of suspected alcohol and drug use by ninth graders, they wanted the class teacher Mr. Rollauf to follow up urgently. A notice from the criminal investigation department regarding a lawsuit instigated against unknown persons who had broken into the school reminded her of the police at the Remington High school in Baton Rouge. A complaint from the Kindergarten teachers about two children who were behaving inappropriately. They didn't know what to do about it, they were afraid. She decided to bring the petitions and complaints from residents about the cigarette butts polluting their area and a letter from an attorney about the critical wording on a student's grade report to the staff meeting tomorrow.

Peter Hilmann's grandmother had sat in her office for quite a lengthy period yesterday, complaining about the insolent, indolent young people today who had it far too good.

"Can you imagine?" she said. "My grandchildren have the most awful behavior. You buy gorgeous, expensive wrapping paper, and they just tear it to apart to get at the presents! And of course they don't just want one thing for Christmas, they've got hundreds of wishes. And they pout if Santa didn't bring them everything they wanted. Chocolate? They say they don't like it and they just throw it away! They've got it far too good, they don't know the true value of anything! Hopeless. No idea about the work that other people do anymore! Things were different when I was their age!"

Breathing deeply, Katharina sat at her desk to immerse herself in the daily work of dealing with complaints. She had to hurry, as she was expecting her colleague Rollauf in half an hour for an urgent one-on-one teacher conference.

Her gaze hung on the big dark poster with white letters that she herself had hung on a crooked nail a long time ago:

'The children now love luxury,
they have bad manners,
contempt for authority,
they show disrespect for elders
and love chatter in place of exercise.'

When had the philosopher Socrates lived?

450 BC? More than two thousand years ago? There was another one from around that time – Aristotle, born at least 150 years later, who was purported to have uttered his own wise words on the subject of youths:

'I see no hope for the future of our people
if they are dependent on the frivolous youth of today,
for certainly all youth are reckless beyond words.'

Complaints about the younger generation are as old as humankind, and in spite of all these wise sayings we haven't been destroyed yet, thought Katharina. So much today is different from back then. And yet everyone knows that our youths are ultimately a reflection on our current society. Katharina was certain she remembered the young people from before the reunification as being different. Was that really the case? Or was it just the knee-jerk of an old mind to view the younger generation through a critical lens?

"And yet, modern kids are what we make them" she murmured, and simultaneously realized a contradiction to her own thoughts. "We? After the reunification? Or someone else? They'll never be what we were. That's hard to grasp."

What she called "teacher conferences" affected the harmonious atmosphere at the school like healing water from the legendary fountain of youth, source of eternal youth and eternal life. Without them, Katharina's field of work and influence as principal would have lacked a vital driving power. The hours of her time and energy that she invested went far beyond what was defined as a work day by the new educational bureaucracy in Germany. She spent endless amounts of time working with each individual teacher.

"Why are you doing this?" asked Jürgen Misslich, the experienced long-time principal of the neighboring school in Heidesande, with whom she was on friendly terms. "You're working yourself into the ground."

"Ensuring the emotional stability and support of teachers is of utmost importance at this time. Much more important than writing reports to the school board."

"No one's paying you for the time you spend doing that."

"Time is needed to change things."

"You can't really change grown adults."

"But maybe I'll get a thank you."

"Pah. At the end of the day you'll just get a kick in the pants from above, because your school's students aren't testing high enough, even if they're turning out into damned fine people. Whether the teachers feel like they're in good hands or are just sliding by on the bare minimum, neither the school board nor the government are interested."

"Whether they're interested or not is beside the point."

"If you say so. Then what?"

"Well, on the one hand, I want to hear about all the problems with students and families that I can't see for myself, honestly and in as much detail as possible in these conferences."

"It's privacy, my love! According to law, not everything is your business."

"But I need those details in order to take the right measures with children and avoid making bad decisions in terms of psychological support."

"How so?"

"In isolated cases I'd have to lever out bureaucratic regulations to be able to aid in a personal capacity."

"That's ridiculous," Misslich interrupted her. "This never-ending female emotional intelligence! We have staff meetings. Parents don't want you to know about all their details and problems. Everything is kept private. I'll say it again - privacy. We don't live in the GDR anymore, my dear colleague." He smirked and winked. "And as long as our teachers are portrayed as slackers and idiots by the media, complicated kids and especially their families aren't going to want anything to do with your 'psychological support.'"

"That's for sure. It's unbelievable how destructive the media can be," Katharina agreed. "Always desperate for a sensation, they resort to making fun of teachers."

"They're taking away the essential image of a role model that kids can look up to. But the positive image of teachers has clearly been destroyed and replaced with artificially created idols who appeal to questionable instincts." Misslich had gotten himself riled up again in his overly critical view of the world.

"Questionable instincts?" Katharina looked at the figures on the private TV networks in front of her.

"Look at the aggressive, homicidal heroes in kids' movies! Their hearts beat faster at the sight of gory murders and robberies, torture and pools of blood. Rivalry, jealousy, and rape are fascinating the primitive urges in our children." Misslich's rant burst out over Katharina in an angry torrent. "The sex industry has been developed to a perverse perfection! These blonde girls, with their enormous silicone breasts and long hair oozing with sex, make every fiber of a male brain quiver. They act silly and show the rampant sexuality inherent in using drugs and alcohol." Misslich was on a roll now. "And that's what our children see day after day on their computers and TVs. The numbness to human suffering drilling into their subconscious ..."

"You're right, Jürgen," said Katharina, trying to calm the irascible stream of words. "But unfortunately we can't do much to change that. These teacher conferences aren't about the unfortunate role that media plays in educating children, but about the health and wellness of every one of my colleagues."

"Mutual respect and friendly back and forth, eh?" Misslich joked. "That sounds just like a normal teacher meeting."

"Not at all, my love! In a one-to-one conversation I can address their success stories and teaching progress as well as their real worries and needs, privately and honestly. That way no one feels like they have to expose themselves in front of a huge group."

"When would they feel like that?"

"Like if angry parents are picking apart their teaching."

"So what if they do? What else?"

"Or an unprofessional reaction to misbehaving children."

"You're not saying someone at your school has lost their temper, are you?" Misslich's steel-blue eyes bored through her with sharp humor.

Katharina was undaunted. "No, but used the wrong words! And you can't just give them a warning then."

"Hah, I've seen parents retain a lawyer just for saying 'You idiot!'" Misslich grinned.

"You see! And I'm sure they got justice. If the atmosphere at the school isn't right, the teachers and their nerves all go to hell in a handbasket."

"Bunch of hooey," said Misslich in his manly self-assured way.

"It's not hooey at all," Katharina said matter-of-factly. "You know perfectly well that if anything is awry in the chain of teachers, we're only as strong as our weakest link. And then the kids will steamroll us every day with problems. Students can be terrible that way. We try to create a comfortable learning atmosphere with them, with established rules and boundaries, but they'll turn into a mob in a flash."

"You may be right. Our teachers have burdens that stink to high heaven. We thought it would be very different after the re-unification." With these words, Misslich reached a hand out to his colleague. "Take care, Katharina, and I wish you much success with your next teacher conference."

Throughout the school year, Katharina found time (undisturbed if possible) for every one of her forty colleagues. Over the years these mutually critical conversations became a truly safe space for ideas and suggestions for improvement. The school's overall climate was one that emanated dependability. And over time, the principle of democracy and confidentiality became something that was taken for granted. Heidrun Meschke, whose meeting time had at first been pushed back because of an illness or some other impediment and then later lost in the heap of appointments, voiced protesting reminders. "I haven't had my teacher conference yet, please don't forget!"

Katharina sometimes laughed out loud when new colleagues were deployed to her school and privately asked around the faculty, with perhaps a hint of misgiving, what they should prepare for these discussions, just to be safe.

One teacher, on the occasion of her fiftieth birthday, had brought in a couple bottles of champagne for a morning toast in the teachers' lounge. When Katharina discovered this, she shared a story from her time teaching in the 70's.

"We were still pretty young, and we had a champagne toast in the staff room for someone's first baby during the long recess. During the next hour, when one of the students was standing up to take attendance – that was how we did it back then – he suddenly said, 'Mrs. Stern, is it your birthday today?' I held my breath. 'No, why?' – 'You're so cheerful today.' It was funny, of course, but the worst thoughts were running through my head. What would he say at home? Parents are so judgmental. You become vulnerable. I'd never be able to respond confidently to a lazy student's fat, nagging, whining, shrieking mother like my old deputy principal Strenge. 'You can kiss my ass,' she screamed at him. He grinned and answered, in quite a friendly tone, 'That seems a bit much to ask, given the size of it.' Anyway, since then I haven't ever had a glass of champagne so long as students were still in the building, and later insisted that my colleagues refrain too, for the same reason. So I ask you not to consume any alcohol in the morning, even if there's something to celebrate."

At the next teacher conference, this colleague brought Hans Müller with her, the friendly yet forceful staff council representative who had been elected by all as their staunch defender. He eventually left the room shaking his head.

"What I'd like to know is why you're so worked up about being told off for champagne," he grumbled.

"The principal said I drink alcohol at school. I need a witness if she tries to lambast me here," she said bitterly, "plus then I'm insured legal protection."

She didn't yet know the function of the teacher conferences at the school in Pammerow. But there were reasons for that. Once bitten, twice shy. Katharina couldn't fight off a hidden smile.

"What could have changed these teachers so much after the reunification?" she pondered, feeling dubious of the newfound freedom everyone had.

"What happened to them before?" asked her inner voice.

Katharina didn't try to puzzle through that though, though for a moment the names of Hollenkamp, Wagner, Rutzlaff, Lola Herr, and the old superintendent surfaced from the storm of her subconscious to flash through her mind.

Things were much better for the teachers than they had been before; the lessons they'd previously had to inject with the GDR's political agenda were no longer around in the same way.

"For us, that was the biggest moment of joy and relief in our whole careers as teachers," she wrote ecstatically to her friends in London right after the reunification. "Getting rid of this mandatory political loyalty to the working class, the Socialist Unity Party and their political objectives has cut my time expenditure on lesson planning in half. I no longer have to contemplate how I can artificially politicize my lessons in case a higher up sits in. Or in case anyone sits in, never mind who. I'm suddenly free to use anything the world has to offer in my English class. My own personal wall has fallen. Since the few months before the wall fell, I've been following the news stations on TV and the radio with more interest than ever before. Everything is suddenly completely different. It's all slowly coming to light what I didn't want to believe before, because the truth was just a bother. Any weak protests I had subconsciously were always suppressed, pushed off to the side, always defeated by downplaying what was going on in the limited scope of political information available. I thought the people who claimed to be suffering so much here had to be exaggerating. But all of a sudden, those indescribable conditions are in living color right before my eyes. I never believed it before!"

In her dreams of heaven, Katharina could not, nor did she try to, imagine all the marvelous things that lay beyond the horizon for schools and teachers in her country. In 1989, she felt free beyond words, full of ideas for her new life!

Monday, October 28th 1996

Karl's driving by himself to the psychiatric clinic in Rostock-Gehlsdorf. They spend an hour waiting for the doctor to come around and give them permission to leave for a few hours.

They drive to the Honda dealership to look at a modern new car for Felix. Even a 75 PS seems to be too big for such a small guy. Why are we doing this to ourselves? Felix is terminally ill. We're trying to replace the clearly hopeless situation in front of us with optimism for the future.

My day was exhausting. Six hours of teaching, a test committee meeting with the state institute, a festive event with all the entrepreneurs in the region, and finally an emergency conference of the youth club, in my position as municipal chairperson of the social committee. I'm investing my last bit of energy in saving the world. What did this day do to save me?

Tonight I feel like my nerves are at their breaking point. Slightly jittery, easily excitable, on the verge of tears. It seems I can't just skip a reassuring visit to the clinic and not worry about it. Fear is stirring in my subconscious that we haven't overcome our problems –an MRI will be taken on Wednesday after the radiation is over, the results of which I'm very anxious to see. Will the radiation prove to have been successful?

As a small child, if some catastrophe was lurking on the horizon or if some heart's desire wasn't being fulfilled, I sometimes prayed, 'dear God in heaven, if you're really there, then prove it to me now and give me a sign. Then I'll believe in you.' I called on him to get pregnant with Felix. What would I beg dear God in heaven for today, if I were sure he was there? What would I offer him for the life of my child? If I could turn back the wheel of time, what would I give up in exchange for a positive outcome?

The word from the thousands of throats in the Leipzig Monday demonstrations resonated in Katharina's memory. "Tra-vel free-dom!" How deeply she had felt the frisson of these words in October! The opening of the border should have brought Katharina the freedom to travel that she'd always dreamed of.

She felt the long-suppressed drive towards distant lands rise up inside her. Suddenly a need awoke in her that had been resting in deep slumber. All at once a great other world had opened up, with an unlimited culture, conflicting histories, endlessly wide geography which she felt she had to hustle to catch up on. Suddenly she was aware how little she had known of the world outside her small village before the reunification in 1989, in spite of her letter exchange with a 'free' part of the globe.

But the news in her letters from London was changing in alarming ways, the problems with Mark taking on a more concrete form.

"Listen to this. Colin answered my questions. I just want to read this part out quick."

"October 12th 1991. It doesn't make me happy to write about what we're going through, as we're ashamed of him and his horrid behavior. But at this point we've decided that he has to leave our house again. Maybe you can imagine what that means for us. He is our only son, the son we've always loved and still love. It brings tears to our eyes to think of it. Taking him back into our home was a big mistake. We spent two years living in a nightmare. We couldn't go on living with his violent tendencies.

Let me sum up in a few sentences what we've gone through in the last several months.

Mark began to fight furiously over small things, and would scream at us in rage, especially when he was drunk. It was getting out of control, to the point of violence. Sometimes he punched me and I had to get medical treatment. He even hit Vicky and kicked her, like when she wouldn't give him her car – when he already has his own. Last fall the police came round because he'd started a pub brawl. He got in trouble with the police multiple times. He beat his girlfriend. She got pregnant last February, but she broke it off with him over her qualms about his feelings, which you can't blame her for. When she was here once, he beat her for no apparent reason, dragged her down the stairs and trampled right over her in a rage as she was lying on her stomach in front of the front door. He pushed me over the car from behind, shoved Vicky and his girlfriend to the ground again, and my elderly parents happened to be visiting, they sat frozen in terror. Finally I called the police. That was in June. June became July and he didn't want to go to therapy. After the next big confrontation we ordered him to leave.

The worst is over now, but I feel dreadfully guilty to have failed as a father ..."

"I'm speechless," said Karl. "None of that makes any sense. What could have changed the boy so much? He was such a nice, likable fellow when he played table tennis with the kids here on their visit."

Two years later Katharina was shaken to read in one of the London letters that the worst was in fact not yet over. "Colin's describing their awful Christmas holiday," she told Karl as they sat cozied up to a glass of champagne that evening, enjoying the last few moments of Katharina's birthday in peace together.

"January 1st 1993. Christmas. Mark came, and he looked like a walking skeleton, with filthy clothes and long, uncut, uncombed, unwashed hair. My elderly parents were deeply shocked to see their grandson looking like that at Christmas. An already thin guy, he'd gone from 76 kg to 66. He doesn't seem to have gotten any sleep for a while, if the deep dark circles under his eyes are anything to go by. He sat there for about an hour, barely moving, not saying anything, while the others tried to besiege him with food and drinks. Then he went to bed without a word and emerged again almost 24 hours later. Merry Christmas. Nevertheless, everyone in the family tried to suppress that image and have a good Christmas morning. Like every year, they opened the presents under the tree and sat around the table for the traditional turkey dinner that Vicky had lovingly prepared.

On Boxing Day, when friends and other relatives showed up to exchange gifts, Mark looked somewhat human. The guests were still quieter than usual, subdued by Mark's exhausted, emaciated appearance. They ate and drank more than they should have, as tradition demands in Great Britain on Boxing Day, and played cards long into the night, while the older ones watched Christmas programs on their favorite TV channels. A successful holiday; the guests didn't leave until 2 in the morning and even Mark became a little sociable as the evening went on.

The next day, Mark started talking confidently about finding a room in London and looking for a job. He said the people he'd kept company with in Oxford had gone half mad, except for two of them who were completely mad, and he didn't want to go back there anymore. Once again, he had left the hostel where he'd been living. We listened to him and hoped for the best. Within a week, he'd actually found a room and talked optimistically about a job opening. He said it would be impossible to find a room or a job in Oxford, but in London there were opportunities. This attitude was encouraging, but then he stayed moody all week, and his attitude changed. He couldn't sleep at all and he walked around the house in the middle of the night, not particularly quietly, I might add. He even snarled at his mother in a rage just like before, so that she was fluctuating between fear and panic. We consoled ourselves with the fact that his lifestyle and ours just didn't go together, that he recognized that and was looking for his own room and a job to pay for it. On New Year's Eve he told us that the landlady wanted 100 pounds deposit for the room, as well as 50 pounds in advance for the first week's rent, and he still needed 30 pounds. He said he felt a bit under pressure. I gave him 50 pounds, which seemed to satisfy him. The next Saturday

Mark moved in to his new room. He came into my office, gave me the address and phone number, and marched off, his knapsack on his back. I promised him that I'd bring all his things in the car, including the TV, as soon as possible. And Mark thanked us for having taken such good care of him over Christmas. On the one hand I hadn't believed he would get a room so quickly, even though he'd hoped to. And for five minutes after our son had gone, I felt ecstatically happy. That whole week we felt like a huge weight had been lifted, especially when we weren't being woken up by him all night. We felt this surge of relief that he was gone, and with him, all the tension and worry over what he was going to do next. But then I suddenly burst into tears when I realized that I was happy our son had left us.

A week later, we learned that Mark had never arrived at his new lodging, and instead gone back to Oxford that same night to be with his drop-out friends and return to his old life. He called once to tell us, after he'd collected his 100 pound deposit from the landlady ..."

"This is unbelievable! What the hell does 'drop-out friends' mean? Junkies? No work, no home, and addicted to drugs? We always thought nothing like this could ever happen in our circle of friends! And who's to blame? Who's really responsible? This wouldn't have happened under socialism," said Karl.

Summer fluttered into their home along with the next letter, which surpassed Katharina and Karl's wildest imaginings of parental unhappiness.

"London, May 28th 1993. We were both feeling newly encouraged Mark turned up again when two or three weeks ago and claimed he'd gotten off the drugs. He looked much healthier than at Christmas. We had even considered taking a couple days holiday in Wales and leaving him at home with Udo for company. You remember cheerful Udo from our old Potsdam course. I'm sure you've also heard that he's been trying to find a new job in the neighborhood here in London, after he was let go from his teaching position in Germany for supposed connections to the Stasi?

Udo's been hard at work since he arrived in the middle of March. Every Thursday he went to the library to study the 'Times

Educational Supplement' and the 'Guardian,' both of which have classified ads for teaching jobs. At first he wasn't getting any results, but his CV and his self-confidence slowly grew. Two weeks ago he finally was invited to his first interview. It was with a school near Hastings, where they're mainly looking for a German teacher, but who could also possibly do a little Russian and Latin. Vicky and I were worried about his chances, because even though he's a capable man, this would be his first time in a competitive job interview. That means being peppered with penetrating and possibly uncomfortable questions by a group of people who know the English education system inside and out. It goes without saying that he passed his test with flying colors and even outdid three other candidates (one of whom was from East Germany) and received a great job offer in one of the nicest and most coveted parts of England.

All this good news was too good to last, and we should have realized that fate was setting us up. When we arrived back in Victoria after our trip to Dover, Jane was already waiting for us at the train station. She reported that when we had arrived in Belgium on Thursday and Vicky had called home from the hotel and talked to Mark, she heard that Udo had come straight from Sussex – very excited over his job offer (the interview was in the afternoon and we had left in the morning). Mark had hung up the phone, come back into the living room, and told Udo "Mom says good luck on the job."

After Udo had gone to bed, he was woken up again at 5:30 in the morning by a crashing noise. He came out of his bedroom to see Mark swinging a hammer over his head as he yelled 'Out of my way, Udo!' Then Mark began to systematically destroy the house. First he smashed the telephone, so that Udo couldn't call anyone. With his hammer he shattered the upstairs windows, having already smashed the ones on the lower level before Udo got out of bed. And then he smashed everything breakable within his reach. He destroyed the TV, the VCR, the CD player, the tape recorder, refrigerator, washing machine, the freezer, and everything else except for a mirror. He ripped the electric cables from the ceiling and the walls, wrenched them from the outlets and left huge holes in the plaster. He shattered the lamps.

Even small things were not spared. The cups and the dishes on the kitchen cupboards were almost all broken, he flung eggs on the floors and left behind some sort of omelet made of glass and porcelain. Sadly even your gifts to us were lying in shards on the floor, the rum pot, the spice jars from Rostock, the beautiful German cups and the German flower aquarium.

The only thing that got him under control (Udo stood on the stairs and begged him to think of his mother, which had no effect) was the arrival of the police, who our neighbors had called. Unfortunately, to get in the house and detain Mark, they had to break down the front door, but in the end they overpowered him with eight cops, a few of whom were armed with protective shields to distance themselves from his potentially deadly hammer.

Poor, gentle Udo was completely distraught and had to be consoled by our neighbors with a cup of strong English tea. He was plagued with guilt and shaken with fright. 'If only I hadn't taken this job! If only I'd been brave enough to stand in Mark's way! If only I'd been able to think of something!' But the police told him that even they wouldn't have stood up to a drug addict on a mad hammer rampage without protective shields.

We told him it was mad to regret his job, because the problem was Mark, not Udo. It wouldn't have helped anything if a smashed Udo was on the list of 90 things that had been destroyed.

Jane and Udo had already cleaned up most of the wreckage on Friday and Saturday before we came home Sunday. Udo must have done a fantastic job; he managed to glue the presents I received from my Potsdam group back together, even the ship from 1979. He had rebuilt the bookcase as much as possible and put the books put on, and cleaned the carpets and floor tiles. Even so, we were in for a mighty shock when Jo drove us back in the car. The police had nailed corrugated sheets over the windows and door, so that the house looked like a squatter's building in West Berlin. The three hammer blows aimed at the TV had only produced three round holes in the screen. At first glance everything looked like it had been demolished, but upon closer inspection we found plenty that hadn't been destroyed. Most things made of wood were fine, for example.

Monday morning we went to court and Mark was ordered to a hearing on June 7th. He had shaved off all his hair and has turned into a total skinhead. He was served a restraining order from coming near our house. I'm trying to put broken things back together and build them up again. But it's hard, because insurance doesn't cover damage done by someone who legally lives on the premises. When we tried to talk to Mark, he ran away. Now he's gone back to Oxford. He told Jane that he had tried to get off heroin (we didn't even know that he was on that sort of awful drug), but he would get so depressed some nights when he went to bed that he'd take a 'bad' drug and ended up going over the edge. Well, that's hardly a good reason. I don't know how I'm going to tell my parents about this new development.

As I write this, the wind is whistling into the house through the corrugated sheets. We've survived. We're still planning to visit Germany in July. We've developed a sort of Mark-immunity."

"I don't believe that," said Karl thoughtfully. "But they do need a strategy for protecting themselves; it's not just about Mark anymore. Maybe they mean it."

New horror stories kept emerging from the city that only a few years ago had been Katharina's idea of heaven on earth. Storm clouds were throwing dark shadows over her heaven.

"London, July 9th 1993. Mark was finally placed under arrest by the police last week and is now in prison in Bristol. Now he has to face up to all the charges that have been collected on police records relentlessly over the last year since he got on 'hard drugs.' So he'll probably have to stay there for a couple of weeks. We're trying to be hopeful and optimistic about the situation, he's getting medical treatment for depression and addiction as long as he's there. On the other hand, drugs like heroin are very, very tough and stubborn. Realistically he's got a long road ahead of him before he can lead a normal life. It's not just about drugs. It's about having lived with chronic depression for seven or eight years, and that he's spent the past four years living with all the corrosive effects of long-term unemployment. We're not holding out hope."

"He belongs in a hospital, not a jail," said Karl.

"London, May 5th 1994. Mark showed up again last Friday at his grandmother's, in Hay Town. She called us Sunday morning while he was in bed to ask if we wanted to meet up with him. He hadn't shown any interest in calling or visiting us. We decided not to go. Last year he told his grandmother that his probationary officer had advised him to 'get himself clean' before seeing his parents again. Independent of that, Vicky had decided herself before not to see him again before he himself tried to. Last May she drove to Hay Town and he refused to speak to her because he 'was too ashamed' and got angry. She claimed she would respect his wishes and left. On the other hand, we would rather see him again if he's back to the old Mark. So I suggested a compromise; we would ask his sister to meet up with him. We called Jane and she was on board with the idea. She drove to Hay Town for tea on Sunday afternoon and had a long conversation with Mark. We didn't hear any real news though, because Jane's been afraid of Mark's aggressiveness for years. And so she only talked to him about personal, non-controversial topics. She didn't ask him about his plans or his life in Oxford. She found out that his probationary officer was a woman (Vicky says that could be bad news if she notices his obvious hostility towards women, but of course it depends on how sharp, intuitive, and smart this probationary officer is). Mark also told Jane that he was thinking about going to Amsterdam and cleaning windows or moving to a rural part of Wales. She presented these to us as 'optimistic thoughts' on his part, but unfortunately she didn't realize that over the last few years at home he had expressed these plans for Wales and Amsterdam several times. The part of Wales he wants to go to is hub for hippie drug activity, and Amsterdam is internationally famous for drugs and prostitutes. However, the last time he went to Amsterdam he was deported out of the country on a narcotics offense by the Dutch police. And it's madness to talk about cleaning windows where everyone lives in flats and he doesn't have a ladder. In any case, Sunday evening or Monday morning, I'm not sure when, he left Hay Town and went back to Oxford. His grandmother always tells him he can only stay for two or three days. She knows he'll always need drugs sooner or later. If someone sold him 'bad' drugs, like at our place in May, her house might also end up being demolished."

"What a hopeless situation," said Karl. "Who can even help in a spot like this?"

"London, January 25th 1993. When we last went round the pub for a Guinness and a couple rounds of pool, he actually told me that he started cocaine at the beginning of summer in 1989. Cocaine brings about extraordinary highs, but then hangs around to cause extreme paranoia and hallucinations in those who are addicted, which can often end in violence. 'That's how I am,' he said resignedly, 'that's how it is.' We were flummoxed. He's not just addicted, he's truly dependent on cocaine, but in his view, neither he, nor I nor Vicky could do anything about it. 'That's how it is.' As parents we've spent years wracking our brains in increasing despair about what we should have done better – without knowing that he was taking a chemical that so completely destroyed his healthy brain and his normal behavior, that there was nothing we could have done as soon as he swallowed or inhaled the bad stuff."

Karl broke into Katharina's reading. "You see, that's exactly what I said back then, the kid's probably taking hard drugs. That's the only thing that could have changed him like that. He'll kill himself with that stuff if he doesn't get off it soon."

"It goes on from there. He seems to be wandering in and out of prison after prison. Never for very long. No one there even cares that he's sick, clearly very sick. It says here that during one of those drug trips he shouted to his parents from the back of the car, 'I'm mentally ill, you know. I could just drive at 70 miles an hour ...'"

"That's practically a hundred kilometers an hour," Karl interjected, doing the math.

"...and yank the hand brake on this car and watch it turn over a few times. It wouldn't make a difference to me, I have nothing to lose.' When he got out he started kicking against the car, and when he couldn't find a bottle of wine he thought was in it, he lost his head. 'If the police come now, I'll kill both of you, you're both already fucking dead.' He punched through the glass on the car door that Colin and Vicky were hiding behind. The police arrested him."

"What a disaster," said Karl.

"You know," Katharina murmured to herself, "even I get scared, reading this. If they'd been better informed about the effects of these drugs in 1989, maybe they could have done something. Today there's help lines you can call in any hospital or library, where you can get advice on drug problems."

"But then when his window cleaning company went under and he was jobless, he basically turned into the ideal target for drug pushers in a big city like London. Back then, as parents, they knew just as little as he did about the dangers. No books or papers ever really explained what kind of effects illegal drugs can have," said Karl.

"But today it's too late for Mark, isn't it? A sick brain can never be healed again. But it can destroy everything: the boy, his love, his friends, his family. And all because of these hard drugs."

"No, it's not just the shitty drugs. It's a shitty society that lets someone make money off the Drapers' misfortune. Lots of money," said Karl.

Katharina nodded pensively, thinking of her school. "Isn't that an isolated incident? Mark's descent started at the same time as our newfound freedom, in 1989, because he was too free. Children can't cope with unlimited freedom. Especially when the grown up world underestimates the dangers and doesn't set any boundaries for the child, out of love."

"We saw him in December 1989 though! We didn't really notice anything. Did we, Katharina?"

"Just that his life style and his judgment seemed a bit extreme, but we wrote it off as a peculiarity of the English way of life."

"But it must be possible to rehabilitate Mark," Katharina said to Karl, "he'd be going through drug withdrawal and depression at the same time, would that even work?"

"What kind of letter are you holding?"

"London, February 19th 1996. We're so sorry to hear the bad news from Pammerow. It sounds like Felix has diabetes, but I assume it can't be that because it's the first thing doctors look for these days. Hopefully you've got a couple of good answers to this by the time this letter arrives.

Last Sunday we went on a spontaneous trip to Bristol, after a very dubious phone call from Mark. He's staying in a home run by the church. Think what you want, but the church are the only people who offer help for drug addicts and homeless youth. The government here is only interested in cutting back on funding for social services so they can slash taxes and win upcoming elections with a lower tax plan (like in 1979, 1983, 1987, and 1992). At least there he's warm and gets three hot meals a day. The problem is that other druggies live in these shelters and they all pose a temptation to each other. And the local drug dealers are only too happy to prey on these people. We didn't think Mark would accept medical treatment. In the past, he refused every piece of advice. But this time he was so near the end of his rope that he willingly went to the 'Bristol Drug Project' and signed up for a doctor. We found him in a very bad way. He could barely walk. You'd think he was a decrepit old man. The whole time he was shaking and his tongue seemed crippled. His speech sounded confused and muddled.

He called on Friday and his voice seemed clearer. He had started a detoxing course through the Bristol Drug Project. It would be really great for him to participate in that. I should probably explain to you that these detox courses are a hard program for addicts. They have to join a therapy group for six weeks, after which they have to check in to a psychiatric clinic for two weeks to go 'cold turkey' (which means to stay absolutely drug-free, which is very painful and awful). Then they move into a special compound for at least six months, far away from the cities (e.g., the Welsh or Scottish mountains). There, they're part of a group of people, every one of whom suffers from drug addiction and wants to escape from it. The basic idea is for all of them to make good friends over the six months, to share their pain and suffering. So at the end of the course they might have a dozen lifelong friends, who helped each other in the struggle against drugs and themselves when they were tempted to fall back. If they make it to the compound after the cold turkey stage, their success rate is 80 to 90%. It'll take a very long time, even for Vicky and me, but there's a small glimmer of hope keeping us upright."

CHAPTER 6

The seven years following the opening of the border flew by. Katharina's first trip to England only fanned the flames of her yearning to travel. Having spent thirty years' worth of vacations in the GDR almost exclusively on camping grounds in her own country, she now wanted to grab up all the unseized opportunities that this new world had to offer, and she wanted to do it as fast and furiously as was possible. All the beautiful names of famous cities that she'd read about in books were suddenly within her tangible reach, not just images evoked by stories she heard from other people. She wanted to see some of the new world. London had been a shot from a starting pistol. Next she was off to other parts of the United Kingdom, Belfast, Edinburgh, and Cardiff. Her most sensible option in the long run seemed to be taking shorter trips to the world's capital cities, since Karl wasn't a big fan of long trips and the children were slowly growing past the age where they just wanted to be around Mommy all the time. Katharina's vacations were no longer about rest and recuperation. Within three years she conquered Rome, Vienna, Paris, Amsterdam, Stockholm, Brussels, Bern, Copenhagen, and Washington DC. That also included five days spent in New York, which clearly was not enough time for exploring America. She would definitely have to go back, thought Katharina. After all, they spoke English and their educational curriculum was kept up-to-date and realistic.

America was a long ways away from Pammerow. America was also a long ways away from the anxieties that plagued her. She'd never covered America in her teaching. Those two ominous lectures about the US from the tenth grade English textbook, which she'd often cut short in favor of preparing for tests on other material, vanished into the ether after the reunification. Her lonely GDR English textbook had been booted off the shelves in her office in exchange for colorful new ones filled with texts she didn't recognize. The schools in the old federal states had taken this opportunity to update their old textbooks, which she was supposed to throw out since their content was about ten or twenty years out of date. Never one to throw out a source of knowledge, she initially hoarded the old sets in her new office. But a year later they were still lying around gathering dust, because the western publishing houses had very quickly flooded the market with modern material. At first she still tried to buy any books that had anything to do with English, as she had done during the time of the GDR. In the GDR, there was no English book or textbook available that she hadn't collected on her shelves – altogether, the collection took up less than three feet of space. But she soon realized the futility of her endeavor, if she didn't want to have to install new shelves to house the plethora of books being produced by their new society.

Losing the textbook whose texts and exercises she'd memorized by heart meant she also had to update her knowledge as a teacher. What she didn't know about the world seemed to be endless. She'd already completely changed the material she taught on London after her first real visit to the place. Her concept of heaven on earth became more realistic.

America's time had come. At least, the US's time had come. It was time to see the schools and students, and especially the teachers. She had no idea.

The German Marshall Fund of the United States, in cooperation with the German Pedagogical Exchange Service, made the impossible possible for Katharina.

She applied for a six-week teacher development trip through Washington DC, New York, Sacramento (in California), Baton Rouge, New Orleans (both in Louisiana), and Bloomsbury (Indiana). Katharina was overwhelmed by the glamorous sounds of these geographical names, which before now had only buzzed about in her imagination. They had existed only in the pages of atlases and on the screen at the movie theater, and nowhere else.

Beautiful and dreamy, like heaven.

Katharina's stipend for the school trip to the US was partial reparation for having been sealed off with the east after World War II, in the area known as the Soviet Occupation Zone.

While the other occupation zones had been able to benefit from the American Marshall Plan and blossom into commercially successful states, the last piece of reparations paid for the damage done by WWII to the former Soviet Union.

"You may not have been able to enjoy the advantages of the Marshall plan, but now we have the money to include the east in our teacher development programs, in the interest of fostering a good relationship between Europe and the United States," said an associate of the Pedagogical Exchange Service.

The application process was extensive, as the limited budget would allow. Her briefings, and the extra trips she had to take to Boppard for exam-style interviews, made clear the pressure the organizers were under to ensure the success of this trip. It was a mission for the good of society. Their expectations were under intense scrutiny.

"I did it! I've been chosen as one of six teachers from the eastern states!" Katharina exulted, when she received her acceptance papers from the Pedagogical Exchange Service.

"What are they expecting from you?" Karl asked her at home. He was certainly pleased for his wife's whirlwind of excitement, but remained impassive and objective with his feet on the ground.

"That was all covered at the introductory meeting, wasn't it?"

"I mean, what are your actual objectives?"

"An American named Linda was very emphatic – she said the most important thing is to socialize and have personal contact."

"That's great. What for?"

"To exchange experiences between schools and training facilities, or the offices and communities that they belong to."

"And you think the Americans will be interested in Pammerow or your GDR experiences?"

"You don't have to be so sarcastic. I don't really know either. In any case, I'm bringing a bunch of slides with me, and with each picture I'll the American children a bit about how we live. What sort of pictures would you take? I already took one of our kitchen, the bathroom, my desk, our living room, classrooms with students and their trendy outfits, the class schedule, the school, our car, Rostock with the old church and the trolley, the Doberan Minster in Bad Doberan, the Molli steam train in the middle of city traffic ..."

"Why do you need those?" Karl pulled a skeptical face, because to him this seemed like the last thing you'd have to bring on a trip to America.

"I'm supposed to bring to light the issues in my own country. Apparently no one there knows anything about East Germany. Linda says a lot of the, haven't even heard of Germany, which I find hard to believe. But which issues should I talk about? How I've been steadily putting on weight for years? I've been writing it down, and at the end of every year my stupid scale says I've gained at least two pounds."

"Americans eat fast food and drink soda, and that accent leaves nothing to be desired," Karl retorted. "Compared to that, your 150 pounds is nothing!"

"Oh yeah, that reminds me of our other crucial job. In making these contacts, we're supposed to try to get rid of our prejudices. Linda's exact words were, 'spread the image of America as a diverse country and break down clichéd perceptions – '"

"I don't think you're going to learn much of anything new. You can look up everything about the US in books. The media keeps us as informed as we need to be. Just enjoy it like it's an interesting vacation. Meanwhile, I'll keep our house and home running."

"When I come back in six weeks, I'll be wiser. Then I'll tell all."

When Katharina returned to school six weeks later, she was now an Honorary Mayor of the City of Baton Rouge, which was akin to being an honorary citizen and she brought the little gold key to the city of Baton Rouge back to Mecklenburg-Vorpommern in her carry-on.

All Karl said was "What the hell is this supposed to be?"
So her impressive accolade did not go to her head.

"How did you end up doing that?" Angelika asked her on the phone; they were still great friends from their time studying together in Berlin. Friendships formed in those younger years have something of an implicit quality and lack of complicity that is hard to achieve later on, thanks to life's experiences and disappointed confidence or unwanted scandals. This was something

Katharina had noticed. Sharing a common past was a powerful connection. Lifelong friends from childhood and youth will even embrace each other's weaknesses and mistakes without a second thought. They belong together, and that's that. Through time and distance, Katharina's old friendship was still essentially unchanged over the years. Although they both lived in different places with their respective families, in completely different worlds over a hundred miles apart, they still felt the same closeness when they saw each other or chatted on the phone, as though nothing had ever been between them.

"It was quite a surprise. I now know that I went to the US with completely false perceptions. Not just because it felt like I discovered a whole new world every day, but because American teenagers and their teachers have zero grasp on what's going on in Germany today, much less in the east of this country."

"I can only attest to that," Angelika interrupted her. "It was exactly the same for me when I tried to visit America shortly after the reunification. In one school, the teachers were astonished that I could speak English. They thought everyone in the GDR spoke Russian."

"You see! The media has manipulated people into believing these half-truths with their ideologically biased coverage. They've made Russian out to be the native language of the East Germans," Katharina ranted. "Things were even crazier on my trip. I visited several different German classes there to give lectures in English. Not a single student could show me where Germany is on the globe when I asked. They pointed at Egypt, China, and the north of Sweden. At least with the adults I could say Rostock is 'near Hamburg and the harbors' to help them figure out where it is. I didn't even try to describe where Pammerow is. But everyone's eyes lit up with understanding when I was trying to describe the area I come from and mentioned Berlin and 'the fall of the wall' in 1989. Then they had me painted as a poor oppressed woman who had to live behind barbed wire, and they felt sorry for me!"

"I bet they asked how you could stand it."

"That was precisely the one question I was always asked, all over the country, by students as well as docents at the Bloomsbury university, by teachers and their relatives in Sacramento and at many schools that I visited in Baton Rouge, always the same things over and over again. Why didn't you protest in all those years? Why did you stay there and not try to escape? Everyone should have tried to escape. Surely no one could stand such an inhumane system. They always wanted me to confirm that I'm so much happier now with my new freedom and that it must seem like heaven to me."

Angelika said nothing from the other end of the line.

" ... And there was real interest. I was totally unused to having to field so many engaging questions from students. There were no awkward pauses like we have sometimes when guests are visiting the classroom at home, if no one has already written down questions and prepared them with the class. I'd barely finish telling one story, when I'd be bombarded with a bazillion new questions. I've never seen a classroom atmosphere like that."

Angelika was still silent.

"You'll never believe it, I was passed around as a consultant to answer these questions. Whether it was at family celebrations, teacher assemblies, evening parties, speeches at schools – there was a backlog of curiosity about people from the old GDR, about what we went through. You won't believe it. I've never in my life had to answer so many questions at once. Everywhere, at every opportunity," Katharina wanted her friend to understand her excitement and astonishment.

"No, I believe you, it was the exact same for me. The likes of us always believed our lifestyle was boringly normal. Sure, the world was closed off to us, and we were all made into back-country hicks, whether willingly or not. But what is it exactly that makes people on the outside describe it as 'the golden cage'? What did you say to that?" Angelika asked.

"Do you want to hear about the gold in the cage now? – I talked about great things were for children, how everything that was really important only cost a few cents. You remember, the price of rent or kids' shoes or bread. There was almost no crime, I could come home from dancing alone at night with no fear, my grandma never locked her doors in the countryside. And the kids played together without a mother always hovering around trying to protect them. Zero percent unemployment, which of course no one appreciated ..."

"Yes, I know," said Angelika, unimpressed. "But for me it was still a cage, even if it was golden."

"I certainly didn't want to sugarcoat the GDR, I just wanted to try to explain why I and so many others never protested on the streets before 1989, especially not the village road. The first time I dared to go to a Monday demonstration in Leipzig was to protest not being able to travel. There were so many people there. My fear of being reprimanded was gone. I've always tried to please everyone."

"Yes, well, that's typical for us only children."

"That's how I was raised, as a polite girl. Never questioned any authority, I was always more likely to doubt myself instead. I must have been the one who was wrong, not the specialists who had learned and studied everything. They would know best what is right."

"Spare me the self-pity, please. Did you tell all that to the American schools?"

"No, of course not. No one would have understood, anyway."

"And what does all that have to do with being 'Honorary Mayor of Baton Rouge'? Angelika broke in impatiently.

"You know, this city in Louisiana was one of a kind to me." Katharina awkwardly tried to begin her explanation. "The population is about 700,000, and they're all from about fifty different countries. Can you imagine? You wouldn't believe the tension, because 40% of the people there live below the poverty level."

"Surely you've read about immigration in the history books!"

"Yes, but I had no idea what that really looks like in a relatively small area. In Mecklenburg-Vorpommern I hardly know any foreigners, except for two people from Vietnam."

"True."

"Fifty different countries in one city! There's a lot of interest in maintaining international relationships, even with Germany."

Angelika didn't like such high numbers. "That still doesn't answer my question!"

"Here's the answer to your question. The American professor Miller and the incident with the baseball. You know everything that happened then, in 1986," Katharina shot back briskly.

"Yeah, I kind of remember. Long time ago. What about it?"

"In one of the speeches I gave to the city and school represent-atives in Baton Rouge, among other things, I told them what happened to me."

It suddenly came back to Angelika. The disastrous memory of Katharina's political naiveté in fraternizing with the so-called enemy shot abruptly back into her consciousness.

"I don't believe it! And then ...?"

"Of course, I told the story with the necessary humor and dis-tance after ten years. It was a big surprise to me when the audi-ence got riled up and angry on my behalf; I was used to the way Germans sit calmly and impassively during speeches. It came out of nowhere. They just started pelting me with questions right in the middle of my talk. A few of them were making wild ges-tures, which was probably the typical American exaggeration of emotion kicking in. I still try to downplay everything a bit. But it was only one of many stories about what happened."

The cautious tone of the elementary school teacher on the other end of the line, who had visited the States almost once a year since the reunification, began to hint at understanding.

"I can imagine it. They couldn't believe what a violation that was. You were basically punished for trying to make friends and establish personal contact with Americans."

"Right," Katharina agreed. "And just like others who heard the story, everyone there decided they wanted to respond by giving me a thank-you. Ten days later I was invited to a function at the old capitol in Baton Rouge to run the German flag up next to the American one – I felt very strange about it, you can imagine. I've always hated running up the flag, and the very first thing I did as principal at my school in 1989 was get rid of the formal roll call. But Americans have a completely different attitude towards their flag. When I visited friends at their homes, they actually put up the German flag in front of their house as a gesture of hospitality. Can you imagine that, Angelika?"

"Unbelievable," she marveled.

"The star-spangled banner was hanging up in every classroom. I thought I must be seeing things when I went to sit in on my first lesson, and every morning the teachers and students get up from their seats and put their right hands over their hearts, their eyes on the American flag, and recite the Pledge of Allegiance. It almost sounded like a prayer."

Angelika interrupted her bewildered description. "That's exactly what I saw in Washington. I know the words by heart now. 'I pledge allegiance to the flag of the United States of America, and to the republic for which it stands, one nation under God, indivisible, with liberty and justice for all.'" She recited this in English, followed by a perfect German translation.

That was Angelika. She could already recite the pledge of allegiance on command. She was a perfectionist in everything she did, a tendency that had been inextricably bound with an ineffable zeal since the days of her earliest childhood. Whether that was entirely healthy remained a question to be asked later in life. Or so Katharina thought.

"Well, I don't know it by heart," she giggled, "but it may well be part of the new cultural studies unit for our English class."

"Even though in my opinion, the part about 'one God' isn't true.'

"No, of course not. American traditions. This inflated sense of patriotism is a bit disconcerting to my German psyche, which was taught for forty years that we were to blame for Germany's past, as the generation that came after – WE started the war, after all. Germans have been burdened as a society with collective guilt."

"No wonder. They even have a functioning national anthem. By comparison, in the 60's we weren't allowed to sing the line 'Germany, united Fatherland' in the anthem by Johannes R. Becher. And then when our new freedom came with the new old anthem, we could only sing the third stanza of it because the Nazis played around with it too much. – Well, that's an entirely different topic."

Katharina burst out laughing. "At the beginning of the 70's when I practiced the national anthems of Great Britain and the US with my choir, Hollenkamp practically jumped out of his skin. Wagner made me realize that I'd better leave it alone. I hadn't even thought it through."

"But you were always crazy like that. You couldn't go around teaching the American national anthem in the GDR!" Angelika corroborated the old memory.

"Anyway, since then at international sporting events I can match the lip movements, the winner and the melody with the right country," Katharina noted proudly, since otherwise she was clueless when it came to sports.

"So you hoisted the German flag at the old capitol in Baton Rouge, and then you received honors?" Angelika came back to their original point.

"Yes, I was conferred the official document with the title Honorary Mayor of the City of Baton Rouge with unusual solemnity by the chair of the International Relationships Committee, Mona Olsen – who also happened to be German. Then came the symbolic presentation of the key to the city."

"Key to the city?"

"Yeah, it was a teeny tiny silver key. They don't have any medieval city gates like we do in Europe. This key is supposed to open all the doors to the city, the key 'to the heart of our people,' as Mona put it. The Mayor of Baton Rouge, Ed McHugh, gave me the task, and I quote, of 'fulfilling the responsibilities of the office conscientiously and performing all duties assigned by him.'"

"That sounds good. Does that mean anything specific for you?" Angelika asked.

"Naturally I have to make the acquaintance of many new faces in America. And she emphasized establishing connections to this part of the world, where they know just as little about us as we do about them. The only way to be a part of it is to help to build the bridges we need between our nations."

"Why is this Mona Olsen living in America instead of Germany? Marriage?"

"It could be marriage, but she didn't seem to have family at the moment, she lives alone. I casually asked her why she didn't move back to Germany, even though her parents and family live there. Instead she lives in this very puritanical part of Louisiana, where the schools are totally backwards – imagine, there are twenty-six teenage girls at that school this year who are pregnant and don't know how they got that way!"

"They don't know how ...! I can't even believe that!"

"It's true! Sexual education isn't allowed in the classroom. Improper according to the morals from the olden days. Even the roles of women there are pretty questionable, in my personal opinion."

Angelika added in her own experiences. "You can't say toilet or potty there. If you have to go, you have to say that you're looking for the bathroom or the restroom or you want to wash your hands."

"And American romance movies hardly show any skin. The scene fades to black just when it's getting good. They go right from kissing to babies."

"That sounds like that I believed when I was a kid."

"Exactly. Well, in any case, Mona rattled off three basic reasons that I never thought of when people asked me why I wanted to travel."

"What were they?"

"First, she talked about the limited living space in Germany, everywhere is too small and there's always too many people in a tight space; second she mentioned all the restrictions and rules – there's too much you're not allowed to do, too much bureaucracy, which serves itself first and then everyone else."

"And the third reason?"

"Yes, the third reason was something I never even thought of. Health."

"Health?" Angelika repeated, disbelievingly.

"Temperatures there are significantly higher. People don't suffer from high blood pressure as much because their veins aren't constricted from the cold. Plus the extra hours of darkness here in the north have a negative effect on people's moods. So the Germans are said to be closed off, and characterized by our climate and weather as pessimists who frequently suffer from depression. All you have to do is observe people from all the different nationalities at an American airport and then later land at a German airport. And compare their faces – which I happened to do."

"And?"

"It's true."

Again there was silence on the line.

"Whatever. I've got plenty of verve. It's not like that was my last trip to America. Next time I'll be bringing students with me."

"By all means, have fun with your new extra duties." Suddenly Angelika's interest was waning. "How is Felix doing?"

Katharina took a deep breath. "It's hard to say. We're going from doctor to doctor. They can't find anything. He's lost a lot of weight and has dark circles under his eyes. He's been having to drink a ton of water and he keeps going to the bathroom at night. The final year exams really seem to be stressing him out suddenly. It's frightening."

"That doesn't sound good at all. Anyway, I wish you all the best. Good luck recovering from jet lag. Call me again. And then take care of your son like he's the whole world!"

Tuesday, October 29th 1996

This time I'm driving by myself to Gehlsdorf and waiting another three hours until for the doctor to come around at 4.

Torsten, the one with epilepsy, is sitting by me – a handsome dark-haired young man, telling me his story. He's lived with chronic epilepsy since childhood, but his severe breakdown is what landed him here in the mental hospital. It happened after four years of living with his American girlfriend, Evelyn. He had loved her so much, but had no idea what was really wrong with her, how seriously sick she was.

It was the most extraordinary story that I've ever heard, besides Felix's complications, I'm trying to remember it word for word.

"When I first met Evelyn at work, she had just fled in a confused rush from her husband's family in Spain after three years of marriage. She was driven to despair by the insular traditions of their small Spanish town and the role they expected her to play as a woman. She felt at home in the world, not confined to one country. Evelyn needed to be in a big city in order to maintain the expensive lifestyle to which she was accustomed. She spoke five languages fluently. Brilliant! It just came naturally to her. She was from Florida and belonged to a multicultural family of immigrants. But this ability for languages developed from her tremendous studiousness, to learn something and study it – even the language of the country she was living in. Her straightforward, charming charisma fascinated me. It was love at first sight. In her desperation to get away, she had rented a furnished room for 1200 Euros a week here in this foreign country. Naturally I wanted to help her find a fast way out of this financial situation. How? I couldn't find

her a simple apartment fast enough. So I suggested that she move into my small apartment right away, until she found something suitable. This turned out to be an extremely naïve mistake, but in the beginning I was very happy living with her, although she suffered from severe insomnia at the time. I eagerly helped her; she was constantly broke from spending thousands of Euros on language classes. She wanted to study more and looked online for certificates and tests she needed from foreign universities. Everything cost a lot of money.

Her ambition bordered on insanity, the very personification of perfectionism. An 'A' was never enough, it had to be distinguished with honors, she regarded anything less as a personal failure. With her well-spoken charisma, she very quickly made friends with others. She pulled people under her spell, made friends fast, and came across as entertaining, charming, and powerfully eloquent. I couldn't help but notice that she often displayed exaggerated happiness and energy when it was totally inappropriate. Her endless need to talk and her excessive temper were things I didn't recognize until later. She had trouble falling asleep, and after three hours of sleep she was wide awake and fully of energy, even at night. She was always working at her computer, writing, studying, communicating, making lofty plans. Evelyn felt magnificent and spent this time generating an astonishing number of ideas and more energy. She threw herself into debt due to her love of shopping. But she never felt like she was at home. She didn't feel comfortable in any apartment, within a year she was on her third one – always dragging me with her, because she didn't want to live alone. Always just a little bit better, bigger, or more expensive, which put a strain on her budget. If I tried to bring it up, she would wave it away. "Let's not always talk about money.' She could be very persuasive. She always managed to get new lines of credit. The crash came in waves. After all these great flights of fancy through the high heavens in her fantasies, her mood suddenly took a nosedive. The awareness of being 'poor' because she couldn't manage her money, drove her into a fury and an endless depression. Soon she was out of a job. I always helped her out with money. She always felt unfairly treated by life. Whether it was Spain, her family, or her company – she invariably saw herself as the victim, and everyone else as the perpetrator. She was never, ever, guilty. Within a year I lost all my savings that I'd collected over the past few years. It was my fault. I could never say no.

She screamed at me over a misunderstanding, locked herself in my car at a rest stop in the middle of the night and threatened to never unlock the doors and that she was going to kill herself. I only obeyed because I didn't know what else to do. At first I interpreted this episode as nothing more than the misbehavior of a spoiled only child. I felt so helpless and afraid that I couldn't act anymore, only react. I couldn't fight with her because I just wanted peace and always ended up trying to pacify her and calm her down again. But I felt myself start to lose my dignity, my self-confidence, my health, and my money. I lost my friends, my place at work, and my joie de vivre. How was I supposed to comprehend what was almost incomprehensible? When I finally convinced her to go to the doctor with me to treat her insomnia, I began to understand.

The psychiatrist's analysis told the story of my life with Evelyn. One minute she'd be on top of the world – and the next, down in the dumps. A tricky disorder called 'bipolar disorder' or manic depression. How does someone end up such a condition? Stress? Overload? Genetics? The doctor described the disorder's symptoms, which no one would ever have interpreted as 'sick.' The sufferer invariably behaves selfishly and only in their own interests, takes no consideration for their surroundings, shows no charity or understanding for others. They have no sense of discernment, they don't apologize. In the depressive phase, they're full of accusations, aggression, and threats. They manipulate their surroundings and play everyone against each other for their own benefit. Everyone who gets in their way is made into an enemy. That explains everything. In any case, I'm completely done and can't go on. Burnout, depression. Did you know there are four million people suffering from this disorder in Germany alone? And no one talks about it."

The three hours of waiting went by so quickly for me. All the different stories of sickness go far beyond anything I could imagine. I'd like to have found out if these disorders are curable today. But then we went straight to Grandma and Grandpa's for two hours. Back again at 6 pm.

For now, this is supposed to be his last night in Gehlsdorf, after seven long weeks of being cooped up! Even if it is in a golden cage, where as a minority he gets the best care with food, clothing, lodging, and medical attention. But what person doesn't prefer the freedom to choose themselves where and how they want to live, as long as they have the capacity to choose?

(Excerpt from Katharina Stern's speech to 700 students and teachers at Redemptory High School in Baton Rouge, April 1996)

"When I was born, it was three months after the founding of the legendary German Democratic Republic. In other words, I was born into the GDR, grew up in the GDR, and never knew anything else. You ask me why I didn't protest at being locked behind a wall on pain of death? You ask me if I didn't realize sooner that the GDR was poor, dishonest, and miserable?

Well, no one told me it was supposed to be miserable, that we were poor and being lied to all over the place. The generation before me talked about a completely different time that was miserable. With fifty million casualties.

Whom did I believe? Everyone gives the benefit of the doubt to the people closest to them, their fathers or grandfathers, mothers or grandmothers, their own flesh and blood. We believe their assessment of history. Not propaganda or the beliefs of someone else. During the search for the truth, it's natural for us to put our trust in the people whose love and care we've witnessed firsthand, and who have never led us astray from our best interests.

My parents were very young when they married, only 20 and 23 years old respectively, and they were happy together without needing much money. As an electrician, my father earned 200 marks a month at the time – about fifty dollars in American money – and my mother often waited until pay day to buy groceries. After the war they had 'met in October, got engaged at New Year's, and married in May,' as my mother put it; she was fond of telling the great fairy tale of her love with 'a poor refugee from the east.' And they still love and need each other today, a few days before their golden wedding anniversary, to the point that neither of them likes to be without the other. Some couples don't manage this today, they spend so much time talking about the material objectives of the marriage, until their love drains away with freedom and fear of responsibility.

I experienced a carefree childhood. In Kindergarten I loved playing with tons of other kids. For me, school meant all kinds of achievements and kids' summer camp was fun. My grandparents, aunts, and uncles all showed me the same care and sympathy.

The German border didn't concern me as a child. The building of the wall in 1961 in Berlin barely made it into my sphere of awareness, although naturally my elders had to experience the painful separation of big fugitive families from the east during this event.

The workers' and peasants' state, which called itself the GDR, provided support for children from working families. School wasn't interested in the pockets of parents. My parents never had to pay a cent for my education or my university training.

The GDR called itself 'the land of the working people.' It goes along with the Indian philosophy that land, water, and air belong to everyone. I never saw property as a status symbol. Money had no particular worth that would cause someone to commit heinous crimes in order to obtain it. So the crime rate remained negligible. I lived in the country, where many don't even lock their front doors.

The equal status of women was self-evident; it wasn't even a question, and to me the law regarding that seemed redundant. I never had to accept a material compensation that differed from my male colleagues. The only time I felt needled by the outrageousness of the patriarchy and rebelled was when the vicar at my own wedding wanted to use the old cliché 'wilt thou obey him and serve him all of your days.' He was just an old man from an older time.

You talked about being locked up in a cage? That thought never even crossed my mind as a child, because everything inside the borders of the GDR was child- and family-friendly. Things were good for us, we thought. Having to wait ten years for a car meant we had time to save up to pay for it. (We wouldn't have been able to afford one at all if it was there immediately.) Not having bananas and oranges available at the counter every day, but only on special occasions, meant we enjoyed our Christmas feasts all the more, because it was one of the only times we got to enjoy tropical fruit. The lack of telephones meant we met up in person more regularly.

Now seriously – the world remained closed to us and we were

all made into hicks, willingly or unwillingly. But why was our country described as a golden cage from the outside, and not a black prison? I'm trying to give you an answer to your question while at the same time make it clear why we didn't all just riot in protest.

It starts with the way the GDR treasured its children; no child should become the monetary burden of their parents. To that end, there were special rights for women in the workforce. Twelve weeks paid time off after the birth, and a thousand marks cash to welcome every newborn into the world.

As a parent now, I cherish those good intentions all the more than I did back then. I know today as a citizen of a so-called free society that children don't just represent the future of a country, they are the core of all happiness in ourselves and in our society. A society that makes it too hard for young people to raise children without detriment, that doesn't support their children and doesn't invest everything they have into educating their offspring, must age, and ultimately must stand back and watch helplessly as their spiritual values dissolve into nothing and material wealth alone can't make them happy.

As an example, children's clothing represented almost no cost factor for us as parents due to the extremely low prices, which by the way are very different today. And as I already mentioned, even the crime rate in our youths was nothing to speak of, we only heard about drug problems from the media.

I'm going to show you an overview of our personal expenditures from the time (with a net monthly salary of 1500 East German Marks, approximately $375):

- Monthly rent for our three-room apartment with bathroom and kitchen: 36.00 M
- Daily cost of Felix's daycare with breakfast, lunch, and milk: 1.40 M
- Monthly cost of Olaf's Kindergarten: 10.00 M
- Daily cost for hot lunch: 0.50 M
- Daily cost for fruit or chocolate milk: 0.25 M

The cost for electricity, water, and heat were always fairly low – maybe a tenth of today's prices. We were able to buy any essential groceries for very little money. A bread roll for 5 pfennigs, a two-pound loaf of bread for 63 pfennigs, a three-pound loaf of bread for 93 pfennigs.

Public transportation didn't cost much. A trolley or bus trip was 20 pfennigs for adults, half that for children, and free for kids under six. The list goes on.

Universal healthcare was available to everyone without having to undergo any inspection; we thought it was self-evident that medical care should be free.

The GDR was a literary community, books didn't cost much, same for the children's textbooks, if parents wanted to buy them.

The thing that no one back then was truly able to appreciate was the zero percent unemployment rate. Everyone possessed the unconditional right to work, and the directors arranged a job position for every person. But with that right came the obligation to work, so that no one was living off of the labor of others.

The strong ties we had to our friends and neighbors were especially noteworthy. Our community was one of trust, we celebrated together, and we all helped each other in solidarity, trying to balance out the invariable scarcity of spare parts, luxury goods, or tropical fruits. There are plenty of amusing stories I could tell ..."

In summation, a golden cage. The birds within were content with their lot, until they became conscious of another, freer life, and then they struggled against the bars. Or when the cage became too small for their growing wings and they'd been told to swim instead of fly. That was what Katharina thought of it.

Wednesday, October 30th 1996

Felix has to go in for an MRI at 11:30 in Schillingallee. Grandpa is going with to supervise him, so he doesn't have to wait by himself for so long – sometimes it takes hours and then Felix suddenly forgets why he's sitting there and wanders away.

But the transport works out, he'll be taken from here out into the south part of the city to (hopefully) his last radiation session. Dr. Liber-

nicht schedules an appointment for a follow-up visit on January 31st 1997, which seems like a surprisingly long time to me. Three months to wait and hope?

I pick Felix up from radiation, and once more we drive together back to Gehlsdorf, where Professor Ruhe is expecting us for an exit interview. As always, in the last few minutes right before our meeting, I can feel the knots of fear constricting my throat. Professor Ruhe sits like a god in white behind his desk and declares the main results.

"It's clear from the MRI that 90% of the tumors is gone. There are some visible remains, which are assumed to be the debris from the destroyed tumor, and that will have to be 'eaten up' next time. All in all, a successful radiation therapy."

My heart stops.

Felix is unaware of the significance of this statement. He is exhausted and almost falling asleep on his chair.

New appointment with Professor Ruhe is January 9th 1997, 5 o'clock. We present Dr. Engel with a home-grown baobab as a farewell gift and the nurses with a thank-you box of chocolates.

Felix is looking forward to going home, and keeps asking for reassurance.

"Today is Wednesday? And we're going home now and then I don't have to go back?"

Yes, an incredible burden is falling from me – I could almost cry. My nerves have held up astonishingly well for the last eight weeks, even if I've lost thirty pounds.

But today, for the first time, I've finally received positive confirmation that we are no longer looking at a matter of life and death.

I've been existing on this wild fear that I've been trying to repress since August 12th 1996, since I furtively opened the envelope from the doctor and read the 'brain tumor' result. Are we really meant to have gotten so lucky with this tumor, which Professor Nahm in Greifswald estimated as having a 60% curability rate? And pinpointed as 90% curable by the university in Tübingen, which only started research in the last six years? Will Felix be part of the 10% who have to resume treatment one day, with chemotherapy, in case germ cell tumors are secreting (spreading again) – which the doctor said might happen.

The MRI also showed that during the operation on September 4th in Greifswald, a five-millimeter long lesion on a tract of the hippocampus (the tract that transfers short-term memory into long-term) was visible. That's what caused Felix's problems with retaining memories over short periods of time. Hopefully that will be able to heal somehow, the damage to his memory has made him rather helpless.

Many questions remain open. How do we proceed? I'm not yet convinced that the doctors found the right combination of meds. They're on their own quest. I'm hoping everything will become normal with time, which heals all wounds. Doesn't it?

Katharina paid particular attention to the American youth on her trip, observing them from the perspective of a school principal. At first glance, they looked exactly like the teenagers back home. Almost all of them wore jeans of all kinds, t-shirts or sweatshirts with and without symbols, pictures, and letters. Even the sneakers of different brands were very familiar to her. But upon closer inspection, there was much that was different. In a classroom at Florin High School in Sacramento, for example, the children all had highly diverse skin colors. Their parents, grandparents, or other ancestors were Vietnamese, Japanese, Mexican, Filipino, Chinese, Irish, British, and African immigrants who had brought their cultures and religions into the country. Achieving mutual understanding required quite a bit of tolerance here. And it didn't work entirely without problems. Despite the noticeably happy faces – the difference between America and Germany seemed to boil down to their grouchy expressions, one needed only to study the faces and their nationalities at an international airport – despite their remarkable ease in dealing with each other, she sensed the tensions between the traditions. Katharina was always astonished to see so many young girls in school who were already pregnant.

"At our school we have 26 young mommies between the ages of fourteen and seventeen," the students at Baton Rouge High in Louisiana told her, a school with twelve hundred students.

"How can it be that so many teenagers, themselves practically children, are pregnant at a single school? Is it an infectious trend? That must be unique in the US!"

"Not at all. The schools nearby are the same way. The girls aren't very happy about it and many don't even know how it happened." Katharina listened to them carefully, because even she had had a situation like this in her class ten years ago, but it was still only the one incident in all her twenty-four years of teaching. "Maybe you don't know this, but at most American schools they're not allowed to teach sex education in biology or natural science. It's because of the different religions that forbid talking about it."

"Our laws are very strict about that," a student remarked. "For example, there's a law for youth protection that forbids 17-year-olds from staying out later than 11 pm. If someone is caught on the streets past that time, they can be arrested by the police."

"And you can't drink beer until you're 21," added a tenth grader.

The cafeterias at high schools and even universities weren't allowed to sell alcohol. Katharina was able to follow the debate in the daily papers. The attempt to lower the drinking age to eighteen failed miserably. Within a short time, the accident quota of teens behind the steering wheel grew by 200%. Very strange. At this age American teenagers already knew how to drive a car – the school parking lots were full of cars owned by students, which they were allowed to drive when they were fifteen or sixteen. All American students had twelve years of mandatory education, so they didn't leave school for the first time until they were eighteen.

The eighth graders sneered at Katharina for asking about the problem of smoking among teenagers, which at been increasing for years at home since the reunification.

"You know, we're past that age. The little kids in fifth and sixth grade, sometimes even in third grade, brag about it. But then it just goes away. Smoking isn't cool, it just ruins your complexion. Well, to be honest, we've been trying way different drugs ..."

Katharina ended her interview with mixed feelings. Although she hadn't actually seen many smokers in her six weeks – in this country only about 10% of people were smokers, but she had seen before her eyes the steadily increasing rate of drug-related deaths among youth.

In these six weeks, Katharina observed the good and the not so good. Mostly she noticed that the young people were generally open-minded, cheerful, and engaged. Her students at home were still wary against getting too involved in discussion from when she had had the American professor as a classroom guest for the first time in Pammerow. Or maybe this was a new thing? The suspicion occurred to her that it could also be the disinterest of a new, post-reunification generation that only cared about having fun.

She asked a group of students at Redemptory High school in Baton Rouge, "How is it possible that your school has such a great working atmosphere?" In the hours she spent with them, everyone always attended to their homework, they kept their files ordered neatly and imaginatively, and they spoke pleasantly. Lessons were marked by active cooperation, attentiveness was unenforced, and during recess they sat chatting on benches in the yard or playing ball on the tarmac near the school building.

"It's very simple," the students told her with knowing pride, "it's because we have fair punishment." She was taken aback. "If we haven't done our homework, we have to stay late after class and do it over again."

"Staying late as a punishment?"

"Yes. If someone's acting up, they can also get put in detention."

"Are there protests?"

"We think it's fair – and so do our parents."

"But what if someone maybe doesn't like to study?"

"If someone doesn't like to study at all, they get kicked out of school."

Katharina raised her eyebrows. Something like that would never be possible in Germany because of their human rights laws.

When she spoke with the principal, the real reason for the industrious atmosphere became clear.

"About 70% of all students in Louisiana attend private schools," the American principal informed her guest. "At this school, parents pay three thousand dollars a year for their child to attend, and this is a fairly inexpensive school."

"That much money?"

"There are parents who pay up to $10,000 for expensive schools. Anyway, 80-90% of our schools are private. Education has a high price. It's a very precious commodity."

Katharina's school at home, where she was principal, guaranteed the right to a free education, an uncontested right for one hundred years in Germany. That was where her convictions stood.

"Yes, you're right, education is very precious," Katharina agreed. "But I see that from a different perspective. Everyone has the right to education. It's a human right. No matter what you pay for it. We're not living in Africa. The fundamental right to free education is what makes our society into paradise."

The other principal smiled. "What costs nothing is worth nothing." Katharina excused herself and thanked her politely for this opportunity to visit.

The privately owned Redemptory High school in Louisiana made her contemplative.

Her students at home had been steadily slouching lower, in both posture and performance, ever since the arrival of their new freedom in 1989. Was that supposed to be the solution for a good working atmosphere at a school here in Louisiana? Based on the motto 'what costs nothing is worth nothing?' She sensed a quiet anger growing in her subconscious. Because even at home ran in blind beliefs on the meaning of a status symbol always more around her old fundamental right betrayed people out of this heaven.

At the public schools in America things looked different. Katharina read in the New York Times that 130,000 children were bringing deadly weapons into school EVERY day, and not just in Chicago, New York, or Detroit, but even in well-protected communities. Incidents of death just happened. Nothing out of the ordinary.

She had rarely felt this tension at a school, but she saw firsthand how teachers and students protected each other. When she left school grounds during a break, she saw a security officer with a sheriff's badge, a radio in his hand and a gun at his waist, as he patrolled amongst the students as a matter of course.

American was a long ways away from Rostock. She thought about that for a long time in April 1996.

Thursday, October 31st 1996

Today is a holiday. It was actually the mistake of a student that drew my attention to the topic of Reformation Day. He wrote that in 1517

Martin Luther 'nailed his 99 prostheses to the palace church in Wittenberg.' Sometimes I think wistfully of the thesis on the sale of indulgences when I know I've made a mistake. Then I wouldn't be free of mistakes, but at least I'd be free of a guilty conscience.

Thinking about that doesn't make me laugh anymore. These exceedingly important daily work problems eat up our interpersonal relationships and leave no time for ourselves.

Life doesn't give us a test run. We have to do everything the first time the way we see it in hindsight. I've never heard someone say on their deathbed, 'if only I'd spent more time in my office. Or at school. Or in the field.' If we'd paid more attention and spent more time with our kids, would we have realized sooner that something was wrong with Felix?

Felix sleeps for a long time – his memory and cognitive performance are especially weak after sleep.

His temperature has been consistently high, today it's over 99 F. Is it the flu, or his body reacting to the healing from radiation? Felix has been complaining of a stomachache since Monday. He's not eating much, he has no appetite. Why? He's not feeling well.

CHAPTER 7

I'm not sure how to make this clear," said Heidrun Meschke. She was a seasoned teacher, grayed over the years, and had always been highly respected by her students. "During my first few years teaching in Pammerow, I always ended up putting my foot in my mouth at *Parteilehrjahr* meetings, and when it came to injustice in the school, political or not, I couldn't keep quiet there either. But I still garnered a certain esteem from parents and students. Every June 12th on International Teacher Day, when all our hard work is officially recognized, my students often brought me flowers and little handmade surprises, and my classroom looked like a sea of flowers. And that came from the heart. It wasn't done out of mischievousness. But now? Take a look at the papers. No matter how good we are, we teachers are being portrayed as the assholes of the world, as the idiots and lazy slobs of the nation."

Katharina felt obliged to correct her. "Heidi, you know that the press is free to write whatever they think will sell now. They need attention-getting headlines, and scapegoats. Teachers have become the scapegoats of the nation."

"Yes, I know. It's madness," Heidi replied. "Any good psychologist knows kids need positive role models who they can look up to. Instead, there's a confused, overwhelmed mother out there writing an 'I Hate Teachers' manifesto, who probably comes from her own troubled home and is trying to work out all her interpersonal relationship issues by writing a book. And that sort of thing will get published, too, because it'll generate a sensational headline and make money!"

Katharina nodded in agreement, although she hadn't taken the content of the book seriously. It voiced such extreme hatred and its arguments were so devoid of logic that no sensible person could possibly believe it. But not everyone was a sensible person, thought Katharina, which was what the media was counting on. Out loud, she said, "And if the most important person in a child's life is openly vilified like that, then they'll lose all respect for the importance of education and good behavior."

"The crazy thing about it is that there are hardly any other countries in the world where teachers are manipulated to have such a horrible public image, like here in Germany. Tell me why that is, Katharina. Everyone knows that kids all over the world learn best when the teachers are respected and education is valued highly."

"I don't really know the answer to that either. I met plenty of students on my trips through schools and universities in the US and interviewed them. In Sacramento, they spent their breaks sitting in the halls or the yard, studying!"

"We've always had our sign out there. Keep off the grass!" the teacher remarked drily.

Katharina smiled, her eyebrows raised. "A boy told me that he spent eight hours in class every day, then played on a sports team after school, and worked at McDonald's at night to make some money."

"That seems a bit intense to me. Nobody can keep that up."

"They can. And it was by no means uncommon. The principal of the school in Sacramento mentioned he was especially surprised by how industrious the children in Asian immigrant families were."

"China is on its way up in the world. That's an international fact at this point!"

"The Asian community isn't just Chinese anymore. In any case, the parents in these families showed a lot of respect for their children's individual teachers, and they placed a huge significance on education and personal effort. They were willing to spend a third of their income on tuition."

"Well, that's certainly understandable. They wanted to make things better for their children. That sort of motive has a very profound effect on people. I've heard of it too. These children end up having incredibly strong motivation and an amazing learning experience."

"Well yes, but unfortunately you can't compare those conditions with ours, Heidi. I'm sure Asian traditions are a factor, too. But it shows us that parents and family traditions are a deciding factor in whether or not children value school. As a teacher you can offer the world to your students, but the parents won't even notice that you're spending valuable hours of your own life. No one can be forced."

"And our people won't accept that either! Why not? Has our entire civilization come down with a case of lazyitis? There we are, putting ourselves out there in our free time and working our tails off fostering talent and providing support for struggling learners, with theater groups, student papers, school band, student radio, library, folk dancing groups, yoga, Swedish, Norwegian, English Is Fun, spelling practice, table tennis, cooking and baking, Russian and French, manners and comportment, career training ..."

"Stop, stop." Katharina tried to curb her tirade and inject some civility back into the conversation with quiet humor. "It would be different in Africa, too."

Heidrun tried to answer the question in her spirited, emotional way. "What costs nothing is worth nothing. The state guarantees our children the right to an education, but uneducated families will spin that into malicious coercion and a restriction of their personal freedom."

"True."

"Did you know that Lena posted a bunch of vitriol about me on a website – I think it's called *schülerVZ*, some social media site for students – because I griped at her about not doing her homework?"

"No, what did it say?"

"Stuff like 'slut,' 'puke whore,' 'someone should hang her from the closest lamppost,' 'spank her ass,' and that sort of thing ..."

" ... That can't be true." Katharina was disgusted.

"Other students showed it to me out of concern and said I should put a stop to it!"

"Yes, of course. But how are we supposed to make that happen – we don't know the first thing about computers."

"Do I have to just let it go?" Heidrun asked indignantly.

Katharina deliberated. "We have to fight back!"

"I'm already starting to shake just thinking about it!"

"I think this girl is mentally ill! You can't take it personally!"

"I've gone out of my way for her, staying late after school to write her letters about her troubles."

"You shouldn't do that, Heidrun!"

"You know, this is making me feel horrible! I can't even sleep anymore."

"Enough is enough. You can't take this to heart! Your job is to give the kids an education, nothing more."

"Well, education isn't worth anything anymore today. Kids just see it as restricting their free will, because they've been raised with no boundaries whatsoever. My blood is boiling."

"Calm down!"

"School isn't worth anything anymore. Neither are teachers. Not even kids, what with the focus on materialism. Everyone's out to sell themselves for whatever they can get. And can you explain all of that?"

"I can now," said Katharina. "After almost forty years and 41,657 hours of teaching at this school, after seven Education Secretaries in this region, six of those in the last twenty years"- she paused to breathe - "after 1,497 kids and their mothers and fathers and entire families, after seventeen years of being a teacher in the GDR, after 1,534 hours of individual teacher conferences in twenty-two years as a school principal ..." by now Heidrun's face was beginning to relax, "after 3,211 hours of sitting in on classes, after 1,567 hours of impressive development meetings, after hundreds of hours of classes and lectures in London, Edinburgh, Sacramento, Baton Rouge, Milwaukee, Oslo, and ..."

Her listener's eyes were wide. "And?"

"And after living through two decades of emerging media indoctrination in two different political systems, I actually can explain it."

"Did you add all of that up?"

"Just for fun."

"I don't believe you!"

Katharina looked her colleague square in the eye. "And after hundreds of letters from London."

"I don't understand that part. London? Is that true?"

"It certainly is. But no one believes me," she finished, winking.

"That doesn't sound very upbeat." Heidrun blew her nose and wiped away the tears that were rolling down her cheeks.

"And first thing tomorrow we're going to figure out the solution to your harassment problem."

Felix spent the night at his grandparents' house so he wouldn't be alone while we're all working. He sleeps the whole time while he's there, his memory is doing astonishingly poorly. We go shopping together. He keeps scolding me for not obeying traffic laws – I think he could drive a car again. The only problem would be if he forgot where he was going while he was on the road. Or if he forgot where he parked the car.

Tonight his fever is going back up. His weight has stabilized around 174 lbs, so I'm wary of going back to the doctor so soon. But the fever seems dangerous to me. Is this a new crisis? If only I had more confidence in the doctors, who themselves are still looking for answers.

Absently, my eyes trace the outline of my beloved little bronze statue, heavy enough to keep papers from flying away. The lovingly depicted 'Bookworm,' from the Spitzweg painting, has climbed down onto my desk out of the cramped space of his dusty old library. He stands, lost to the world around him, on the stairway to heaven, which has one less rung on my desk than it does in the original painted version. The bibliophile studies all the endless stories written by life. One book is clamped between his knees, another pressed under his arm. The enraptured scholar holds an open book in each hand, trying fervently to track down the answers to my burning questions. This ladder remains the only illusion that one can be getting closer to heaven even when the floor is lost from under their feet.

In 1997, in the endocrinology department of the Rostock University clinic, Professor Mann's specialist knowledge was put to the greatest challenge yet. What all would go wrong with a person whose pituitary gland no longer worked? Which hormones would have to be replaced, and in which specific circumstances? How? In what quantities? He took Felix into the clinic every day and tested the reactions of what was left of the pituitary gland, always in the hope that not everything had been destroyed by radiation. Always with the thought that the abused cells could recover at least partially. Inexplicable fevers kept cropping up.

Felix didn't sweat, although the temperatures outside climbed to 86 degrees in the shadows. A regular heat build-up seemed to bring him to the brink of death.

Discussion always came back to cortisone, to alleviate stress, aldosterone for mineral and water retention as well as sodium and potassium, thyroid hormones, testosterone, and growth hormones – with utmost caution, lest it grow into dormant tumor cells again – everything would have to be artificially replaced. How could a young boy go on living like that?

"What are you and Karl going to do on February 12th, for your silver wedding anniversary?" Katharina's mother asked worriedly, because a family celebration meant a lot to everyone. These occasions were a chance to bring together even the most distant relatives and friends, who sometimes hadn't seen one another in years. Funerals shouldn't be the only time they all got to meet up.

"We're basically stuck, as usual. I wouldn't be able to just celebrate twenty-five years of marriage like nothing was happening," Katharina answered. Her mother nodded and her father chimed in his agreement.

"We're not in the mood for celebrations either. What's going to happen with Felix? What do you think?"

"I don't know."

"What did you find out when you went to the Youth Office yesterday?"

"Felix was declared to be underage."

"Underage? Why?"

"In his relatively helpless condition, any stranger could manage to convince him that he has to sign something important that he's forgotten about. In this world, the door is wide open for deception."

"Does that mean he's getting a legal guardian?"

"Yes, that would be me, starting now."

"But this doesn't have anything to do with the tumor anymore, does it?" Katharina's father was always in the know. For twenty years he'd been preoccupied with the precise details of his own sickness. Now he kept himself just as thoroughly abreast of the details of Felix's plight.

"No, it's because of the damage to his short-term memory."

"Will that damage be permanent? You should have it declared as a doctor error, if it is. For insurance."

"Oh, just leave me alone. I've got other things to worry about right now." Katharina didn't want to hurt anyone, and she kept herself from reacting hysterically. "Besides, I can't blame the doctor now, he didn't try to do it."

"But if it's the right thing to do," her father pointed out.

"Is there really anything right about this situation?"

"Fair point. So now you're his guardian in all legal matters, and he's not allowed to decide for himself anymore?"

"That's right."

"But you seem to be okay with that."

"Should I not be? When this all started, I thought the most I had to hope for was five months left with him. Today the professor gave me hope for five more years, and then after that we'll have to see."

Saturday, November 2nd 1996

I wake up Felix at 10 o'clock, so that his medicine doses can be spread out throughout the day. If not for that, he would have slept in. I ALWAYS used to have to wake him up, even if it was coming on noon.

Although he's been weakened by the fever, I let him get out of bed. Suddenly I'm letting him do everything I'd normally never allow. Fine with me if he wants to drive to Rostock with Christine (former classmate) and have a good time – I don't know myself anymore.

She picks him up at 2 to meet with their other old classmates at CONTI – an Italian ice cream shop. She brings him back at 5.

In the evening, a bunch of people from his old school show up to visit him (Olaf, Christian, Maria, Robert, Thommy, and Martin). The troop chats with him for a surprisingly long while, although it can't be that interesting to spend an evening with a sick buddy. They really care about him a lot. Although we're feeling uncertain about it, we let Felix go with them to a late showing at the Hansa Film Theater, despite his baffling fever. Christian brings him back at 1:30 in the morning. Completely contrary to my child-raising sensibilities! Why am I doing this? Is it because my subconscious knows that these happy outings could be his last? I'm losing my mind!

Felix was surprisingly alert and didn't fall asleep during the movie.

"We have another letter from the Drapers in the mail," Katharina called out into the living room that evening, where Karl sat cooling off in front of the TV, exhausted from work. He was ready to relax and do nothing at all. "Do you have time to listen?"

"Sure, go for it." Karl nodded.

"London, May 5th 1997. Another seven weeks' anxiety with Mark are behind us. I think I told you that he suddenly turned up at my parents' house and convinced them to be his guarantors. He was detained by the Birmingham police as a vagrant for 'acting suspicious' and they charged him with 'possession of an offensive weapon' (a bottle). The case was originally supposed to be handled in court on June 6th, which is next week. I desperately tried to get him away from my parents as fast as possible. Not just in case he has a severe drug episode again, but because at 81 and 86, my parents' health isn't strong enough to take care of a 29-year-old wretch. My mother has already broken her back twice, as you know, and my father has severe asthma. Just as we expected, Mark didn't help them out at all. He left them to do all the cooking, laundry, and washing up. He spent most of the time in his room watching TV or going out to have a smoke. He was under house arrest, by order of the police, and had a curfew of 8 pm. He had to report to the police twice a week. But Vicky and I had decided two years ago to follow the advice of the experts and have as little to do with Mark as possible until he makes his own choice to get off the drugs and return to the normal world. It was a necessary decision to protect ourselves and give him a clear path to follow, because all the arguments over how we should help him have been breaking our hearts since 1985, and we still haven't been able to do anything. So what were we supposed to do? We couldn't go to my parents, because that would have broken our vow. We couldn't help Mark out of trouble again; he had to be the one to handle it himself. But my parents expected us to help him. You can imagine the kind of pressure that put on us. Suddenly there was tension between me and my parents that we'd never had before. My parents couldn't understand why we wouldn't come and visit them. 'He's still your son, not ours ...' etc. Of course, I talked to Mark over the phone and let him know that I was worried about my parents' health, but from his view, he had nowhere else to go but prison. In prison, he claimed, he would probably get right back on the drugs, whereas staying with my parents would put him in the perfect situation to get clean. Finally I wrote to the lawyers and the court, explained my dilemma and asked them urgently for a legal solution. Two weeks ago they let two of the three charges against Mark drop, which eased up the conditions for bail, and his new parole officer found him a hotel where he can stay until the trial on June 6th.

I hope you're all doing well and that Felix is making progress. I haven't written anything about it, but that doesn't mean that I'm not thinking of you and worrying. I'm collecting medical information relating to brain diseases for you and will send another letter soon."

"Mark's brain is just as sick as Felix's, just in a different way," said Karl.

The international press had a field day in September of 1997, with the headline 'Deadly Traffic Accident in Tunnel – Tragedy Surrounding Diana Spencer – English Royal Family in Distress.' Katharina and Karl heard the news on the radio in the morning as they were eating breakfast together. Katharina shook her head, stunned. A rant was forthcoming.

"I still remember seeing this happy 19-year-old Kindergarten teacher in 1980, shy but standing proudly by Prince Charles's side amid the flurry of cameras and journalists. Anyone who saw the wedding on TV would think the two of them had found heaven on earth. Now she's dead, at just thirty-six years old, with two little children. It's the media that killed her."

"What do you mean, killed her? Are you saying they arranged it on purpose?" Karl retorted cynically.

"How can you say something like that?"

"No one cares about this ballyhoo about the English royal dynasty. Didn't you say yourself that it's a wonderful tradition that's survived to modern times through the children of the older generation?"

"Yes, but nowadays it's impossible for a modern young person to be able to manage the English royal family and the insanity of the press. Don't all the Queen's children end up running aground at some point? Aside from the old royal couple themselves, none of their marriages has lasted very long. Princess Di's accident is bringing it all back to me."

"So, no happy children in the royal palace, like you used to think? How did you come to that?" asked Karl.

"Colin said, among other things, that the British papers have spent the last two weeks covering up their guilt in the death of Princess Di. They're holding on to the fact that the driver was drunk, because he's being used to throw the trail off the paparazzi."

"That's for the royal family to worry about! We've got other problems."

"It was the freedom of the press that killed her, in the end."

"Don't get philosophical on me! What does the new letter say about Mark?"

"London, September 15th 1997. Mark turned up again the weekend before last, because he wanted to go to our family doctor. I think he also wanted to suss out whether he was welcome here, what with winter coming up. Vicky and I managed to stick to the plan we agreed on. We gave him a decent meal and then brought him to a hotel for the night (he arrived early in the evening from Cornwall, where he's been living since leaving my parents' house in May). Eventually we found a guest house with a B&B nearby where he could stay for a week. In the evening we went out to restaurants with him, or he came to eat dinner with us. One night we took him to the movie theater. On Monday I went with him on a ship tour down on the Thames, and we ended in Brent Cross with a lovely ice cream.

The problem is, as long as he doesn't completely cut himself off from drug culture (he may have gone off the drugs in Cornwall, but he still hung around with 'druggies,' since he is one, and took soft drugs) and doesn't decide to return to normal society, he still can't spend the night in our house. We will only help him pay for a couple days in a hostel, so he has a chance to ask social services for help. We give him no more than five pounds cash. That's what the drug-counseling service advised and we've done well with it. If we had just known about Mark's drugs earlier and got advice sooner. (By the way, Mark claims he is mentally or psychologically ill and gets disability money for a severe mental disturbance, with no unemployment support or social assistance. He says he was already mentally ill when he tried drugs for the first time, while we're more inclined to think that it was the drugs that messed with his brain. On Wednesday night we got another touch of danger from the past. Mark showed up at our house drunk, wanting to watch soccer on TV. He hadn't touched a drop of alcohol before that, not even wine with dinner that Vicky made. Luckily we don't have SKY TV, and I managed to convince him to come to the nearest pub and watch the game there. You know our pubs all have TV screens. Before he could drink another drop of alcohol, his head fell onto the table. I called Vicky to bring the car and take him to the guest house, which was quite difficult, as he protested angrily and called Vicky a 'miserable bloody cow' several times in the process. The next day he called me and apologized (again) and we agreed that he needed to see a doctor and he should go back to Cornwall now. I brought him to the train station and put him on the train. He hugged me and said 'Please tell mom I'll get out of this thing someday, somehow. Tell her I'm sorry. Tell her one day I'll make it.' He thanked me, especially for the boat tour on the river, and the train took off."

"Mark is going through the same damned fate as hundreds of thousands of young people in this western world that we call home now too. Our kids will pay the price for their freedom," said Karl.

Sunday, November 3rd 1996

I wake him up at 11 today. He remembers the title of the movie and some of the plot of 'Last Man Standing,' which he wasn't a fan of and found fairly unintelligent. He remembers his friends from the other night too.

Other than that, he remains sluggish like the other days. What could this strange fever mean? He's behaving so unusually, out of nowhere. For example, he was going to help his brother Olaf with something on the computer, which he always used to be excited to work on – but he ran into a problem that couldn't be solved with a lot of patience and brain-wracking. So he just swore, gave up right away, and couldn't by induced to try it again. Professor Mann said he's no longer capable of handling stress. That's why he's going to be taking the hydrocortisone hormone.

At the time I asked Professor Mann, "What can you compare this to? I feel like I need hydrocortisone every day at school. Why doesn't anyone come up with something to help principals?"

Professor Nahm had smiled and said, "You have a healthy pituitary gland, and that can help you calm down from any accumulation of stress. But Felix can't calm himself down after even the smallest bit of excitement, and so if his brain is tapping a nail into the wall, much less chopping wood or doing heavy lifting – he is not able to recover by his own means. He needs a measured dose of pills ready at the right time. Severe cortisol deficiency is life-threatening, and his mental equilibrium can only be stabilized through hormone medication. This condition can pose a risk of suicide!"

I can barely make sense of this situation. Who else is going to be able to understand this condition if I, as his mother, can hardly believe that I'm looking at the shreds of his ability to exist?

What could happen if he's startled by something? Or if he has to complete a test? Or an argument arises?

Physical strain of any kind reduces his cortisone level, which results in his having to make superhuman effort; he becomes torpid and unmotivated.

Sunday, November 10th 1996

Young people don't wax philosophical over diseases. Olaf and his friend Stefanie bring Felix back home late at night without a care in the world. They had a lot of fun ice skating together at the ice rink.

We take his temperature right away – his fever is gone!

It's really gone all of a sudden! Completely gone! I'm all aflutter inside. And Felix simply presses the thermometer into my hand and says with a smile, "It's gone."

Over the five years of hope that Professor Ruhe had granted them, the Sterns' life began to normalize.

"How do you manage with your short-term memory loss?" his old friend Thommy asked, after it had been a year. "Don't you end up forgetting a lot?"

"That's two questions at once," Felix answered. Hair was growing on his head again, darker and somewhat softer than before.

"The forgetting hasn't changed a jot from last year. But I just live with a notepad and pencil by my side and immediately write everything down that I don't want to forget. Like with phone calls. If you call me and I don't write anything down, I've already forgotten why you called me."

"And conversations with the doctors?"

"I do it then too. My brain doesn't seem to keep anything in it unless I write it down."

Thommy nodded understandingly. "And what about getting into the business program at Rostock University? What are you going to do now?"

"I'm not sure, but I really want to try going for a degree – I've got to do something sensible."

Felix started his degree program purely for mental reasons. He needed something to do, and he needed self-affirmation. But his memory wouldn't allow it.

"Mom," he complained, "I can hear and understand all the content of the lectures completely, and I write everything down as much as possible. But the next day when I read through my notes, I can't remember having heard any of it."

"I'm secretly hoping his condition will get a little more normal over time," Katharina said.

"Studying doesn't work like that in the long run, though," said Karl. "Felix, didn't you also apply for an apprenticeship at the bank before your operation? You were going to do that along with your degree program, and I don't think you declined their offer yet."

"It's worth a try," Felix nodded.

He seemed to get along at the Deutsche Bank branch for six months. But he didn't talk about it at home. Suddenly he was let go, as soon as the trial period was up. The managers had noticed that he was always asking about things that had already been explained to him.

"Who hired this idiot?" the instructor demanded. The personnel department verified that his application had had outstanding credentials when they chose him.

Karl and Katharina were deeply concerned to observe his depressed reaction to this turn of events.

"Felix's whole world is falling apart, because he doesn't understand that his nature is still in a state of constant change," Katharina fretted in commiseration.

"It's true," Karl nodded. "He even said there was some controversy with a customer who he perceived as being rude to him?"

"There was. He didn't have enough of the cortisone stress hormone, and he couldn't keep up the polite façade you need to work in a bank."

"You need a polite facade?"

"Of course you do. It's part of the business in a bank, even if a customer is behaving rudely."

"I suppose so. That's not going to work too well with his excessive sense of justice and lack of self-control."

"Not at all. And aside from that, I think he's suffering a lot from the fact that he's not as high an achiever as he used to be."

"Yes, that's a crash he's going to have to adjust to as a healthy person, for now."

"Karl, did you know that Felix needs new health insurance?"

"Why?"

"When he was admitted to the bank apprenticeship program, he had to cancel his own home health insurance. He had to give up his share of my private health insurance."

"Had to?"

"Yes," Felix confirmed. "I had to fill out so many papers, I thought it was just a given. I never even thought about it."

"We don't really have any experience in this area," said Karl.

They didn't realize this had been a mistake until he lost his position with Deutsche Bank. Katharina's insurance would no longer take him back.

"That's private insurance for you," Karl scolded. "All they care about is making a profit, not sick people. I would never get private insurance myself!"

Katharina shrugged. "We were thrilled not to have to go through a huge bureaucratic process at his operation."

"What reason did they give for refusing him?"

"He's been highlighted as a very expensive patient, too much of a financial burden for private insurance companies. They won't do it without enormous premium payments for a 'new admission.'" Insurance is just a business, a necessary evil for those who are sick. Thought Katharina.

So Felix was out of insurance, which brought him privileged treatment with a few medical experts. Katharina appreciated that Professor Ruhe and Professor Mann remained in charge of his treatment in spite of that. A small remnant of humanity in the cruel system of plutocracy.

In the meantime, the failures to which he was unaccustomed gave over to a distinct depression. His mood sank. He tried to make himself useful in the household. He took over the complications of tax filing. He kept the family computer in good condition. But in order to keep himself from hanging around the house jobless and completely losing his ailing mind, he took what was called corporate job training. He was working alongside youths who didn't want to learn, or couldn't, who hadn't graduated from school.

"This is the school for my life," Felix tended to say, shaken. For the first time, he was getting firsthand experience of kids who were 'at rock bottom,' as he called it, 'who don't have any parental guidance or support from their families.' Their work attitudes and scatological vocabularies went far beyond anything Felix had ever encountered. This situation was made twice as bad in Felix's cortisone-lacking brain, because it couldn't manage diplomacy. His sense of justice bounces collided with overwrought teachers and difficult students without brakes or tact, and it was objectively impossible for him to grasp appropriate boundaries.

"A lot of times the lesson can't even be finished," he noted several times. "I really feel bad for the teachers."

"The material is far beneath his level, but he's still turning a brave face and going to this school anyway," observed Katharina.

"So he isn't sitting at home by himself," said Karl.

"I'm still worried about his development."

"Why are you worried now?"

"Felix is distancing himself from everyone else in the class. He's turning into a loner."

"Do you really think so?"

"Has it occurred to you that he doesn't appear to have developed any feelings towards the opposite sex?"

"Yes."

"That's because of radiation contamination from the medical treatment."

""We'll have to get compensation for that then."

"It also seems like not only his memory, but his entire personality has completely changed."

"What do you mean?"

"His natural gregariousness has given way to a more timid reclusiveness."

"Now don't use such big words."

"He's completely isolating himself from the outside world. He's not making friendly connections with any new people."

"But he has plenty of friends."

"He only keeps contact with his oldest friends, the ones who stuck by him during his time of greatest need. No one besides them knows what's wrong with him and he doesn't want to tell anybody."

Felix argued. "I have to live my life as normally as I can, and I don't want anyone to be sympathetic. Whether I manage it, or I never do." There were tears in his eyes.

He managed to finish a skilled laborer certificate in information science, with a 'good' rating. This was because of his functioning long-term memory and his extensive grasp of world knowledge, which made up his personality – long before the operation, which changed his life so much.

Over the years, his left brain had apparently been able to take over some of the functions of the damaged right side. Felix wrote down a lot so as not to forget anything, but his power of retention lengthened with each passing year.

"I'd be interested in trying to start again with the degree program I gave up."

"If you really want to, then try it," said Katharina. Privately, she was doubtful. But his strong will triumphed over the circumstances. He received a place at Rostock University and successfully graduated. Learning and studying worked surprisingly well with the memory aids he used, even if, as someone whose success had previously come in the form of A's and B's, not all his dreams could come true.

He filled out at least sixty applications after that, and just as many letters of rejection rattled his newly restored self-confidence. But at last he managed to get an internship in Frankfurt, and later a steady job with a computer firm in Hamburg. As a bachelor, the little two-room apartment was all he needed.

Friday, May 24ᵗʰ 2002

Every time Felix has to come to a doctor's appointment, he comes from Hamburg to Rostock to stay with the doctors, whom he knows well, and for their side they supervise him with scientific interest.

Although Felix's circumstances are relatively good, I'm nervous again. Aunt Charlotte, who would be eighty in October, appeared to me in a dream. She said "the cancer won't kill me." Crazy.

The enormous walnut tree in the garden has begun to bedeck itself with deceptively tempting greenery. But soon enough, that greenery will leave us in darkness for all its budding life. It's taking away our hope and light, says my father. The tree has to go.

The precarious five years post-cancer have gone by, and it's time for Felix to reintroduce himself to Professor Ruhe in Greifswald. The results will be unveiled: has anything changed? Are any anomalies or metastases visible? We suddenly find ourselves suppressing our anxiety at home.

I'm driving Felix to Gehlsdorf to see Professor Ruhe. I feel an unpleasant trace of the old fear rearing its head. One patient in a thousand. Will he even recognize us after five years? I'm not expecting a long conversation. At least, I'm hoping it won't be long.

We enter his room, where he's sitting rather unspectacularly in the armchair in front of his desk, legs crossed. Hundreds of scenes from the horrible months in 1996 swim before my eyes. Absently I stare at a potted plant on the window sill. It's grown beautifully and its shining green leaves are full of life. A baobab. I take a deep breath, the words of my grandfather returning to me. Then I look probingly into the face of the doctor. Does it betray any sign of bad news?

"Stern," I introduce myself. "Do you remember Felix at all?" In the same moment I realize how dumb the question was, coming out horribly stilted instead of relaxed, as it should have been.

Professor Ruhe just smiled. "Of course, I remember Felix very well. We played table tennis here quite often!" Strange that he remembers

Felix by that, because the professor played table tennis in his youth and was a regional champion or something like that. He pronounces the deeply profound words calmly.

"Now, Felix, we've looked at the new images from your CAT scan and MRI. It looks good. Everything is in order for now! You can come in for a follow-up in another five years." Felix nods, as though this is all perfectly obvious.

Can I really believe any of this? It's all happening so fast. Sometimes stress causes one to react inappropriately to positive news. But maybe we'll survive in the shadows of the walnut tree, and let it stand.

CHAPTER 8

The daily joys, headaches, and emergencies involved in being a school principal filled Katharina's life to the brim. From the first part of her day in the morning, to the last thing she did at night. There were only twenty-four hours in a day.

But learning to live with her son's sickness, one that made her acutely aware of the mortality of existence, effected a drastic change in the way she perceived her own harried life. Suddenly the things that used to rattle her weren't as important anymore. A great inner calm poured over her in the face of all the thousand trifling details she had to deal with at school.

That evening as she sat working at her desk, Katharina's thoughts were occupied with her conference with Rosi Schmidt, the class teacher of 5C. She replayed the day's events in her head. By now it was no longer possible to trace everything from the grueling school day all the way to her return home. But an old question, one that she'd been suppressing for months due to her own lack of power, returned to her today after her conversation with Rosi Schmidt. What was going on here, damn it, what was wrong here?

Katharina had already heard the hard numbers, when she'd had the teachers analyze the social structure of all the grade levels in the school. An unusually high number of children were acting out. They weren't just isolated incidents. Different from what she had been used to in her time as a teacher, just a few years ago. The children couldn't focus on a single subject for more than ten minutes. During gym, it took shorter periods of time for them to become wiped out. They constantly had to go to the bathroom. They showed almost no interest in learning. They brawled with one another, "for fun," they said, but no mercy was shown to the losing party. If someone was already lying on the floor, they would be brutally kicked. No compassion, no sympathy, no pity, no boundaries, no regard for human life.

"*Gebt den Kinder das Kommando!*
Sie berechnen nicht, was sie tun!"
The German singer Herbert Grönemeyer bawled from the ra-

dio, which Katharina always let play in the background while she worked. *"Let the children take over! They're not so calculating ..."*

"Kinder an die Macht!"

"Power to the children!" If only the man knew how delusional his lyrics were!

Having a wide lexicon of bathroom humor and being able to turn any subject into a sex joke meant being cool, the kids explained to their teachers. They couldn't pay attention, had absolutely no ability to concentrate on the spoken word. Their tolerance for frustration was almost nil. Their test scores were sinking lower and lower. They couldn't read. More and more parents had their children tested for reading and writing disabilities so they could drop bad grades off the report card. Over thirty such disorders were on file as having been supposedly confirmed at her school. A flicker of doubt as to the validity of these tests entered her mind as she eyed a withered baobab on the school psychologist's window sill.

Cases of diagnosed ADHD were piling up in every grade level. Two or three students with attention deficit hyperactivity disorder in every class! Did the diagnostician realize that they were diagnosing every one of these children with a brain disorder? Katharina couldn't believe that every tenth student in her school allegedly had a brain disorder!

Incidents of suicide attempts by mentally disturbed teenagers were piling up ...

She hoped her teachers' analysis would yield the answer to the question of what could account for all of this. Was it the quality of their teaching, as the educational experts who conducted school evaluations would have her believe? If she came to understand her teachers, would she, as a 55-year-old principal, no longer be able to understand her students? Katharina didn't want to become detached. She feared succumbing to the standard generational divide to which even the Greek Sophocles had fallen victim – the younger generation is weak in the eyes of the preceding one. They didn't work hard enough, had no interest in learning, and no respect for their elders. That was how it was thousands of years ago. They smoked, took drugs, and drank themselves to death. That, too, had been the case long ago. What was new was their spending the day sprawled in front of the TV or sitting at the computer with unfettered access to information and the depths of human imagination, which they were incapable of dealing with. And that, Katharina reflected, was the heart of the problem. What else could it be?

Rosi Schmidt seemed to have been very anxious to have their meeting. "I have so much to tell you. I just have to tell someone."

There was an unusual flicker in her gaze, and Katharina observed the teacher's glinting eyes and shaking hands with growing trepidation. What was wrong with her class? What was wrong with her? She wouldn't be the first ...

Rosi Schmidt's analysis sheet for the fifth grade lay before Katharina. Of these twenty-three children, eleven had already survived the battlefield of their parents' divorce. Over half of them no longer knew a home life of harmony and stability under care of both mother and father. With surprise, she saw that things were no different in any of the other grades, all the way up to tenth. Half of them were children of divorce.

Rosi Schmidt explained to her what that meant in a long talk. Katharina had taken notes so that she wouldn't forget a single detail. Mentally she replayed through the conversation, rehashing the teacher's every sentence – and her own reactions.

"You know, children of divorced parents aren't the general rule in my class. Imagine, five of those kids are still wetting the bed every night. Yes, you heard right. Five. One of them even soils their pants regularly. I probably shouldn't even be telling you this, as the principal."

"Why ever not?"

"That sort of thing falls under the jurisdiction of Germany's new privacy laws. But I just have to get it off my chest. These children are eleven and twelve years old! Tell me, what am I supposed to do on a three-day field trip, where the children are all meant to get to know each other better? Put plastic sheets on all the beds? Bring diapers? Our social worker, at any rate. I'm not touching anything here anymore unless she's there."

"Please try and stay calm!" Katharina noticed the nervous twitch in Rosi Schmidt's eye for the first time.

"My little Peter Hilmann, the one who soils his pants, you

know, has parents who are separated, they both have good jobs with the police, so they're educated and so forth. They've just had a new house built so his mom can find a new partner. That's romance for you."

"Yep, that sort of thing is happening in a thousand different places in Germany."

"And what happens with the kids, each time? The separation is wreaking havoc for poor little Peter. His dad is demanding unconditional custody rights and making his wife's life a living hell."

"Oh dear."

"Apparently now they've found a 'solution' for the kids – Peter has a little brother, too. Two days of the week they live with Dad, and the rest with Mom, with special arrangements for weekends."

"Who comes up with such a thing?"

"Two days of switching location every week! Sports equipment will be missing because it's in Dad's living room while Peter's living with Mom at the moment, or his missing homework will end up buried God knows where amid the chaos."

"That explains a few things."

"Everything is higgledy-piggledy at school. And I can't even conduct a decent parent-teacher conference. I really need to talk to his mother in order to help the child, but he won't allow it."

"He won't allow it?"

"He insists he has to hear everything and stalls every meeting. I finally just went to visit the mother and called it a 'private cup of coffee,' so I could talk to her personally."

"You can't do that!"

"What can I do, then? Just stop caring about all of this?" Again the nervous twitch in her eye.

"It's the law."

"But laws can't encompass every possible special circumstance. This is about living beings, children, who don't always react according to plan!"

"Mrs. Schmidt, when teachers rely on using their own common sense to make decisions regarding students, they can wind up garnering complaints if things go south. For example, giving out a B in gym class, when the father says his child should have earned an A because he's a fantastic soccer player outside of class. If you can't back up a decision with specific reference to the education laws, it'll be illegal."

"Yes, that's all illegal, that's what the father told me too! You should have seen the first night of parent-teacher conferences! There were sparks flying around the room when the mom sat in one corner of the classroom and he sat in the opposite corner. But he kept staring at her, ready to open fire at any moment."

"How awkward."

"His cell phone kept ringing while I was talking, and he took the call right in front of all the other parents and just chatted away up to the very end."

"And you didn't say anything about it?"

"I can't very well try to discipline the parents too! But I've never experienced such defiance at school, and disrespect towards me. What am I supposed to do?"

Katharina sensed the teacher's feelings of powerlessness, and let her talk further.

"We put together a great barbecue afternoon with all the kids and parents, and neither of them showed up. The reason? They wanted to go to an over-30's night at a club." Rosi Schmidt paused briefly to let the effect of her words sink in. "You know, their child isn't getting any attention, love, or security."

"What makes you say that?"

"He clings to me. Every single break he comes up to my desk, wanting to tell me something."

"Has his academic performance been poor?"

"Yes, but Peter is highly gifted in math. On the last test he hardly made any mistakes, even though he was sick the two weeks before that. His spelling is perfect and he has a great command of syntax for his age. There one puts their ears back." Rosi Schmidt wasn't really beside herself, her heart was just over-flowing with the sad stories of her students' fates. She wanted her principal to tell her what role she was supposed to take on in all this. What she was used to, what she had learned twenty-five years ago, was that every child needs love and care. If parents couldn't provide that, the job fell to the teacher. But somehow it had been easier to keep up before, and now incidences of upset children were piling up in her class.

"You may also know about the tragic case of my student Paul, his mother has been in a vegetative state for four years."

"I remember, you mentioned that once."

"Being without a mother is hard enough for such a young boy and his little brother, two grades behind him. But the circumstances are tragic because his parents were on the verge of separation four years ago."

"Four years ago?"

"Yes. One evening they said they were going to split up. The next morning, their mom was driving with the kids to Berlin, and there was a horrible accident on the way. She's been in a coma every since. Can you imagine what the kids are going through?"

"Not at all."

"Their father, of course, refuses to accept any support from his mother-in-law, who as their grandmother has been trying to help her daughter's children. She takes the kids to the hospital so they don't forget their mother. The children aren't even remotely mentally capable of dealing with the fact that their mother's been lying there dead to the world for four years."

"This case should really be supervised by a psychologist!"

"He doesn't want to do any psychological processing, at this point he wants to throw away the furniture."

"Oh dear."

"There's obviously another woman in the picture, which is par for the course in this sort of situation. Agenda full of hiding and covering things up."

"Maybe that would be good for the children."

"The other problem is that their father isn't around to drive them three times a week. So they have a neighbor to do it, who of course doesn't spend the night with the children. That's what they agreed on with the Youth Office."

"Have you dealt with a representative of the Youth Office?"

"Of course. But they say they can't do anything else to help. You can hardly imagine it – the child literally begs for affection and constantly clings to my skirt. He shows distinct signs of depression. Paul's behavior has gotten so out of control that he – and now his little brother, too – is beginning to tell tales, in order to get attention."

"What sort of things is he saying?"

"He said once that he fell off his bike, and a man molested him."

"What's that supposed to mean?"

"He was so convincing that I contacted the police. He kept up the act for days. Then he sheepishly admitted he made the whole thing up."

Katharina was speechless.

"Or he said his father got into an accident with a truck. Every day he told me that his father was in the hospital and he hadn't had time to do his homework."

"So he didn't do any homework."

"It was crazy! In the end, none of it was true. Mrs. Stern, I'm feeling completely overwhelmed. What should I do?"

"There's not much you can do. Ultimately it all comes down privacy. You really can't even talk about it, much less intervene. We're not living under socialism anymore."

"But I can't just let these kids run up against the wall, Mrs. Stern!"

"You're right. Let's come up with something tomorrow at the team meeting."

"Do you think we'll find a solution?"

"It won't be too hard to come up with open rules," Katharina tried to calm her colleague. "These aren't singular cases, even if they're distinctly different from each other. There's also jittery little Nina, who since her parents' divorce – similar to the Hilmann kids – has been spending one week with Mama and the next week with Papa, always switching back and forth. So she's missing her work apron because it's at Mama's house, or she doesn't have a signature because no one knows where her notebook is."

"Yes, but ..." Rosi Schmidt looked at her with wide eyes.

"Don't you dare say anything publicly! Our new freedom doesn't reach that far! Even if the child is terribly confused and falling apart. You'll get slapped with a lawsuit before you even know what hit you. These people have perfected the art of claiming their right to sue. For the right price, there are lawyers who would stoop to taking this kind of case. I could name you countless examples just from the past few years."

"But this is unbearable, Mrs. Stern! We're in desperate need of radical change in a couple of the more obvious regulations, in order to do our jobs."

"It's not that simple with the regulations," Katharina argued.

"But not all children and problems can be fixed by a single, general rule. I need freedom to make decisions at school according to the individual case, or else I'm going to go crazy. None of these rules handed down from above that are so far removed from reality they're barely feasible."

"What do you mean by that?" Katharina asked.

"Well, it's not my fault that Mecklenburg-Vorpommern's school graduates have the worst scores in all of Germany!"

"No one's saying that!"

"That's not true. The teachers are to blame, aren't we? And our horrible classes, according to the evaluation."

"They didn't say that."

"The media is tearing us to pieces!"

"I know."

"It's also not because I can't or don't want to come up with really good lessons! There are too many special cases of troubled students. Far too many. You can't help all of them. Our work has become so meaningless." A glimmer gave away the tears in Rosi Schmidt's eyes again.

"You know," Katharina said, relenting, "Even I had to come to terms with the fact that all my old ideas about being able to change the world for children were nothing but an illusion. There's nothing we can do anymore to help guarantee success for our students."

"I agree with you there. That means our work has no purpose anymore."

"What on earth is the matter with you? Do you know the story of the thousands of starfish who were thrown up on the beach by the big waves after a storm?"

"No, why?"

"The starfish lay on the beach, unable to make their way back to their life in the sea, and dried out in the sun. An old man, who was out for a walk with a friend, carefully took one starfish after another and set them back in the ocean. His friend shook his head and said 'What difference is that going to make? There are ten thousand starfish stranded here. You can't save all of them.' The old man took the next starfish, threw it back into the water, and said, 'It makes a difference to that one.'"

Rosi Schmidt smiled and nodded. "Maybe you're right."

Suddenly her thoughts returned to her class. "The crazy thing is that in all of these instances, they want for nothing! They all have houses and two cars. They all go on vacation several times a year. But they don't get on with their life and with their children."

"Is that really true of all of them?"

"I only have one student in my class whose mother who isn't as well off. She works at the federal property office as a case worker, which they only hire university graduates for! Her neighbor earns more money on welfare than she does as a working mother of two children. She also does painting on the side to make ends meet. She graduated with a business degree in real estate, but she hasn't been able to find a job in that."

Katharina sensed her old suppression mechanism kicking in.

"Oh, I don't believe that. You probably just misunderstood something. Try to calm down a bit. Apart from that, nothing has happened."

She was deeply concerned for Rosi Schmidt's condition. Her reaction seemed excessive, her gestures were erratic, tears shone in her eyes. She was overworked. Hopefully not about to burn out. That would be the third among her colleagues. Katharina was annoyed that she couldn't come up with something sensible to offer her colleague besides empty clichés to try and soothe her.

'Apart from that, nothing has happened' – that was what Rutzlaff had said too, that one time after the baseball incident with the American professor, to keep her calm. But by now she knew what had happened afterwards.

The teacher Ulrike Möwe, from Wiesenborn, and her husband had tried to enjoy the privilege of being able to visit her grandfather in the former West Germany for his birthday, two years later. Happy to have gotten written permission, they got on the train. At the border, they were suddenly asked by border patrol to disembark. From then on, her inner attitude towards the politics of the GDR disintegrated over time.

The husband of Eva Zauder, the English teacher from Clockshagen, received an unknown form of punishment for his wife's naïve activity, and had trouble sleeping for years after. He passed away a few years later from cancer. Her son followed shortly after that. Sunk in depression, he took his own life.

Dörthe Pagel, the teacher from Sonnenhagen, never managed to displace her constant fear and anxiety. She always felt as though she was being watched, and her insecurity in public ultimately had an extreme effect on her mental health. The ability to speak her mind soon deserted her. She died years later of an undiagnosed brain tumor.

Heide Schmidt from Weisertorf? She also spent the rest of her life in the grip of a secret fear. Instinctive repression was her only saving grace, bringing her relief in her stressful life as a teacher.

All the others, for various reasons, left the work force several years early.

Rutzlaff himself was probably enjoying a well-earned retirement in the best of health. Thought Katharina.

She would have to do more to protect her own colleagues. Rosi Schmidt had more to share with her boss in this private conversation, something to do with a horrible website and Heidrun Meschke in tears.

"Next time ..." Katharina had to break off the conversation. What should she advise her to do? Hundreds of stories just like this were all over her school now. And not just at hers, she'd heard from colleagues at others. As a teacher she wasn't allowed to intervene, according to law. What insanity! What was wrong here? A decline in moral values? In her heart of hearts, she knew. Every society has the youth it deserves. Where had she read that before?

Friday, May 19th 2006

Ten years. Has it actually been ten years already? I haven't written anything in a long time, even if Felix is still secretly my problem child. His life is going off in a different direction than Olaf and Stefanie's, who are already married and have made us grandparents twice over.

Felix has become more independent, since he was able to have his status as a minor lifted several years ago. I think there was some truth to the words of Professor Nahm, his surgeon from Greifswald. Over time, the other half of the brain can take over the previous functions of the damaged side.

Felix is coming into Rostock from Hamburg for a doctor's appointment, and every time he goes to Professor Mann. Afterwards he's always supposed to tell me what the doctor said. But he just shrugs and says "Everything's fine, Mom."

Professor Mann, from the endocrinology department at the Rostock University clinic, observed his long-term patient carefully and thoughtfully. "How are you? How are you getting along with the medication?"

"I think I've gotten a handle on it over the years. Like if I have to spend two hours waiting in the hall here, my cortisone level is practically zero. Then I'm just at the end of my rope and can barely keep it together to be polite."

"Well, waiting for the doctor is annoying, but your problem is that you can't calm yourself down due to your lack of stress hormones. Small annoyances that fade away quickly in healthy people have a more long-lasting effect on you."

"Yeah, they do. Recently someone ignored my right of way on the Südring, and the car took a hit. I was doing pretty badly for a few hours, I was panicking and I couldn't calm myself down even though nothing serious had happened."

"You drive a car?" Professor Mann inquired, concerned.

"Yeah, for ten years now. Thank God I took the driver's license test before my operation. Afterwards, my damaged short-term memory and the stress from the test would have made it a catastrophe."

Professor Mann nodded knowingly. "Incredible. Haven't you gotten into any other stressful situations?"

"A hundred times a day. Rude customers at work, clearing up disputes ..."

"How do you handle that?"

"My mind still works. By now I can tell exactly when I really need to take a cortisone pill to relieve the pain from stress. My ears turn beet red when it's time. Or else I just feel really flat, and lose all my drive. Unfortunately the cortisone makes me bloat up if I have to take it too many times in one day. And then I don't look as good. That's why I try to cut back on the pills and just endure it for as long as possible."

"But you can't do that!" Professor Mann said in an unusually sharp tone. "Do you have any idea how dangerous that is for you? Do I have to lecture you on why you are not capable of making it through an accident without medication? Are you not aware that the cocktail of hormones that I've concocted for you together with researchers from international universities is the bedrock of your life?"

"But I really do look better when I don't take as much cortisone."

"That helps nothing. Every pain, whether physical or mental, has an effect on you of varying strength, which cannot go away on its own. You will be emotionally devastated if even the tiniest thing goes wrong."

"I'm always aware of that," Felix affirmed.

"Do you have a girlfriend?"

Felix shook his head no.

"In case it ever comes up, we need to have a talk about extra medication. For the testosterone, there's a long-acting patch. No more injections, which are painful and hard on your skin."

"Okay," Felix smirked.

"Does everyone in your life know what's wrong with you?"

"Why should I tell everyone? That won't make it better."

"Right then." Professor Mann took a deep breath, sensing that the conversation and the time spent waiting had already put his patient into a depressed mood. "Keep your weight under control, and keep in touch when you need new medication! Otherwise, we'll see each other again in three months."

As the young man closed the door behind him, Professor Mann paged thoughtfully through his patient files for a few minutes. Felix Stern would have to live the rest of his life with artificial relief for handling stress. With help from his medication, he could manage well. His surroundings would have to adapt to make things easier for him, if he were going to be able to succeed in all areas of life. And that remained the bigger problem. The doctor knew that no one could truly understand the problems with the pituitary gland and arrange to work around them, without having experienced it firsthand.

He carefully moved the pot of impatiens, overflowing with vibrant red blossoms, to the side and opened the window. Outside, the dark-haired young man crossed the street with quick steps and readily came to the assistance of an old woman who was uncertainly tapping her way across the cobblestones with a cane. Helpfulness was becoming his trademark.

Professor Mann took another deep breath and called in the next patient.

Thursday, May 25th 2006

Today is the Ascension, a day off for me with no strings attached.

Felix writes a lot down so as not to forget. His new computer science job in Hamburg requires him to travel regularly, especially to England and the US. The English that he learned from the Drapers as a young boy (better than mine, according to Vicky) is coming in handy now. The Drapers have long since relocated to London, and had to sell the house that held all their bad memories. After Jane's baby was born, Mark threatened over the phone to come after the whole family with a knife, and they fled in terror and left no forwarding address.

Felix has become more self-sufficient by now. He accomplishes everything just fine on his own, living in his little two-room apartment in Hamburg.

I recall my grandfather's maxim for life:

Trust in yourself, take life and your circumstances as they are.

That calms me down. I don't know where he got that saying from.

The word "trust" stirs a memory - "prust," from the English sentence in that strange letter back in 1982, the one even the Drapers couldn't figure out. Could whoever wrote it have picked that up somewhere, in their stupidity?

Perhaps I'll stop keeping a diary.

CHAPTER 9

Monday, April 17th 2009

I happened to find this diary on my bookshelf today – next to all the other ones from twenty-seven years ago – and flipped through it. It hasn't been filled up, just like the old ones. It's still waiting for news. Today, of all days, I find myself once again remembering the anonymous letter from the days of the GDR, the one that threatened bad luck unless I sent it on to twenty other people in need of some good luck. I didn't send the letter, not even to the Drapers, and since then my superstitious subconscious has been keeping track of all the misfortunes.

Today is the second anniversary of Mark's death. He died shortly before his fortieth birthday, full of pain and despair in Bedford prison, when someone screwed up in the office and denied the methadone treatment he'd started, forcing him to go cold turkey. Someone found him hanging from torn bedsheets off the bars of his cell. I was still recovering from a bad fall and wasn't able to make it to his memorial service in London.

Mark has been gone for two years now – a horrible tragedy, one of many in these free times of alcoholism, drugs, drug crime, unemployment, deteriorating illnesses, and gambling away money on the stock market instead of investing it in our young people. But now I understand that not all the socialist descriptions of capitalism in the GDR were propaganda.

Wednesday, June 25th 2009

That crazy old letter! The first line is still a mystery after twenty-six years. Something with "all together" and "the good" and "the way" and "trust." Sounds like an English Bible verse – but I didn't find anything on the internet. Instead I find the unfortunate Michael Jackson. Dead. Drugs. Medication. Stress. A rich man speeding towards heaven after having lived through hell. How disillusioned I feel about the happiness of such people!

We're already in the twentieth year since the reunification, since the opening of the gate that I believed, from inside my golden cage, must lead out into heaven on earth for all people. I will have to tell my grand-

children that however hard I try to peer back behind the gate, I still have yet to see anyone. A figment of my imagination from old times?

What will I say about the freedom we won in my speech at the twentieth anniversary celebration in our newly built auditorium? I probably won't say how much I've whittled away my own health by fighting the new bureaucracy to add a new auditorium onto our old school, wasting unnecessary strength and energy. I won't say how astonished I am that so many of my most active, most exuberantly venturous teachers, brimming with idealism, wind up burning out in their teaching careers and suffering from undiagnosed depression. I won't say that all those years we spent struggling to gain independence and freedom in decision-making in the schools even after the reunification ultimately came to naught because of the lawmakers. They cast a suspicious eye over any freedom we demanded, because apparently the only way to maintain freedom is by force. The more of it they allow us, the more control mechanisms they have to implement based on their own self-importance. Personal responsibility is a foreign concept for German bureaucrats.

I will say, "We were never again as free as we were then."

"Hey Mom. I'm going to be back in Pammerow for the weekend. I wanted to visit my old friend Thommy, you remember him?"

Of course Katharina remembered him. He was part of the circle of friends who had stood by Felix's side offering help and advice even when Felix's memory was so full of holes. But that wouldn't warrant a phone call. He came 'home' almost every weekend, as he called it.

"Oh, and the other thing I wanted to say, I'm bringing a colleague with me from the firm in Hamburg. She wants to see Rostock and Warnemünde, but she only speaks English and no German. Is that okay?"

Aha. So that was why he was calling. "Of course. We have foreign guests to stay all the time. It's no problem, Felix. I'll get the guest room ready."

"We don't need a guest room."

Katharina was silent. What kind of arrangement had he just finagled? He wasn't seventeen anymore, when it had been fine for all his friends to sleep on air mattresses in one room together at a New Year's party. Even with the medication from Professor Nahm, Felix's lack of hormone control rendered him somewhat simpleminded, and combined with his lack of experience, he had a habit of crossing the normal boundaries of discretion. Somehow she would have to explain the impropriety of what he was proposing, and prepare a second room in spite of his request so that his colleague wouldn't be caught in an unexpected quandary.

"We won't be back from Thommy's until late. You don't need to wait up for us. Then we'll see you at breakfast." And with that he hung up.

"What should we do, Karl? This could be really awkward for his colleague."

"Who cares?" Karl muttered from behind his paper, where he was studying the farm weather report for the weekend. "He's old enough to know what he's doing."

"But he'll make a fool of himself. We'll have to explain it to him when they arrive."

"It's not that big a deal. It's already pretty late. I've got to head out early in the morning to teach my workmate how to do her job. I'm not going to wait around all night before I can go to bed."

On Sunday morning, Katharina realized that her son's arrival had escaped her, even though she was a light sleeper and had plenty of experience in going right back to sleep when her sons let themselves in late at night, back from their days as adolescent club-goers. Karl came back in from the field for a mid-morning break. "Isn't he up yet? It's already ten."

But no, there he was. Felix was just now coming in with a mischievous smirk, unaccompanied.

"Where's your colleague?"

"She's still sleeping."

"Did you offer her the room upstairs?" Katharina asked, first thing.

"No."

She raised her eyebrows. Felix was radiant, although his facial expression attempted to conceal the exuberant joy belied by the rest of his body language.

It was another hour before the young woman appeared for

breakfast. She came out of the bathroom looking groomed. Her dark eyes were freshly made up and fringed with long dark lashes, and her glossy black hair looked just like Snow White's. Her clothes were discreetly fashionable, a short jacket over a plain black skirt. High heels gave her legs the elegance of Hamburg, the big city.

She was smiling, and carried a small flower between her long sleek fingernails as a thank-you for having been put up for the night.

A bit of chit chat in English. A cup of tea. A breakfast roll with salami.

"We're going to take a stroll through Rostock. I want to show her our lovely neighborhood by the sea, and the sights. We'll eat in the city. We might see you again tonight before we head back to Hamburg."

And with that, the two of them took their leave. Felix seemed transformed; he was almost unrecognizable.

When they had left the house, Karl and Katharina looked at each other with wide eyes, stunned.

"What the hell was *that*?" Karl stressed the last word, stretching it out.

Katharina repeated him, irritated. "What the hell *was* that?"

On the same day, Felix sat down in front of the computer to look for a cheap apartment for the young woman. He immediately canceled her 995-Euro arrangement for her, as even a single day more would be too expensive to pay. Was it her lack of experience in a foreign country? Or lack of caring, even if she had a credit card? She was in prime position to plummet into debt. He offered her a room in his own small two-room apartment, just for a couple days until she found something of her own.

His good-natured sympathy, blind trust, and own lack of experience led to her staying there forever, in a surprising turn of events. She couldn't raise money for her own place.

Tuesday, July 20th 2009
Once again I'm turning to this diary. The last time was almost a year ago. I don't trust myself to discuss my worries openly. First I

have to straighten things out with myself and sort out my thoughts.
Trust – have trust?

Why does the suspicion strike me that this girl's behavior can't be
entirely normal?

And so love seemed to grow. Her insomnia continued. The nights
became day, and during the day she slept, if she could get away
with it at work.

In the beginning she was able to stay on at the German branch
of the company, but her boss was friends with her Italian still-hus-
band. Conflict was inevitable. Jeanne couldn't and wouldn't live
that way. After a few months she quit, not bothering to account
for the emotional and financial consequences.

Unemployed and unhappy, she sat alone in Felix's tiny apartment, filling out applications and coming to the realization that
in order to get a job in Germany, she'd have to master the language first. So he got her a second laptop and some expensive
German language classes at the Goethe Institute, which cost
hundreds of Euros.

In the course of her personal expenditures, Jeanne somehow
managed to spend all her money in a very short amount of time,
everything she'd brought with her from Italy, as well as every
cent that she'd earned here, or rather, received from the unemployment office. She was overcome by the pressing need to buy.
Everything that appealed to her, everything that was modern.

Felix loved driving. His family had given him the money for his
Honda three years ago. Now they were jetting off on trips with
the car every weekend.

For Felix a whole new world was opening up; after his illness he
had practiced restraint and saved his money. Now they traveled
to far-away countries together. Flying became a regular matter of
course. He accompanied her on short excursions to Italy to help
retrieve the luggage and belongings from her former marriage
home.

Within just one year, they'd whiled away happy hours in Rome,
Montreal, Moscow, London, and Krakow. Felix, who was normally so frugal, spent his money lavishly, even though his position with the company was suddenly terminated (for reasons

unknown, he claimed) and he found himself living off of unemployment overnight. After just one year, everything he'd saved up had disappeared. Twelve thousand Euros, gone just like that. It was admittedly unpleasant for him, but he loved her. Her every wish was his command. And she had high standards. She was a woman of the world, and subsequently needed to be out and about in it.

Jeanne searched frantically for ways she could make money. She nearly agreed to work for a wealthy sheikh, who was prepared to pay handsomely for a woman.

When Felix had to travel to Munich for a new job, she threw a fit. Why couldn't she fly with him? She could stay in a hotel and wait for him. He understood that she didn't want to have to endure the loneliness of the tiny apartment, but he couldn't let her pressure him when it came to official business matters. He had just found a good job, and had obligations to fulfill. Apart from that, his bank account was empty. His refusal resulted in a scene right out on the open street, accompanied by floods of tears. When Felix came home from work at night, she was keyed up from her day of not working and always yelled at him; he would turn right back around and go for a walk. By now his stress hormone pills were taking effect, and he was able to tolerate the situation in his home.

Somehow she never quite made herself at home in the tiny apartment. Six months later, when some friends came to visit for a cup of coffee, she had to ask Felix to show her where the instant coffee was kept.

A cat, they thought, might help relieve some of the loneliness of having no job. The animal passively allowed itself to be loved, kicked, thrown, and cuddled. In particularly critical moments of despair and mania, she asked Felix to have the cat euthanized. He didn't do it, but he cried.

Jeanne filled out applications for jobs all over Germany and was ready to move anywhere to earn money. But the companies showed no interest; either her German wasn't good enough for a paying job, or she didn't meet the qualifications in Germany. She had spent her whole life studying and learning, but two Bachelor's degrees and five languages still didn't add up to a Master's degree, which in Germany was only enough for mid-level-paying jobs. These she refused indignantly. "I'll get a Master's degree online. About 5000 Euros? I guess that's pretty expensive, but I've already been accepted by the University of Cambridge in England."

Wednesday, July 21st 2010

She's not a girl anymore, she's a young woman, but she behaves like a girl. Full of grand ideas for projects and trips she can't afford, unconditionally demanding things she can't really have, and when she's refused she breaks down in tears and aggressiveness. Extreme mood swings from zero to a hundred, from laughing to crying fits, from vibrant joy to throwing temper tantrums. She wants to sleep half the day away, even when she's visiting us, then she's energetic in the evening. At night she wanders around the house, unable to sleep. No consideration for others. Spoiled only child? Canadian lifestyle? No sensible person could tolerate living this way!

I'm suggesting that they consult a doctor.

Tuesday, August 17th 2010

A call from Felix, early in the morning. Their visit to the doctor resulted in a diagnosis: bipolar disorder. The doctor had described the symptoms to them as "up one minute, down the next." That explains everything.

Everything? What sort of a disease is that? Manic depressive? I've heard of this before. From a young man in Gehlsdorf and his girlfriend Evelyn.

Felix feels relieved. His darling girlfriend has a mental illness, it's not a character flaw that makes their coexistence so complicated. She can go to the hospital, take medication. Thank God. She's just sick. Just like he was. She just has to take medicine for the rest of her life, just like him.

"For heaven's sake. This is a very serious illness, it completely changes a person and makes living with them into hell," the old woman cried, visibly agitated. "Now the girl's peculiar behavior all makes sense ..."

"Oh please," Katharina interrupted her mother. "Everyone gets depressed sometimes. Don't exaggerate! I've had the same symptoms, when I was younger. You know, when I was pregnant for the first time and moved out of my life in Leipzig and Berlin and into this teeny tiny village in Mecklenburg. Where I didn't know anyone and was far away from my whole family."

"Why did you have to move so far away from us, anyway?" This accusation always sprang to her lips, bidden or not, the moment her beloved daughter was faced with any sort of trouble. The disappointment of having her only child end up moving almost 250 miles away was seared into the old woman; Pammerow was at least six hours away from Leipzig – which in the 70's, during the GDR, was a distance that meant practically the equivalent of a trip around the world, making allowances for the traffic back then. And to make matters worse, it was the countryside, out of which she herself had moved her family into the city back in the 1950's, in order to spare them the hard life of a farmer.

"Why did I move? For love. And it just happened to be this place, because someone wanted to retain Karl's farming business and helped him get a one-room apartment. An apartment was like gold dust in those days, there wasn't enough living space anywhere."

Her mother strayed from the subject, distracted by memories of the time.

"Yes, well. That's a reason to marry in the middle of icy February, even though there wasn't a single flower to be found in the dead of winter! And then you spent the whole time shivering miserably from the cold in the tiny chapel. It was fourteen degrees out, and the Gustav-Adolf Chapel wasn't heated."

Katharina felt obligated to explain to her mother, forty years after the fact, why she hadn't waited until summer to get married.

"Getting married was the only reason administration would accept for not taking a job placement 'where the state needs you.' I had to agree to that in writing before I started at Humboldt University. If we hadn't gotten married, we would have had to keep up a weekend relationship for three more years, living in different places. I would have stayed near Berlin."

"Why Berlin? You could have come back to Leipzig."

"No, don't you remember? My contract to teach English and German in Oranienburg had already been drawn up. So I had to get married at twenty-two years old, in the middle of the freezing winter of 1972, and then we were allowed to move into the attic of one of two apartment blocks in Pammerow. Do you remember what it looked like? Being students, we didn't have any money. We made shelves for a cupboard out of old fruit crates ..."

"And laid my old tablecloths over them so no one could see the mess, like it was hiding behind a curtain."

"That's right," Katharina laughed. "There was just one room. Some nice farmers gave us two old mattresses when we got there, so that we had a place to sleep, and an antique wardrobe from the Wehrmacht, which was gathering dust in a barn somewhere."

Her mother chuckled to herself, falling into the familiar rhythm of these old memories. "You took a saw and some red paint to it and made all the furniture for the kitchen and bathroom. There were six cups hanging on a hook glued on to one of the doors, and sometimes it fell off if the load was too heavy."

Katharina nodded. "Happy times for us. It was the first place we owned together by ourselves. Everything we made there together told its own little story."

"It was so snug we had to sleep on air mattresses in the tiny kitchen when we visited you for a few days."

"The whole thing only consisted of about ten square feet of floor space, with a sloping roof and two rooms. The old boiler only heated the bathtub, and there were two private walls framing the toilet."

"You never had the luxury of a separated bath and toilet again after that, did you?" her mother added.

"But fortunately we always had the two," Katharina said drily, coming back to her original point. "And Karl was moved to the National People's Army after just a few weeks. So I sat by myself in this small village, far away from the pulsing big city life I was used to, drowning in the sudden loneliness, while at the same time blindly plummeting into working as a teacher at the school."

"I didn't realize that you weren't happy."

"I won the gold medal for long jump at a Teacher's Sports Day, and it cost me our first child. A miscarriage. Then the depression came."

"No, no," her mother interrupted her daughter abruptly. "You can't call that depression. People just say that whenever they happen to shed a few tears."

"You think so? The new baby was already on the way when Karl had to leave for a year and a half. And Olaf was nine months old before he came back. Are you saying I just shed a few years from being lonely?"

"Oh, stop telling old stories and stay on the subject. I know what I'm talking about. I had a husband who changed completely after thirty years of marriage. You know that. Out of nowhere, he suddenly became quiet and everything seemed to be too much for him. He barely talked, and wouldn't tell anyone why. He couldn't be happy about anything. Just spent the whole day sitting apathetic and unmotivated in his TV chair, and then couldn't sleep at night. Morning was when he felt especially powerless. He had to force himself just to get out of bed."

"And what made it happen?" Katharina broke in.

"There was no trigger that anyone could see. He had always been a reliable, responsible leader in his department. He worked very efficiently and precisely, a perfectionist at work as well as around the household."

Katharina nodded again, thoughtfully. "I remember how he would arrange every strand of tinsel on the Christmas tree just so, and he put two trees together to make one so that the symmetry would be even. Every drawer in the cupboards was in perfect order, and he'd assigned a place to every single object at home and in the office."

"Even years later, after he'd been sitting at home as an invalid for a while, his colleagues would call him whenever they were looking for something in particular. He always knew exactly where it was."

Katharina didn't interrupt her, instead letting her speak. With every sentence she relived the past anew, although she already knew the facts. But now that she had lived her own experiences, the past was suddenly cast in a new light. She was the same age today as her mother had been then. All at once she was unsettled to realize that she now understood her mother's oft-repeated narrative, because she could relate to it herself. She, too, had been stunned recently at her father's funeral, when amongst his collection of documents she found his mother's old diary and letters. Her grandmother described her escape in the days after World War II. Even she, at that time, was as old as Katharina was now. Even she had once clung tightly to her belief in heaven, and was always there in her thoughts. But she had come back because there was no one there. It was reality that killed her. She never grew to be an old woman.

History is made real when we can connect to it on a personal, rational, and emotional level. Thought Katharina.

"The doctors never discovered the cause of his emotional suffering. Our marriage and our family lived in such a harmonious atmosphere, there was no occasion that would lend itself to induce such anxiety," her mother explained again.

Katharina interrupted her train of thought. "Do you think he could have been stressed out by all the years he spent studying electrical engineering at night? That kept him chained to the kitchen table every night after work for seven years."

"That might be it. But he was young, and he enjoyed it. What else could it have been?"

"His horrible experience in the war?"

"No one knows, not even me." Her mother shrugged helplessly. "I'm sure being overworked came into it."

"I think that experiencing those things in his youth was destructive for Dad, and many others," Katharina reflected aloud. "He was never really able to get over it, and it culminated in severe depression, just a few years after the first unrecognized heart attack when he was forty-six."

"That's true, but you weren't there to see it in person. He ended up spending years in the psych ward in Dösen. I went to see him every day after work."

"Did he get better after that?"

"A little. But even after that, when he was allowed to come home again, he was still broken somehow, and never really seemed to be able to focus on work again. Everything he had enjoyed before just stopped meaning anything to him. He was on a lot of medication, and it seemed to keep the depression under control so most people didn't notice it. But I noticed."

"What do you mean?"

"The man who used to be so happy was now incapable of enduring any contradiction or criticism, and he reacted harshly to hearing it. We all but disappeared from the public eye; he didn't want to meet or see anyone. There was no more going to the cinema for us, no more theatre, no more traveling. I put all my own wishes on the back burner and swept any potential controversy out of the way as quickly as possible. I put up with him when he argued and got aggressive, and swallowed down my own protests, because he really was a very good person."

"But that ended up making you sick, too. Didn't you have to retire early for numerous mysterious health problems?"

"Yes, I certainly did. So mysterious that I wouldn't have even noticed them today. I got sick from the permanent stress and had to give up my position at the omnibus park before it was time."

"And you just spent the whole day at home? Alone with him?"

"That's the only way I could be there for him. I put everything I wanted behind the needs of my sick husband."

Katharina was silent. She could remember that her father suddenly seemed to be ailing from some mysterious mental illness at fifty-four years old. But it was hardly spoken of, and then she was living almost 250 miles away from her parents and without her own phone. The mixture of not knowing and not wanting to know, or repressing, was already a part of her system of self-preservation, a means of keeping her own psyche healthy and intact in the face of unfathomable facts. It was the same device that had prevented her from connecting to her father's war stories, oft-repeated and so boring for her.

"But by then I had already been married to him for thirty years of his sickness," her mother suddenly interrupted their mutual thoughtful silence and her hands began to shake, which always happened at the slightest bit of agitation. Her heart and circulatory system were reacting with terror at the news that her beloved grandson's much-awaited girlfriend had been diagnosed with a severe form of depression. "The boy will never be able to cope with it, his life has just started over again ..." Her mother said out loud what Katharina didn't want to think. "He'll wither away. It'll never work, he's already juggling his own medications and disabilities. He can't be solving other difficult problems yet. You have to discourage him from this ..."

Katharina felt a lump forming in her throat.

"I can't do that," she said quietly. "He's so happy. He feels like he's in heaven. He's found the first great love of his life. Because of the brain tumor, he's had to wait more than thirteen years for this. It won't be that bad. He doesn't smoke, he doesn't drink, and he's not on drugs. He's capable of handling his own medication conscientiously, and can lead the life of a healthy person."

But her maternal instincts didn't leave her in peace, and the lump in her throat never fully disappeared. She couldn't and wouldn't admit to herself that she suspected how his heaven would look.

EPILOGUE

Karl says only little girls write in diaries. Nevertheless, I'm reaching one last time into the bookcase for my diaries.

Once again I'm sitting in front of the television along with two billion other viewers. The English royal family is celebrating a wedding in London. William and Kate, a happy couple, an ideal world. At least they left out that clichéd bit about obedience for Kate. There goes Diana's son amid the cheers of a million people the same way his parents did on July 29th, 1981; I still have a tin can depicting their faces sitting on the shelf in commemoration. No one is surprised at this ceremony as they were thirty years ago, which later led William's mother to fall into depression and ultimately killed her – the media, the beginning of the end. All of Britain is rejoicing today. There you sit as a seasoned citizen of the GDR, and you ask yourself, why do they do this?

I have to write this down and wax a little philosophical so that I don't forget any of it. What am I supposed to do? Am I supposed to say everything I know out loud? Sometimes it makes me very anxious. And not just because of Felix.

Am I just overexcited, or is someone going mad here? Grandpa and his depression are springing to mind, though he did live to be eighty-five in spite of his three heart attacks. Am I too sensitive because it's suddenly clear that I've been crossing paths with apparently unknown phenomena my whole life? Meanwhile, Rosi Schmidt is calling out sick. She's completely wiped out. Can teaching a class finish someone off like that? Little Paul from 5C had to go meet a psychologist – for symptoms of depression. Heidrun Meschke cries at the drop of a hat – she broke down in tears after the last instance of students bullying her over the internet. I sent her home. Udo seemed unable to cope with the pressure of the English school system, and he returned to Germany due to depression symptoms and other mental reasons. Meanwhile, things were looking worrisome for Angelika. Excessive workload all the time, insane piles of papers that needed correcting at the high school. 50-hour weeks weren't enough to manage it all. She spent months in a *wellness clinic to try and handle her sudden burnout. She's been at home for six months ever since her relapse.*

Mark Draper? No comment.

And last of all, Jeanne.

After the soccer player Henke killed himself due to severe depression, even the media had to pull its head out of the sand. People are trying to uncover the roots of the disease. I tried to gather information on the internet. There was a lot written there, both sensible and not so sensible. You can easily get carried away in the flood of unfiltered information. No wonder the kids are going crazy, it's too much to deal with! I never got any further with the eternal mystery of the screwy English sentence. By now I've asked every native English speaker I know. Even the Drapers shook their heads. I've searched "God," "way," and "heaven" on the internet, but there was nothing there that could give an answer to my question. Too bad. In any case, the stupid thing from the letter keeps me occupied, and is proof that superstition can motivate the brain and keep the gears turning. Or should I say, blocking the gears? Anyway, maybe I should have thrown out that idiotic letter back then, and maybe then there wouldn't be all these cases of mental illness today. You never know.

That was meant to be a joke. Period.

The former Minister of Education celebrated her husband's hundredth birthday in 2012. He had died twenty years prior, the strident last head of the GDR's controlling old guard. In honor of the occasion, his widow came forward after twenty years of silence and let herself be interviewed by journalists far away in Chile. Katharina saw the outcry that went through the press. The once mightiest woman in the GDR would talk about foolishness, not understanding why people had risked their lives to escape the golden cage. Or something like that. Those weren't their people, she said, but rather the enemy of the working class. Or something like that. In the class struggle, the revolution sometimes ate its own children, she claimed. Or at least they shut them up behind a wall, so that they could enjoy their happiness undisturbed and free of evil outside influences. Or something like that. They hadn't been given enough time to create a whole new socialist GDR.

"Well, what did they expect?" Katharina thought as she read the article in the local paper, the *Ostseezeitung*. "This seemingly intelligent, vicious woman slammed the door on Europe twenty years ago in a fit of pique, and ever since then she's had no sense for the reality of living in Germany, aside from her sympathy for the old guard of aged comrades." Vaguely disgruntled, Katharina took a sip of her coffee. "Cold. – She froze up on the stand before the reunification happened. The only topics she'll argue are the old ones that were hammered in to me by Hollenkamp and Wagner and so many other comrades at the *Parteilehrjahr* meetings back then. What makes her think she knows it any better?" Katharina was getting herself worked up that anyone would take the senile woman so seriously, to the point of letting her take up prime time on TV twice.

"The media probably doesn't want to let the bitter old woman's world get stirred up again because they missed out on a chance! – The paparazzi are always on the lookout for sensations, for a blaze that's been hidden under the ashes of history for years," she fumed. "There's no idea that's so good it's worth people dying for it. And it's even worse if the revolution locks up its own children, golden cage or not."

"Now we know how it ISN'T going, Mrs. Honecker," Karl commented during the broadcast.

In any case, this dictatorial old woman and her unrealistic ideals that had been repeated throughout the course of history were to blame for the fact that Katharina hadn't been able to tear down the veil of her fantasies at the right time, her dream that the wide world beyond the borders of the golden cage must be heaven.

Whom hadn't she presumed to be living in the heaven she imagined? It was Felix who told her first. He knew more than she did, from the delirium during his tumor operation. He had already been there once. They all flashed before her mind's eye. The travelers she envied on the train to Hamburg that rushed through Grandma Hanschke's garden. The happy people living in the land of the free while the Wall still stood. Those who had so many different languages at their command from their unlimited freedom to travel. The wealthy royal children of Buckingham Palace. The Americans who lived amid countless possibilities for expensive education and police in the schools. The successful families who lived peacefully together in a free world without money troubles. The unchecked schoolchildren, free to make their own decision without being patronized by teachers. The young people caught up in the frenzy of drugs. The journalists of the free press. The people who weren't legally obligated to work. And those who were healed of their depression through modern western medicine.

Felix had told her once before, on the morning after the damage to his memory: "There was no one there. So I came back." Katharina felt the trepidation from those times rise up in her chest again like an unbearable knot.

The tiny smartphone rang softly. During his last visit over her birthday, Felix had set it up so she could access her e-mail on her cell phone. As a computer specialist, he took charge of solving any problems his mother had with it. She still hadn't quite mastered this new piece of technology, even though she was constantly surfing the internet, connected to the whole world.

There was an e-mail from Jeanne in Hamburg.

"Felix and I tried to figure out your puzzle with a little help from the internet.

TRUST THAT ALL WILL LIVE HAPPILY TOGETHER AND THAT THE GOOD WILL LEAD THE WAY.

Does that help you at all?"

Katharina rested her head on her hand and stared at the words on the screen in surprise. Sunlight streamed in through the windows, obscuring the letters with its glare. The knot in her chest seemed to loosen. Her gaze landed in the garden, on the newly planted fruit tree in the bright clearing where the felled walnut tree used to stand. She shook her head in disbelief. On the desk before her, the old bookworm statue stood proudly with a hidden smile, for his books had finally revealed the solution to his puzzle, right there on the ladder to heaven.

"Thirty years too late for an old illusion – or maybe early enough for a new hope. Thank heaven."

ABOUT THE AUTHOR:

Brigitte Zeplien

 Born 01/15/1950 in Lützen, near Leipzig (Germany, former GDR)
Married for 45 years, two sons, two grandchildren
Retired school principal

She spent her youth and childhood in the metropolis of Leipzig. After completing her degree in German and English Education in Berlin, love and marriage to a farmer brought her to Northern Germany, where she taught English and German at a rural school near Rostock. She then led the school as principal for 23 years following Germany's reunification in 1989 (the fall of the Berlin Wall). The experiences she had teaching in and visiting schools in London, Milwaukee, Sacramento, and Baton Rouge allowed her to bring new concepts in instructing classes to her own school.

At the end of his last year in school, one of her sons was diagnosed with a brain tumor.

The book "Katharina Stern, or Tell Me If There's No One in Heaven" was her debut novel, in 2012. This was followed by a collection of poems and stories titled "Humor ist, wenn man trotzdem lacht" (Humor is When You Laugh Anyway, 2014). Her novel "Tabu oder Großmutters Vermächtnis" (Taboo, or Grandmother's Bequest) was released in June 2016.

www.brigitte-zeplien.de

This particular book was first published on August 24th, 2012. The hundredth birthday of the German Democratic Republic's last Head of State, Erich Honecker, was commemorated by many, including his widow in Chile, the former Minister of Education; Margot Honecker died recently in May 2016.

But with this literary work, Brigitte Zeplien would like it to be remembered that by forcing separation and isolation on a country in the effort to achieve his political goals, he not only carries the blame for the great monstrosities known to the world today, but also for the painful aftermath and countless individual fates suffered by the common average citizen, which no one talks about.